NICE CHILE

Nice Chile

CHILD OF WOE

A Novel-Fiction

Rebecca Golden

iUniverse, Inc.
Bloomington

Nice Chile
Child of Woe

iUniverse books may be ordered through booksellers or by contacting:

iUniverse
1663 Liberty Drive
Bloomington, IN 47403
www.iuniverse.com
1-800-Authors (1-800-288-4677)

*Because of the dynamic nature of the Internet, any web addresses or links contained in this book may
have changed since publication and may no longer be valid. The views expressed in this work are
solely those of the author and do not necessarily reflect the views of the publisher, and the publisher
hereby disclaims any responsibility for them.*

*Any people depicted in stock imagery provided by Thinkstock are models,
and such images are being used for illustrative purposes only.*

Certain stock imagery © Thinkstock.

ISBN: 978-1-4759-6328-1 (sc)
ISBN: 978-1-4759-6329-8 (hc)
ISBN: 978-1-4759-6330-4 (e)

Library of Congress Control Number: 2012921991

Printed in the United States of America

iUniverse rev. date: 11/27/2012

Part 1

The Row
Savannah, Georgia

1925
"She pressed her feet on the cold damp floor,
and crushed her hands on her heart
Or stood like a statue so still and pale,
lest a tear or a cry should start"

"Rosalie"
Caroline Gilman

Nicie walked along side the weather-beaten picket fence, leading into the Savannah, Georgia slum houses called *The Row*. The stick in her hand sang a song as she walked in its rhythm, striking each board. She had thought about walking on the other side of the road to break her habit, but somehow, there was a certain amount of pleasure gained as she left marks on the fence, stripping and defacing the paint. The large flakes lay at her feet; a signature of her anger. Today, especially, she walked even faster and more furiously, as she left her marks behind. "Who am I?" she wondered. "Why won't somebody tell me?" she murmured under her breath. Again today, five-year-old Nicie had become irate.

Her morning had begun promptly at 6:00 a.m. As usual, she ate a cold biscuit left from last night's supper. This was not a problem for Nicie; she had learned to look forward to her one cold, hard biscuit each morning. She would pinch off a bite and place it in the roof of her mouth where she sucked on it until it dissolved, making sure each piece dissolve before taking the next, storing any uneaten pieces in the pocket of her apron. Granma Goolsby had made her little apron, and had trimmed the heart-shaped pocket with red rickrack that had been taken from the one she had worn out two years ago.

Leaving the house this morning before anyone awoke was not unusual. Even after they awoke, the only thing missing, as far as they were concerned, was the one biscuit. This was not because the people she lived with were stingy; it was because the Depression of the country was in the beginning stages; *The Row*, however, had been in a depression for years. Each family was careful to account for each commodity, using sparingly, "making ends meet," Granma Goolsby called it.

Nicie spit-bathed her eyes as she headed into the eastern direction of *The Row*. Soon she could see Granma Goolsby's cabin jutting out, almost in the road, which had been part of an old buggy trail. Its weather-worn ginger bread front was covered by a rusty tin top, and was in dire need of repair. Stretching into the edge of the cotton patch stood a chicken pen, filled with Rhode Island Reds, Dominiques, and a sprinkle of Game chickens. Granma's chickens furnished most of the eggs for her and Charles Goolsby, usually there were plenty left to sell.

Nicie walked on, tossing the stick into a low hanging branch; smoothing her creased apron with a fluff and a pat as thoughts of discontentment ran through her head. It didn't matter that the bed she had slept in for the last three years was a ragged patchwork quilt that lay in the corner of the kitchen behind the stove. Granma Goolsby had once told her as she spread the pallet on the rough wooden floor, "Nice Chile, you can look at each quilt block. There is a story in each one...a life someone had many years ago when things were hard. My own Granma lived on a dirt floor and raised eight children. I say raised, but some of them didn't quite make it; never had a doctor, that poor soul. Well, she did raise six of them to be grown; two died afore they wuz three and God only knows how many she lost and wuz stillborn. She usta hold quilting parties, making bedding with goose feathers; she even sent my own mama a set of her pillows, and Chile, this here is the quilt, made with her bare hands."

Nicie smiled as Granma's house came into view. She was quite taken with this little old woman with her corn-cob pipe and old fashioned ways; she never knew how she had come to call her Granma. She only knew when Granma looked at her, her eyes would close in joy and a hint of a smile would appear on her small wrinkled lips.

Nicie walked aimlessly; she came to the railroad track crossing into a part of town she had never been and her young heart longed to go...just to see...to pretend to be somebody. After hearing Tollie Crane and Millie Martin's conversation this morning, she felt her heart would fail her now as it beat so fast and long.

Nicie had not meant to be in a place she was not invited, but that was before Wimpy, her puppy, refused to go back home. She discovered too late that he had followed her on her mission to gather poke salat weeds for dinner. Poke salat grew around the mule lot next to the railroad tracks in Booger Hill and Tollie Crane, her best friend, lived on top of the red clay hill nearby. Her house stood tall on brick stilts at the edge of the main road leading into downtown Savannah where Mr. Crane owned a dry goods and mercantile company. Mrs. Crane had been a dancer in New York City; Millie Martin told this story in a whisper once when Tollie didn't come out to play.

Nicie loved it when there were only the two of them together. At times, they would walk down into the freshly plowed fields and pick up broken pieces of glass. Excitedly, they would wash the pieces, turning each piece over with the front down, and would take turns guessing the colors, flowers and designs; the winner would get a handclap and hug. These were very precious moments for Nicie and sometimes her joy would become so great she could hardly contain it. She felt as though she would burst with excitement as the angels sang, "Nice Chile, Nice Chile," on and on.

"Here Wimpy, here…come to me…bad boy; don't you go and get me into trouble again" Nicie called! Wimpy had his nose to the ground, sniffing, tracking and running unabandoned. "You'd think you are deaf, dog! You don't hear a word I say!" Nicie spoke angrily. Wimpy whimpered, stopped and sniffed harder with his tail wagged ninety miles an hour. Outside Tollie Crane's house, Wimpy had chased her cat up the tree but the commotion did not draw anyone from the house. Nicie stood outside looking up, and then walked to the backyard. It seemed like a long way to the top of the back porch and she had never been invited inside Tollie's house. She could not see the people inside, but she could hear their conversation. Mrs. Crane said, "There is no way we can tell her the truth. Poor little Nicie can't help it, no need to go and break her heart." A cold, long shiver ran straight up Nicie's spine, her legs became weak as she felt the blood drained from her face; she felt faint. Surely it was some other Nicie they were talking about; she thought as she regained her strength and left the yard.

She forgot Wimpy and she would forget Nicie, too. "Today", she thought, "I won't let anything bother me." Starting up the path she could see the white picket fence come into view. "Home, where is home? Who am I? I am me" she lipped under her breath. "Just me, that's all." A flicker of Granma Goolsby flashed through her head, "Nice Chile, Nice Chile" she called her.

The next morning Nicie arose even earlier and wiped the sleep from her eyes as she folded the pallet and placed it neatly in her corner behind the stove. She caught a glimpse of herself in the big aluminum kettle on top of the stove. The five year old stared back at her with large, green eyes, circled with black. She licked her fingers, pushing her long bangs forward, and was reminded to ask Millie if she would loan her the scissors from her paper doll box.

Today Nicie would count to twenty-five, and September she would start to school. She could print her name, Nicie, but at the time, she left out the last "I." She loved it when her Granma Goolsby called her Nice Chile. Many times she could hear the angels singing, "Nice Chile, Nice Chile" over and over as a cloak of warmth would envelop her small, undernourished body as the words penetrated her soul.

Wimpy had returned home by himself and was fast asleep on the back doorstep. Nicie reached over for the left-over hardened breakfast, closed the screened door behind her and sat on the back stoop. Wimpy accepted the generous pinch she offered; for his rib cage was indelibly imprinted in her mind. She dared not take another biscuit this morning so she would pick a pear, hanging from the neighbor's tree across the picket fence, and maybe, just maybe, if she went to Granma Goolsby's she would have a little bit of cornbread and a bowl of soup. Granma always made soup from the left-over's of the last few days she had stored in an old tin covered ice box on the back porch. Every three or four days the iceman would come by and leave ten cents worth of ice; left-over ice from the tea glasses was rinsed and used to cool the well water that was stored in the cedar bucket located on the back porch shelf.

Nicie and Wimpy finished the biscuit as Uncle Coot called out, "Good morning, did you have something to eat this morning?" He looked around the kitchen and said, "Well, no, it looks like we won't be having breakfast this morning," he corrected. He reached into the cupboard made of stacked apple crates and retrieved a mason jar. He took out a small piece of beef jerky and said "Here, chew on this; it'll tide you over until dinner". His back was turned from Nicie, and she was grateful that her eyes did not meet his embarrassment. At least he'd thought of her. "Thank you, sir", she said as she walked out of the kitchen.

Wimpy was waiting for her, giving a direct look, he wagged his tail, and lifted his paw. Nicie sat on the stoop, stripping the jerky with her teeth. Suddenly, Uncle Coot peered out over her shoulder, catching her off guard, "We don't have nothing for that dog" and closed the door behind him. In the new sunlight of the morning, Nicie darted onto the cracked concrete sidewalk. Taking her stick from the tree, she jutted it out hitting the picket fence with a force she thought would awaken Auntie Mazie. Suddenly, she threw the stick beside the path as she headed to Granma's house.

The chicken coop sat in Granma Goolsby's backyard and the baby chicks she had ordered from Sears and Roebuck back in the spring had now grown into fryers. Today, not only would there be chicken soup but a piece of fried chicken as well. Nicie could almost replace the salt beef flavored jerky with warm, crunchy, succulent fried chicken from Granma's cast iron frying pan.

She could hear Granma's voice, "That you, Nice Chile?" "Yes ma'am, Granma, it's me and Wimpy", she replied happily, nothing in the world was big enough to steal this moment! It was as if all the angels in heaven had gathered together to pour all the love in the world into this one, sad little heart so Nicie began to hum.

"It that music I hear?" Granma asked.

"No ma'am", Nicie answered shyly.

"Well, it musta been the angels singing. It sorta sounds like their kinda music", Granma replied, as she rung the chicken's neck. Nicie thought her act to be a little extreme but never looked directly at the crime so she said nothing. The moments seemed like hours as she sat and watched Granma sink the headless chicken into a large pail of scalding water, dunking it over and over again.

"Get over here Chile. Pick up some of these feathers, and mind you, don't waste 'em. I have pillows to make this year", Granma demanded. Timidly, Nicie did as she was told, when suddenly; wave after wave of nausea hit her and the last thing she remembered was seeing the large spurts of blood, shooting past her as Granma disemboweled today's fried chicken.

The shock of the bright light from the sun made Nicie blink as she was coming around and, Granma was busily blowing in her face and slapping her hands. Eventually, sitting up, Nicie could see the spatters of blood, like small red freckles covering her hands and arms and, the world began to turn rapidly spinning her out of it, once again.

"Dinner's ready", Granma called from the kitchen. Nicie did not remember being in the house nor how she'd gotten there. Her arms and hands were clean and covered with rolled up sleeves of Granma's nightgown. Granma had made her plate with the wishbone, Nicie's favorite piece, before the chicken killing. The food she had craved and loved now became an object of offense and revulsion; her stomach growled. Pain shot through her abdomen like a blow torch and, she began to heave, to gag and to wretch.

Granma put her in her soft goose-down bed; eventually, sleep enveloped this battle-torn, undernourished, Nice Chile. She slept until the next morning while in her dreams the angels sang, "Nice Chile, Nice Chile".

She awakened long before daylight and felt her way out of the cabin onto the dusty road toward home. Late three times in a row! Nicie's feet tapped softly on the soft dirt road; today, surely she would not get by with excuses.

The sun was not up yet as she slipped into the kitchen through the back door, unfolded her pallet and, lay guilty on the floor. A glance at the closed bedroom door of Uncle Coot and Auntie Mazie's room, assured her they were still asleep. She had never become accustomed to Auntie Mazie's harshness and whining voice and today was not a good time to start.

She must have drifted off to sleep as loud voices awakened her senses. "It's not my fault!" Auntie Mazie shouted. "I never wanted that child. Maybe that's why God didn't give me one of my own!" Uncle Coot's voice was cool and calm, "Shhh, she'll hear you. You don't have to do nothing for her. She stays with Mama most of the time, anyway. She don't ask for nothing so the least you could do is to be kind to her." The same fight continued day after day.

Nicie pretended not to hear as she folded her pallet and left the house without her biscuit; her appetite was gone now. She walked without direction, stopping to pick blackberries here and there. The tendrils flowed gently about her face as she bended over for she had forgotten to comb her hair.

It was Sunday and the church bells across the tracks had begun to chime a familiar tune. She began to sing, keeping the beat of the bells; *"I am me; I am me, just me, Nice Chile."* What a beautiful melody filling the air and, in every bush and tree the birds sang her song in unison.

Walking down the railroad tracks she made a shortcut to the big brick church; "Oh how beautiful and how awesome! God sure has a wonderful home to live in", she thought from her small hiding place in a heavy growth of shrubbery across the road. She watched intently as the fathers and mothers held the hands of their children, as they walked slowly and reverently into the church. For the first time, she had the courage to walk this far across the tracks and to hear the words to the music of the bells, *"Amazing Grace how sweet the sound."* Her small bones cramped from crouching for the past hour, so Nicie got up and started her long walk home. She began to wonder, "Who could this Grace be? Is she the pretty lady who took her children by the hand, or was she the one that had been polishing the shoes of her small son? I sure wish I knew this amazing Grace. Well maybe I'll find her one day." Nicie walked swiftly towards Granma's house and began to sing, *"Grace for every need, Grace for every need."*

Nicie's foot had barely touched the first doorstep when Granma's voice rang out. "Where you been Chile? Sho ain't no use worrying 'bout you. Y'ant got no time frame, girl." Nicie's footsteps quickened, "No ma'am, I mean yes ma'am, I was just walking about."

"From the red clay on your feet, looks like you been across the tracks, clear up to Booger Hill, and then some", Granma said with disgust.

"Got things to do making soap, gotta kettle on now in the backyard, gotta stock up for winter", she complained as she dumped the lye into the pig lard.

"Gotta get you ready for school, now go look and see what I made for you. You need to wash up before you try it on 'cause you can't stay clean for nothin'. Would crawl right into a fresh, clean dress, as dirty as you are", she grumbled.

Minutes later Nicie sat for her late dinner of the wishbone left from yesterday, along with hot biscuits made especially for her. After two buttered biscuits and cold chicken she was full and ready to try on her new dress.

The voile dress, sheer and full-bodied with a dropped waistline, was banded with a skinny sash. Nicie's heart dropped; for this dress was nothing like the ones she'd seen today, as a small parade of girls were ushered into the church. Luckily a pin from the hem struck her bare flesh but, the drops of blood could never measure the drops of tears, falling from her eyes! Granma rushed quickly to care for the small puncture wound, patting her softly; she administered love to this small, wounded child but, was unaware of the true reason Nicie cried. Feeling sad, Nicie murmured, "Thank you, ma'am, its pretty."

Later that afternoon, as Granma made her soap, Nicie took a red crayon and busily drew the dresses she had seen today onto pasteboard grocery boxes Granma had stacked in the corner of the back porch. Under each drawing she printed Nice Chile, and wrote numbers one through twenty-five. On one of the boxes, in large print was "GRACE"; even a neon sign would not have been so obvious.

The coming Depression had already started in the poorest sections of the South. Today, as dusk settled along *The Row,* kerosene lamps were spared and most houses were dark. Tonight, there was no sleep for Nicie as her mind swung back and forth, playing like a repetitive record, throughout the night. She swayed between a long lost dream and the rather alarming vision of reality. Right now she did not have the energy to hurt anymore, for all she wanted was to be like other girls her age; her own bed and at least one dolly.

In the faint distance she heard Wimpy whimpering as the morning seemed to go on without her. Finally, as deep sleep blotted her thoughts, a dream came so revealing it played like a picture show. She was standing before a large congregation wearing a white taffeta dress. The dress was much the same as she'd seen on the movie screen, being worn by Gretchen Young. She pirouetted as the light caught the glistening fabric as it flowed and swayed to the music. She danced and danced, holding onto the hand of her father. As they danced, he smiled down at her, but suddenly, the dream changed; the father's hand, which had held her, gently pulled away. Nicie began to cry out, "Daddy, Daddy, come back! I never got to see your face! Please come back! I was so caught up in the moment; I forgot to tell you I love you. Don't go!" Nicie was awakened by her own cries, "Help me! Help me!"

Her head hurt and she needed fresh air. Crawling from behind the stove she pushed the quilt into the corner as she tried to stand and wondered why Uncle Coot had not come to check on her. A large dose of reality was about to show its ugly head. Auntie Mazie, standing in the doorway of the bedroom, began screaming, "What are you doing you ungrateful child? You sound like a dog caught in a trap; yelping, yelping, yelping." Standing there she yawned, scratched where it itched, and lit a cigarette.

"Go on, get out of my sight. No biscuits for you this morning." Nicie stuttered, "I-I-I'm sorry, it was about a dream, I'm sorry."

Opening the door as quickly as possible she stepped into the sunshine. Squenching her eyes, she unconsciously placed her hand across her forehead, like a sun visor, and walked toward the picket fence.

The June morning was dark and *The Row* was quiet as the barefoot girl walked alone toward Granma's house. Granma was waiting in the big front porch rocker; "What's wrong with you, look bad you do? Come let me see you, girl." Taking Nicie onto her lap, she hugged her with great force and gently laughed. Nicie said nothing as Granma said; "Well there ain't nothing a hot buttered biscuit won't cure! Least-wise you're a bit shaky and I'm gonna put some pounds on them bones of yorn. I've got a surprise, I have, all for you so come and see. Can't wait to look at you, but mind you, finish the biscuit and wipe yo hands good", she demanded.

Still suffering from the nightmare, Nicie did as she was told. She could not smile; her heart was not into it. Wiping her hands on the feed-sack towel, she left half of the biscuit and followed Granma into the bedroom. Lying as if they had just been taken from a Sears Roebuck catalog package, were three dresses. They were just like the ones she had drawn on the cardboard boxes!

"Missy Mock, my ole friend, made these for you. I don't seem to be able to cut patterns for little people, 'cause my eyes ain't no more good for sewing. I saved my egg money to surprise you so, this is your birthday and Christmas present, all in one. Now just look Chile, all you please." A stone cold look of disbelief crossed Nicie's face as she stepped closer to the bed.

She held her hands out, moving them up and down as a magician would wave his magic wand. Looking in disbelief, she gently placed both hands on the dresses, patting them softly one by one. Scalding tears fell, running freely like the creek that she, Tollie and Millie had played in last week.

"Lordy Chile, I never did see a young'un like you afore. Don't understand, I don't...no sir...I just don't understand. Cry will ye? Hope them's happy tears. Yes siree, you is some sweet Chile", Granma chuckled. Nicie buried her face in Granma's flour-sack apron; there was no call for words, even her angels had no words for this occasion. Nicie was eager to start school, which was only three weeks away. Spring had left swiftly and fall was pressing onward.

Lena Goolsby had just sat down to a cup of coffee when Missy Mock came to call. "Sit down, Missy and let me draw you a big cup of coffee." A chill was in the air and Missy shivered as she sat at the small table as Lena blurted out; "The mailman got my message to you, I see. Now what I'm about to tell ye, nobody can know. Seeing as how I trust you 'more'n anybody alive; I have a bone to pick with you. My rheumatism has already kicked in, my eyes ain't no more good, my heart is skipping beats, and no doctor within sixty miles can help me. I ain't skeered for myself a'tall. Its little Nicie Chile, all the way, I'm a talking 'bout. I went an ordered her a warm coat fer winter 'cause she ain't never had one afore. You know I got a nice heavy pair of shoes, too; all for four dollars and ninety-nine cents. I knowed it would be high, but Nicie's worth it, I don't know what I ever did afore she come here. Lord how I ramble on like you got all the time in the world to listen to this old woman's problems."

Lena placed a mug of steaming coffee in front of Missy; her hand trembled causing the hot liquid to spill onto the table. Missy said nothing, but her eyes and ears were affixed on her frail friend as she sat drinking her coffee, sipping often; her ears were tuned to the sweet conversation. She 'crossed her heart and hoped to die' if she told anyone of this morning's events. The two friends, of almost seventy-two years, whispered as they sipped the entire pot of coffee. Once in a while they would stop to be excused; the outhouse was cold as they both sat on the two-throned seats and evacuated the coffee, wiping themselves with last spring's Sears and Roebuck catalog. Missy said, "Look Lena, I always did wanna wipe my fanny on a handsome man; today I finally did." Both laughed a deep belly laugh.

They had stayed connected all these years and could not imagine life without each other. Missy walked slowly, exiting through the front door, heading home. Their relationship had never needed explanation for they had always been on the same page. Lena was tired now; she had emptied her emotions and secrets, leaving out nothing. At last she could sleep; how she had longed to bare her soul to Missy, now as she sat in the overstuffed chair she felt tired, very tired…

Lena slept, and dreamed of two little girls, a plantation, a rapist and a funeral.

PART 2

Lena's Dream
Savannah, Georgia

September 1857

"From the fair and fairly sisters
They were born without a sigh
For one remembered evening
To blossom and to die"

"White Roses"
Sarah Louisa P. Smith

The late summer was hot, giving promise to a cold winter. Lena Mae May's pigtails were flying in the wind; her new slate board and chalk were belted and thrown across her shoulder. She went down the narrow dirt street at break-neck speed toward her best friend, Missy Mock's, log cabin. Missy was waiting for her on the front stoop; she sat quietly letting her fingers trail through her corn rows. Her mother, Oprah, had lovingly braided her hair, reassuring her that she would be in good hands today. "You go Poo", she had said.

Both girls met in the street, laughing, giggling and spinning around as their soft aprons and dresses followed the flow of speed. This important day had finally arrived and they would walk hand in hand to school, at last. The school house appeared in the distance as the bell on a pole in the churchyard began to ring. A tall red-faced boy held fast to the rope as he was drawn straight up into the air with each peal of the bell. Children came from all directions and began to line up underneath the drapery of the moss covered oak tree. The students, their clean, coarse apparel smelling of new materials and lye soap, began to assemble at the front door of the Southern Faith Church. The smaller children were seated on the front benches of the church; its dirt floor was covered with straw to keep the dust from rising. Mr. Pinkton, the principal and teacher for the sixth through the eighth grade, welcomed the students. Prayer was offered for a safe school year before the students were sent to their proper classrooms.

Lena and Missy held tightly to each other as they settled into the same desk. Lena unstrapped her slate from the Revolutionary War belt that was once worn by Great Granddaddy Walter Grant. A tap from the teacher's desk brought the class to attention by Miss Ramsey who taught grades first through fifth. Hurriedly, she started interviews with her students, beginning with the first grade. Working her way down the aisle, she came to Missy; "My name is Missy Mock", she exclaimed as she stood by her desk. "I am six years old and I live with my mother and daddy."

Mr. Pinkton knocked on the door and Miss Ramsey stepped outside the classroom a moment to speak with him. When she returned, she announced; "Missy Mock, you are wanted in the Principal's office, will you come with me, please?" Missy broke her hand free from Lena Mae's and followed her teacher without a backwards glance. Shortly, Miss Ramsey returned to class, "Let's carry on children!" she instructed. "Next; what is your name?" Lena Mae stood and stated, "My name is Lena Mae May." "Where do you live?" asked the teacher. "I live with Mama and Poppie in Georgia", her small voice cracked. "I was six years old when I had my birthday", she said proudly. The teacher heaved a sigh of discontentment as she looked over her wire rimmed glasses at the blond child with pigtails. She then settled in her chair shaking her head realizing she was in Dixie, and names must carry on the southern tradition.

Suddenly, she excused herself and left the room, as a small shrill cry, a familiar voice to Lena, came from some area of the school. The yard soon filled with students who were trying to catch one small six-year old with beautiful corn row plaits. Missy couldn't stop running nor could she stop her loud and mournful wails; there were no tears.

Lena could never purge the pain of rejection and abandonment contained in her soul. She did not ask to be excused from the classroom, as she speedily raced behind her best friend. Ordinarily, Lena could outrun her, but not today. Missy ran so fast she passed her house then turned sharply tracing her steps back to the porch. Mama Oprah had heard her cries and had come to her, holding her baby girl in her arms, kissing and hugging the wretched soul as tears poured onto the large globe pillows of Oprah's bosom. "Hush, baby, hush; Yo mama's here, everything's gonna be alright".

Oprah rocked Missy gently, singing as she rocked;

"Hush 'lil baby, don't say a word, mama's gonna buy you a mocking bird. If that mocking bird don't sing, mama's gonna buy you a diamond ring..."

Missy, in the comfort of her mother's arms, snubbed herself to sleep. Lena sat completely still as she stared at her friend, "Missy never harmed anyone", she whispered. "If they don't want you in school, then I won't go either", she declared as she gave Missy a warm hug and left.

As she walked home, Lena had become irrational; she was unable to comprehend the present situation. "Big people just don't make no sense", she spoke angrily. "God, where are you? Help us!" she cried.

A called meeting was conducted at 8:00 p.m. and as the speaker took the platform, he looked out over the board members and began to recite. "The church, led by John Wesley, spoke against slavery at the Missions of the South Carolina Conference in 1832. The message was this: As a general rule for our circuits and stations, we find it best to include colored people in the same pastoral charge with the whites, and to preach to both classes in one congregation, as our practice has been. We are created equal.

The gospel is the same to all men, to enjoy its privileges in common and promotes goodwill." The Reverend C.B. Mock looked at his audience and cleared his voice as he went on. "Now, I don't know how this affects the school, but peers to me the church owns the school. So, do we believe what the word of God says? Do we go by our conference rules, or will we allow an infidel teacher to take over our church?"

When Charlie Bob Mock was exasperated, he was not a man to be reckoned with. He had come from a long line of Negro ministers appointed to the Plantation Missions. At one point he bellowed, "Look, Board Members, is my granddaughter a Negro? Yes, she is!" His gasping breath barely caught up with his blood pressure. "Is Missy Mock a human being?" he asked. "Yes, she is!" the crowd retorted. "Case closed!" the reverend offered. "Brethren, vote your conscience. May God have mercy on your soul."

By 8:30 p.m., Mr. Pinkton had cleaned his desk and cleared out. One of the board members gave him a buggy ride out of town. "Better leave for safety's sake", some said. "Better go now before the word gets out."

Later, Charlie Bob Mock sat at the supper table in his son Adam's seat. It was not unusual for a minister to take over as head of the table; his son and daughter-in-law, Oprah, had prepared a feast.

Reverend Mock loved his family and he captured their attention tonight as he told stories of the past; about how his forefathers had been banned from Charles Towne many years ago. They were sent into the wilderness island of Hilton Head and Grandpa Benjamin Mock had told him stories of his own father's banishment, and horror stories of starting his ministry. He had aligned himself with an Indian slave, whose ancestors had been captured by John Rolfe, husband of Pocahontas and, many preachers were maimed and killed for sharing Christianity with Indians and black slaves.

Reverend Charlie Bob explained, "My Grandpa, Ben, told of a white minister who had been dragged and dunked in a creek until he almost drowned, but it didn't stop him, for there was fire was in his bones. Old Reverend Sane carried the Bible by night into the deep woods and swamps, where he preached to Negroes and Indians using lighted torches. Sometimes he read by the light of the moon; the same full moon helped them get home. Back then the church found it increasingly difficult to enforce its anti-slavery laws and regulations. It became difficult for a slave owner to free their slaves, even if they wanted to because some unscrupulous slave trader would snatch them up and resell them into worse conditions. You know when you preach Jesus and people take Him as their personal savior, they are free! No man on earth can enslave a soul!"

Reverend Charlie Bob dipped a large helping of peas onto his plate, and ate hurriedly as he prepared to continue with his story. Oprah understood Dah; she filled his iceless tea glass to the rim and added another corn pone to his plate and he belched when he finally became full. Missy had fallen asleep at the table, with her legs locked around the bench; Oprah removed her half-finished plate. She had covered the scraps and left-over's with a muslin wrap, and placed them on a shelf in the coolest area of the kitchen. Adam picked Missy up from the table and laid her in her straw-ticking bed. Taking a wet piece of worn out shirt he bathed her gently, then covered her with a light wrap as he rejoined his Dah and Oprah.

"Funerals were a hard thing", Dah continued. "No matter how I try to give it up, I keep my rabbit foot and blade with me all the time; can't never know when I might need them. Yes, these were some hard times. I remember hearing about hard times…night funerals were prevalent back then. I heard that Reverend Berg, a white minister, once performed a burial rite over a humble slave one night. He left home about sunset on this calm and pleasant evening. He traveled about four or five miles until he arrived, after dark, at the plantation. Outside the house, near the entrance and accompanied by the widow, lay the corpse, in a homemade pine box. Reverend Berg came down from his horse and greeted the grief-stricken woman. He told her to trust in God – 'the husband of widows and father to the fatherless.' He addressed the fellow servants on the uncertainty of life and the necessity of making preparation for death. His message was concerning Jesus, his death and resurrection. By the glimmering of the lightwood fires the burial service took place. Reverend Berg's horse became accustomed to the night burials and took him straight home in the dark." Dah yawned loudly and stated, "If I don't get up and get outta here, my horse won't find his way home."

Outside the door, Adam and Oprah hugged him goodbye. He closed his eyes and placed a hand on each of their heads, blessing them. "Amen", he said. "Take care to get Missy to school tomorrow. Oprah, you may want to walk with her."

As he mounted Oprah said, "He sits tall in that old worn out saddle." Reverend Mock gave a soldiers' salute as he rode through the rows of houses. The horse's hooves kept time to the song he started humming.

Adam placed an arm around Oprah. Together, they walked inside. He bent over the table and blew out the candles, exhaling a sigh of relief. He smiled down at his wife, squeezing her hand warmly. Tomorrow would come in a few hours and he would be back on the loading docks, but tonight he had his warm woman to comfort him.

PART 3

School Starts
Savannah, Georgia

"The Row"
1926

"Mingled drops of smiles and tears
Human hopes and human fears
Joy and sorrow, love and woe
Which the future heart must know"

"Ministering Spirits"
Elizabeth Oakes

A ugust would soon end and playtime would cease, but not today. Today Nicie, Tollie and Millie would play once more.

"Peas' porridge hot, peas' porridge cold, peas' porridge in the pot nine days old; some like them hot, some like them cold, some like them in the pot, nine day old."

The girls clapped their hands speedily in rhythm of the rhyme. Of all their games, Nicie enjoyed London Bridge best of all, Tollie and Millie knew what Nicie's choice would be, and her selection was always the same.

"London Bridge is falling down, falling down, falling down. London Bridge is falling down, on my fair lady. Take the keys and lock her up, lock her up, lock her up. Take the keys and lock her up, on my fair lady."

Nicie never told them she really didn't like the words. She didn't understand them. What she understood was the arms hugging her with joy and laughter was warm and true. After the games were over Tollie Crane invited Millie and Nicie to her birthday party next week. She was the youngest of the three; Millie's birthday was in February, Nicie's in June and Tollie's in August. She would barely turn six in time to start school in September.

The special day had come. Carriages and wagons loaded with children, rattled down the row. Tollie Crane's party was only minutes away. Nicie wore one of her new dresses and shoes; a piece of grosgrain ribbon was tied neatly to the ends of her blond pigtails. Her bangs hang low, creating a jagged curtain, barely about her eyes and she looked like a Shetland sheep dog she had once seen in Auntie Mazie's magazine. Checking her hair, she stared back from the aluminum kettle and it did not lie, it had never lied. Oh! How she wished it would just for today. She was careful to bathe every inch of her body; "A clean dress needs a clean body." Grandma told her.

Planning to go by Granma's house on her way to Tollie's was not an option, thanks to Wimpy. She had started out of the row of houses and close at her heels, Wimpy followed. She scolded him, sending him back home, until finally, he sat in the middle of the road until she was out of sight. The party was about to begin, so she would have to see Granma tomorrow.

The big white house rang with laughter; Nicie could hear it two blocks away and she began to trot toward the music. The adults were sitting on the front veranda; wicker furniture held a dozen people with party hats. Tollie's mother, Crelan, greeted her warmly as she walked up the long flight of steps.

"Nicie you look so pretty! She exclaimed. "Where in the world did you get that lovely dress?"

"Granma Goolsby got it for me." She declared proudly. Millie came across the room as Nicie entered the door. Voices rang in unison "Nicie, Nicie" but, she had not heard some of the greeters. Her eyes were captured by the portrait above the mantel. The beautiful woman looking down from the ornate gilt frame, stared straight into her eyes and soul. Her golden hair parted in the middle and fell in waves, framing her ivory smooth face, her mouth appeared as a soft rosebud, giving her the air of a china doll. Nicie was awestruck! Tollie stood beside her taking hold of her hand, declaring, "She has green eyes like yours, just like yours. She is my Aunt Grace."

"The present, oh Tollie, I'm sorry, I forgot!" Nicie was embarrassed. Tollie hugged her saying, "I'll get it later." She had placed two of her own ribbons in the shoebox her new shoes had come in. She'd colored the box with her new Crayola crayons. "It is Wimpy's fault." She mumbled.

Later in the afternoon the birthday cake was served and Tollie was the happiest girl in the world. She would attend first grade with both her best friends; no birthday present could be better. Crelon Crane hugged Nicie close with a little more than a casual hug. "Thank you for coming, I am proud of you. I am proud Tollie has you for a friend. You may come anytime you please. We have lots of room." Nicie left the veranda, walked down the brick steps, woven in a basket weave; they were placed in a semi-circle, curling around much of the porch. Flower pots were filled with ferns and the petunias were in bloom, as were the marigolds. "What a beautiful home! What a wonderful party." Nicie thought as she looked back. She must get home, Wimpy would be waiting for her and she had saved him a tea cake.

As she entered the backdoor of the house angry words filled her ears. Auntie Mazie was dressed to go out; Uncle Coot was not yet home from work and Mazie was pacing the floor. "That man", she said. "I'm tired of him." Minutes later Uncle Coot walked in and set his lunch pail down. "Sorry Mazie, I couldn't get off early. I tried to arrange to work overtime tomorrow, but…

"But nothing!" Mazie screamed furiously. "You can stay here with your brat, I'm leaving!" She pulled the cardboard suitcase out from under the bed, packed her belongings, and with one fell swoop from the dresser, gathered her perfumes, leaving with a slam of the door. Uncle Coot was pale and turning his back to Nicie, he said, "Maybe it is for the best. She doesn't belong here. She has always wanted to go back north to her family." He turned to face Nicie. "I'm sorry you had to hear all of this. Let's go get some supper. He said, holding out his hand, "Why don't we go to Mama's, I bet she has butter milk biscuits." They agreed. This would give Nicie the opportunity to show off her new dress to Granma. She wanted to tell her about the portrait of Amazing Grace but would do this later, this was a sacred thing. She was not ready to share that moment with anyone. Given time to digest the awesomeness of the moment could take weeks, months or years.

The sun was still high as Nicie and Uncle Coot returned home from Granma Goolsby's. Nicie noticed a disquieting, depressed mood had settled through the entire house. Uncle Coot became mute at Granma's and did not offer any information when asked by Granma if he were sick. "I'm just tired" he said. Now, he had retreated to his bedroom; his affect was low and without looking back, he whispered, "goodnight". Nicie had never seen him like this before; he was always sparkling and positive and his demeanor had dictated elegance and pride. Uncle Coot was tall, slim and markedly handsome; his smile evoked a memory of a rich, rare and old coin and his graying temples exuded dignity.

A feeling of urgency forced Nicie out of the house, for it had become a tomb of circumstances. She walked out of the yard, past the picket fence and she moved without plans or purpose, as Wimpy trotted along. They had long passed the railroad tracks and she could see the docks in the distance as she moved towards Bay Street. A small skiff was tethered to the wharf post and without rationale she and Wimpy stepped down into the small boat and began to row. Uncle Coot had brought her here several times, teaching her how to row and anchor the skiff. Somehow, she always thought him to be vague about Fig Island.

In the distance a small island appeared to move in her direction. She was empowered by emotions that she could not understand. "I have to get away. I make everyone unhappy. Uncle Coot will not want me anymore.

You are all I have left Wimpy." Wiping the tears from her eyes, she sat up straight and rowed harder.

Finally, she reached the island as the smell of bacon frying awakened her senses; they were not alone. Taking Wimpy in her arms, she walked quietly toward a small open fire. The frying pan and coffee pot were secured by the large sandstone rocks and a lone stranger sat hunched over the cooking supper.

Partially covered by a large woven blanket and black hat, pulled completely down over the face, the person gave no sign of seeing Nicie and Wimpy did not make a sound. He was comfortable in the arms of his mistress as she crouched behind a large sandstone hill while they watched the entire meal being cooked and eaten.

Later, the shadowed figure moved rapidly towards a sloop in the far corner of a mangrove swamp. Nicie and Wimpy left in a different direction, for it was almost dark and they must hurry home. A million questions bombarded Nicie's mind as she rowed toward the lights of the dock; finally placing the skiff where she had found it, tying it firmly to the post and throwing out its anchor.

She ran like the wind as she and Wimpy started toward home, the sand of Bay Street felt cold to her bare feet as Wimpy ran on a few feet ahead of her. The sunset on the water gave light to the damp street, as if the underworld was lit by millions of candles of every color; angels appeared and carried them coursing through the heavens. The trip had been awesome, but there was no time to bask in the beauty of nature. Uncle Coot would be worried and the very thought of anyone concerned enough to worry about her brought a smile to her face. One thing was for sure, the angels had sent her on a mission. She could hear their gay laughter as they moved through the colorful sky. "Nice Chile, Nice Chile" they sang to her as she declared their presence!

The house was dark as Nicie arrived home. Uncle Coot's door was closed to his bedroom, so she must not bathe tonight; it would create noise. Slipping onto her patchwork quilt, she felt clean and whole, as if she had been purified by both the water and fire she had witnessed. The secret of her mission was safe; she slept soundly.

Uncle Coot was preoccupied in a world Nicie dared not ask about and she was lonely. Instead of moping around she took the opportunity to steal away daily to Bay Street where she could see Fig Island from the wharf. There were no lights from the island to be seen, but on the fourth day she saw a small trail of smoke accumulating in the clouds. Luckily, she had slipped off from Wimpy, leaving him fast asleep on the doorsteps as she tiptoed out of the yard.

Nicie waited in the shadows of the docks until the whistle blew for the dock workers to change shifts. The small skiff was anchored just as she had left it, climbing in, she moved quickly, like a greased wheel and in moments, she was out of sight toward Fig Island. Her arms felt as if they could not row any longer, but curiosity and excitement filled her and boosted her energy and stamina. This zest gave her the speed she needed to continue on to her destination.

She approached the site of the sandstone stove; its fire was almost out, but a person squatting over the red coals, began to fan the embers into flames with a hat. Nicie was stunned as the long, honey-blond hair fell in ringlets onto the shoulders of a young girl. "A girl- it's a girl!" Nicie squealed loudly, which evoked a stare from the stranger; upon discovery, she turned to leave.

"Come back," a soft voice welcomed. "Who are you? Why have you come?" she asked.

Nicie pivoted on one foot moving forward in the girl's direction, she stood in front of the warm fire which felt good to her chilled body.

"I'm, I'm Nice Chile," she spoke. "I live in *The Row*," she offered.

"Come and have a bite to eat with me, Nice Chile. I'm Taryn August, I live in the city and I come here most every day. That is, while I'm home from boarding school in Atlanta. My dad brought me here when he was alive, he also taught me to sail, fish, swim and cook. Can you swim Nice Chile?" Taryn asked. Nicie shook her head as if to say, no.

"Uh, oh! What are you doing rowing a boat to a place you've never been? I can't believe you would be so careless and put yourself in grave danger. I will teach you to swim and show you the entire island and one day I will teach you to sail in my sloop. You must learn lots of things, Nice Chile; I want you to be safe," her voice softened. "I'm thirteen, I will help you, for you remind me of myself when I was your age; bold and fearless," she laughed. "They say it is not always good to have these characteristics," Taryn finished.

Nicie ate in silence as she thought of all the many things she wanted to tell someone. Things that Tollie and Millie could never understand, but Taryn August would understand. She knew in her heart she had met a kindred-in-spirit that would always stay connected to her with lots to talk about. Too soon it was time for Nicie to go home.

"Good-bye" Nicie said as she walked toward the skiff.

"Good-bye, Nice Chile" Taryn responded. "See you tomorrow and you will learn to swim then."

Nicie settled in the skiff and rowed toward the docks. "Good-bye is only a word. It really means "hello, friend," she thought. "Hello!" she called out as she rowed away, and the echo from the island called back, "hello… hello…hello". Nicie exhaled loudly.

Auntie Mazie had left two weeks ago; a big truck had been sent to pick up the belongings she had stored in the little shed-room off the front porch. Many areas of life were changing for Nicie; Uncle Coot was busy cleaning the little room and with the help of Granma Goolsby and Nicie, they would make a bedroom for Nicie. Uncle Coot had brought in a little wrought iron bed and a small curved vanity that he had made from scraps of lumber from the mill. . Summer was over, fall had blown in with a bang and excitement filled the air.

Granma sewed a pink floral overskirt and attached it around the sides of the vanity. Above the vanity was a large shard of broken mirror, surrounded by bent nails; a matching curtain draped the small south window. Auntie Mazie had left a small kerosene lamp in the corner of the bedroom, apparently an oversight, due to the pile of garbage left behind. Nicie washed the lamp with a small perfumed handkerchief she had recovered and painted pink roses on the base of the lamp with some pink nail polish she had found in the crack of the floor, now her room was complete and tomorrow she would start school.

"Today is the best day of my life!" Nicie squealed. Granma is so good to take her chicken feed sacks and make my room so pretty!"

Morning finally arrived and Nicie had not rested well. Whether her restless night was caused by the unfamiliar bed or the thoughts of starting to school, there was no way to tell. The small fragile girl had not closed her eyes the entire night. Just before dawn Nicie was ready and dressed for school. She would make a cheese sandwich and pack the lunch pail Uncle Coot bought downtown at Mizell's Five and Dime Store. He was able to buy sandwich bread and lunch meats now that Aunt Mazie's demands no longer kept him broke; what a relief!

At last, the first day of school arrived and Nicie walked rapidly past the picket fence on up to the brick-laden streets. The soft cool wind from the Bay stung her face. She had never been allowed to be here alone before. She had been there once with Tollie and Millie leading the way and had sat on the front of the schoolhouse steps, pretending to be students.

She stopped and waited for her friends to catch up and when they did, she quickly showed them the entrance papers that Uncle Coot had filled out for her. "Nicie Grace Goolsby, I have a name! I am somebody!" she squealed with delight; Tollie and Millie giving her a blank stare. In the distance she heard a motor car coming in their direction and as the vehicle slowed and stopped, she saw that Mr. Vincent Crane was its driver, offering them a ride to school. She was happy that Mr. Crane had invited her and her friends to ride along. On the way their giggles were filled with apprehension for this was a Hallmark day! The three had each other and nothing could spoil it.

Later that morning the classroom assignments were made. Fifteen first graders were assigned to Mrs. Mann's room which included Nicie and Tollie. As they heard their names called they reported to classroom A, where Mrs. Mann placed them in alphabetical order and in line. They marched in like baby ducklings following the mother duck, to their assigned seats. Nicie's and Tollie's eyes met across the room, but Millie was not with them; the trio had been separated, their pain and unspeakable sadness was conveyed at a glance. .

Mrs. Mann rang the bell on her desk; "Attention!" she stated forcefully. "I will call the roll and each of you will answer 'here' or 'present'." Nicie's heart cried out. "We're here, but Millie isn't." The teacher gave each student a chance to introduce themselves and when it was Nicie's turn, she said, "I am Nice Chile, I am six years old and I live with my Uncle Coot. He works at the lumber mill in Savannah, Georgia and I can write and do 'rithmetic" she continued. Mrs. Mann said "Let us see; you may show us your name, if you'd like." Nicie arose from her desk, with her heart beating so rapidly she thought the other students could see. She took the chalk from the tray and printed in large letters, NICIE GRACE GOOLSBY, in unsteady letters. "Thank you, Nicie. You may return to your desk." She wrote from one to twenty-five before leaving the chalkboard. "I can count, too" she said, smiling, as she watched the response of fourteen wiggling students.

Today had been the longest day of Nicie's life. There was no sense to be made of coloring pictures and playing with the ABC blocks the other students enjoyed so much. She was bored; "School, school..." she repeated over and again. "Where in the world did the word come from?" Nicie's anger was apparent, causing her heart to beat so fast she was about to explode. "I hate school," she spoke through gritted teeth!

She did not see Millie after school and it was as if she had disappeared from the face of the earth. Millie had not been waiting when the last bell rang to walk home with Tollie and herself. The silence between the two girls had been deafening and they only waved weakly at the crossroads, for goodbye was too final! They turned in different directions; each was left with the same thoughts. Nicie headed for the picket fence; surely there would not be any paint left on it today.

Uncle Coot came through the wooden gate at 5:15 pm and sat beside her on the front steps as he handed Nicie his lunch pail. "Well little school girl, how was your first day of school?" he pinched her cheek slightly. "Just fine, Uncle Coot," she said dryly. Nicie had not eaten breakfast or lunch and she was so hungry, her stomach had become bloated, so they walked to Granma's. Granma had made a large batch of salmon croquettes, so Uncle Coot filled his lunch pail with six or seven croquettes and his pint jar with syrup from Uncle Charlie's farm in Syrup City, Cairo, Georgia. The one good thing of the whole day was this delicious supper.

Many times since she had moved into her new room, Nicie missed the comfort of heat from the stove, for it had broken the chill in her bones. She would not let the thoughts of Millie occupy her own thoughts, so as a deviation, she lay on her stomach tracing the patchwork quilt with her fingers, until the sandman came; exhaustion had won. Tomorrow was another day at school without Millie.

Uncle Coot's gentle voice and light tapping woke Nicie from a deep sleep and she sprang from her bed in a flash. She dressed with haste, grabbed her lunch pail with yesterday's left-over sandwich and headed toward the crossroads, where Tollie was waiting, but there was no Millie or any talk of her.

Today, Mrs. Mann taught them songs and the repetitious rhythm reminded her of the day she hid in the shrubbery and watched the children at church. To her delight most of them were in her class, with the girls wearing the dresses she had once drawn on the cardboard boxes; much like the one she was wearing today. Tollie was excited too and both girls giggled, because it was a good day after all.

As the dinner bell rang, the students went out to the playground to eat lunch. Mrs. Mann had said "You may go when the bell rings for lunch. You have one hour to eat, play and visit. We will resume our studies at 12:30 pm." Tollie and Nicie sat alone eating slowly, until in the distance they heard a loud 'boo-hoo'. Millie cried out, "I want to be with my friends", so the two closed their pails and went over, sitting down close to Millie; this was food for the soul and things were looking up again.

After school the three walked home together, when suddenly, Nicie's voice rang out. "I have a secret; Uncle Coot says that I may have spend-the-night company on Friday night. I wish so much for you both to come, we will have so much fun and we can make syrup candy!" Millie and Tollie were almost as excited as Nicie.

"Yes, we will count and read our new books," Millie said. "But, I don't know how to read much and I have a different book than you."

"Why don't we learn to read both books?" Tollie injected. "Good idea" agreed the other two.

Finally, Friday came and the three would spend the weekend together. Tollie and Millie had never been invited to Nicie's home before, so they walked home from school with her. They loved her quaint bedroom on the front porch; but, as all beautiful situations have a cause, there is usually an adverse effect. Nicie did not have an indoor bathroom or a toilet that flushed with water, however, this was not a problem or the first time the girls had used an outhouse. Oh no, both Millie and Tollie's grandparents had outhouses!

Millie joked, "My grandpa called it "sitting on top of the moon", but changed the word by holding his tongue between his fingers and repeating, 'sitting'. "Shi-----," the girls emulated, laughing so loudly Uncle Coot had to shush them. He had to work Saturday and needed rest and had already helped the girls with the taffy pull, because the hot Cairo syrup had been too much for the six tender hands. He stayed with them and cleaned the kitchen while they ate and enjoyed the special evening.

Nicie went to Granma Goolsby's after school on Monday. As she walked up the front steps she called out excitedly, "Granma, Granma, I'm going to be a fairy in a play! I need a fairy dress and wing, wing, wings..." Breathlessly, she entered the house, but the exhilaration lasted no longer than it took to see Granma slumped over in her chair.

"Granma, please talk to me! Wake up Granma!" she said loudly. Granma did not move and her skin had turned blue. Nicie ran down the road, stopping by each house in the row. "Help, help, it's Granma Goolsby!" she cried. The street filled with neighbors, but Mrs. Bradley had the only telephone around and she lived at least a half mile away, so Nicie ran; she must save Granma. Finally, she reached the home of Mrs. Bradley and knocked on her door. Mrs. Bradley answered the door wearing her housecoat; this had been a daily practice after working all day. She listened to Nicie's story, then called Doctor Moore. Taking the frightened girl by the hand, they speedily walked the distance to Lena Goolsby's house. She observed the crowd standing in the street and said, "Go home everyone, matters are in control." Mrs. Bradley spoke emphatically and some of the crowd disbursed, while others stood in small groups waiting for the doctor.

Dr. Moore arrived an hour later; he and Nell Bradley lifted and carried Lena Goolsby into her bedroom. Mrs. Bradley came to sit with Nicie, holding her gently to her breast; she comforted and calmed the sad child. Nicie bogged her face into the lilac scented warm body of the strange woman; feeling that this woman had been born to hold her this day. Time seemed to pass slowly; an eternity lapsed or so it seemed, before the doctor beckoned Mrs. Bradley to enter. Nicie sat alone, biting her nails, with tears streaming down her face.

Quietly she sang, "Grace for every need, grace for every need."

As Uncle Coot entered the door, his breath was coming fast and his words came faster. "They called me. How is Mama?" his questions magnified the pain on his face. Dr. Moore pulled the curtain, separating the bedroom from the rest of the house, as Mrs. Bradley came to Nicie with outstretched arms. "Poor, poor darling!" she said, kissing the forehead of the tear stained face. Not looking up at Uncle Coot; Dr. Moore took the stethoscope from around his neck, folding it neatly into the leather bag. "She's gone; it was a stroke, but she didn't suffer, she went peacefully," he mumbled as he walked through the back door. The sound of the Model T motor hummed through the late Savannah sunset as he sped down the dirt road. His father had taken care of Lena's family years ago and he has been Carrie's doctor.

The crowd disbursed and sad hearts realized the oldest person in The Row was gone forever. There was one other, of course; her good friend, Missy Mock, but somehow Missy did not count to the white neighbors. Most of them had whispered their disagreements of their relationship for years.

Uncle Coot walked out from the bedroom; for a moment, there was a long, pregnant pause and then he howled. His bellow echoed through the thin walls much like the harrowing wail of a tortured animal. The front porches became aglow with lights as the houses were lighted up like the city of Savannah. Coot Goolsby tried to compose himself, but he could not forget the moment Dr. Moore pronounced her dead. Bands of sweat popped out of his forehead and trickled into his brow. The proper words of comfort never came to him as he wondered, "What will I do? Where will I begin?" Nell Bradley appeared to have read his thoughts and loosing Nicie from her embrace, she moved toward Coot.

She stood steadily, directly in front of him and speaking softly, she said, "I will call Barr's Funeral Home, for it appears to be the best in these parts. I suppose Miss Goolsby will be buried beside her father, Mate at Oaklawn Cemetery and it is well kept?" Her statement was a question, but Coot barely heard her kind words; he was taken by the house-coated woman who wore lilac toilet water. Oh, how he missed Mazie at this moment, he needed to hear a female voice speak words; just any words would do now. "What Mam" he asked? "Oh yes, please do, if you'd be so kind." Doctor Moore had sent the hearse for Lena Goolsby.

Later as Nell, Nicie and Coot walked toward their homes, they both held to Nicie's hand as they walked. Nicie had been comforted through the worst nightmare she had ever known. What would she do without Granma? Tears welled in her heart although they no longer showed in her eyes. She had cried out, but there were no more tears to cry. Opening the door to the shed-room, Coot and Nell put her to bed. Coot brought a wash-pan and soap just outside the room and bathed her hands and face then stepped outside the room. Nell finished the bath and pulled the ragged nightgown over the frail body with beautiful green eyes. Sitting on the edge of the bed, Nell said, "Goodnight, Nicie, I will come for you tomorrow", as she closed the door behind her.

Coot was waiting as Nell came down the steps; unconsciously, she extended her hand in the darkness and Coot took hold quickly. They walked without words, until finally, they were outside the gate. "I'll walk you home." Coot offered. "It is not safe for you to walk alone; it is the least I can do" he volunteered. Nell gave an affirmative nod and it was settled, as they walked side by side, not touching each other. On this brisk and clear night the stars were blinking in the heavens. They appeared to be winking their approval of the couple who had just witnessed sorrow and death, but there was magic in the air. The conversation was light and unplanned; the circumstances evoked a tenderness Coot had never known. Their conversation concerned everyday chit-chat as Coot told her of his latest promotion at the mill; she spoke of her job at the telephone company and the problems with installation delays. "It affects people in The Row at times like this" she whispered.

They reached Nell's house and as she opened the door, she said "Goodnight, Charles." He was ashamed and walked swiftly away, but he had stood in Nell Bradley's yard long after she had gone inside. Somehow he felt when Nell closed the door between them, that at that moment, he would like for her to have left it open, even if it were only a small crack.

Nell stepped inside the dark house and pulled the long light cord which hung suspended from the ceiling. The forty-watt bulb hardly lit the large hallway, but she quickly turned it out again, lest she be discovered peeking out the window at Charles Goolsby. Somehow he looked taller, more broad shouldered and leaner-hipped than the man who cried on her shoulder just hours before; he had the look of an athlete. She had seen him from a distance before, but never up close as there had never been an occasion to meet him.

David, her beloved husband, had passed away three years ago. She lived alone, throwing herself into her work and her job was her life. She had been promoted to Assistant Vice-President of the telephone company. At times her large Victorian home began to rattle and echo her lonely footsteps, so she had moved into the downstairs bedroom. There was a strange hollow noise just counting the steps to the top of the staircase that added to her discomfort.

She took off her housecoat and stood in her pajamas and a thirty-eight year old brunette stared back at her from the dresser. After brushing her hair briskly she began to calm down; tomorrow she would help others. This had always seemed to give her life purpose since David had died. Oh yes, she knew about funerals first hand!

She tossed and turned during the night, however, she no longer felt alone. Morning came in a couple of hours and Nell dressed quietly. She tucked her brown shantung blouse into her slacks, tossed her dark hair free and strode to the carport. She was always punctual; she backed her car out of the port and headed toward The Row. Charles and Nicie were ready and waiting on the front porch of the little log house. The three sat in the front seat as Nell turned the car around and headed toward Savannah. The Chevrolet sped down the road and a cloud of dust was left behind. There was no conversation, it was as if conversation was not needed, because the task at hand took precedence over all thoughts.

Nicie began to show exhaustion from lack of sleep. She had busily traced over the patchwork quilt as Granma had taught her to do at these times. "Granma is not dead. She couldn't be." Nicie had heard the Minister say "People never die if they are good. They only go to sleep." Granma had taught her to fend for herself, so she could cook, sew and patch her clothes, too; a little.

Nell turned the car down the magnolia lined street of Savannah, finally reaching the paved drive leading to Barr's Funeral Home. John Barr, III met them at the door, extending condolences and a hand to Charles Goolsby and Nell Bradley. Patting the head of Nicie, he gently pulled her pigtail, smiling broadly. Tears had filled John's eyes at the sight of her. "Your mother was a friend of mine. I want you to pick out a special casket; I owe her that much." He told Charles.

Nicie walked without direction throughout the funeral home. Her eyes scanned the tapestry and ornate gilded mirrors and she was awestruck. There had only been a few times in her life that she had been downtown. In her wildest dreams she could never have imagined such splendor. "I wish Granma could stay here forever. It is heaven; she told me about the beautiful gold and silver there, just like her casket" she mused. "Oh, my goodness, look at that!" Her eyes were glued to the horse-driven hearse enclosed in a glass case. Its beauty filled the middle of the yard and the memorial read: *In honor of John A. Barr, II.*

Suddenly she remembered a conversation between Missy Mock and Granma Goolsby. John had been a plantation owner and Granma Goolsby and her mother, Gale, had worked in the 'big house' as a nurse companion to Evangeline Tyne Barr, wife of John Barr, II. She's heard Mrs. Eva had fainting spells. It was told that the funeral home buried the poor who were unable to pay. Negroes and whites alike were treated with respect and once they had cremated an Oriental who came over on a slow ship. Nicie did not know what cremation meant but it must have been a dirty word since she had only heard it said in a whisper.

Having been lost in the beauty of her surroundings, her thoughts now focused on Miss Missy Mock; she had to see her! She had to be told of her grandma's death. Charles and Nell were almost at the car when they discovered Nicie at the old hearse. Charles walked slightly behind Nell; she was unaware of his eyes on her. Although she kept her skin clean and moist and walked straight and confident, Nell had never thought of herself as beautiful. David had once called her "a southern magnolia with nerves of steel and a heart of gold."

Charles Goolsby was totally aware of the tall, slim body with astonishing hair and today the sun reflected its beauty. There was something about her that was so very appealing. Maybe it was the way she took control of Mama's burial service. She had agreed with John Barr concerning the arrangements and picked out the best of everything. The burial plot was assured.

Afterward, Nell drove to the Whitehouse Restaurant, "It's time for lunch" she quipped. "We will eat enough to last us until breakfast; are you hungry?" She asked, bending over to catch Nicie's hand. She unconsciously took Charles' hand, as well, as they walked down the street to the café. Each ordered beef stew with carrots and potatoes, black-eyed peas, cornbread, banana pudding and iced tea. What a treat!

Charles was somewhat embarrassed by the overt gesture of Nell. He grinned shyly, hoping it could not be detected, thinking what a privilege it was to be with her. She was a wonderful woman. Taking a deep breath, he looked directly into her soft brown eyes that were fixed on him. The silence was deafening, but Nell broke the silence saying, "I'm glad you approved of the shroud. I thought it most appropriate; it was similar to my mother's. She passed away the year after my David and I miss them both; at times…." She was unable to finish her sentence. Thinking better of it, she decided not to allow her self-serving pain to occupy the pleasant lunch. Quickly she smiled, saying "Isn't this tender beef stew? It is one of my favorites."

Charles looked worriedly at Nell. He was surprised to see her vocalize her sorrow; unsure of what to say, his hand reached over to cover hers. He threw all caution to the wind for he must console her. He needed her more than he needed his honor. Her small hand was cold, unresponsive and he gave it a gentle squeeze then withdrew. Her eyes glistened as she looked up at him, a faint smile crossing her lips; she wanted more, much more. Nicie was so into her food she hardly noticed the developing relationship.

"Yes, the stew is great." Coot agreed. "Next time we can go to a picture show, if you'd like. I've wanted to take Nicie, but for one reason or another, I haven't done so." Charles offered as he took his last bite of banana pudding.

Nicie could hardly wait to get home and it was 3:30 pm when she alighted from the car. She had waited all day to go over to Missy Mock's. She turned to the couple sitting in the car and said, "I must go see Miss Missy; Granma would want me to." Uncle Coot snapped his fingers saying, "Thank you for helping me out. You go, baby girl and tell her the funeral is in the Methodist church at 3:00 pm tomorrow; give her my love." He opened the car door for her and Nicie ran. Surely Miss Missy was waiting for word concerning her best friend.

Missy Mock had heard the news last night and walked to Charles Goolsby's to offer condolences; she needed consolation as well, but she had found Charles's log cabin empty. Reaching up to the front porch, she had pushed a red cedar shingle into place that had fallen. After a dozen knocks at the door, she had realized Charles was probably taking care of Lena's funeral. Stepping from the porch, she gently patted the letter in her bosom. "It's just as well" she thought. "There is plenty of time to read Lena's last will and testament." She would give Nicie the letter Lena had written to her. "I think I'll wait until after the funeral. Nicie will have so much to think about today." Missy was relieved; all the particulars would be put off one more day. After all, the messages in Lena's will were life-changing.

Nicie walked fast as her legs would carry her. There would be tears and devastation for Granma's dear friend. She rounded the curve and saw Missy Mock out working in marigolds and zinnias; she was digging with all her might. The hoe, moving steadily, sang a song making one single sound.

"Miss Missy, it's me, it's me, Mame" she called out. Nicie ran with small arms open, a loud sob rose from deep within as Missy untied her dirty apron, took it from around her neck and shook the loose dirt onto the ground. She stooped and grabbed the grinning child. "It's gonna' be alright, nice chile. Yo' Granma saw to it." Nicie did not respond; she was preoccupied.

Missy placed her arm around her shoulders, beckoning her into the house. She noticed the pedal sewing machine was open and on the table was a bright red dress.

"This is yo' Christmas dress, Chile."

"Yo' Granma asked me to make it a month ago. It wouldn't be right to wear it tomorrow. No siree; just ain't right a'tall. Chile, I been knowin' Lena was sick. She done all she knowed. Jus' plain wore out, she was." Sadness filled Missy's voice.

Nicie looked at the dress; how she had longed for one as far back as she could remember. Now, she could wear it in the fairy play.

"Uncle Coot said to give you his love." She spoke shyly. "I…I … want to know something but I'm afraid to ask him."

"What is it? Maybe I can help you, Chile." Missy declared.

"How far is heaven? Can old people and little children go together there? Is my Mama and Daddy there?" she inquired. "Granma would never talk about my Mama. She always changed the subject. I'm big now; I can read some and can print, too. How big do I have to be before I'm allowed to know?" Nicie gazed straight into the dark brown eyes of her Granma's best friend. If anyone in the world would know these answers it would be Missy Mock.

These questions bombarded Missy and she was not prepared to address them today. She had no clue such important issues would come up, especially at this crucial time. She had put on a fresh apron and was ready to rock the grieving, curious child. How could she show compassion when all she felt was anger, betrayal and loss?

"My childhood friend is gone!" She wailed.

Both their mothers, Oprah and Gale, worked together on White Oak Plantation. They had been together since they were a few years old. She and Lena had always been together; in essence, she'd lost her only sister.

Nicie slipped from Missy's warm embrace. "Run along now, Chile. Coot will be worried about you." If the truth were known, Missy needed her space to reflect on the questions and how she would answer. She was tired and Nicie's never-ending questions had worn her down. Exhaustion swept over Missy as she lay across the bed and dreamed of her childhood. There was a plantation, her mother Oprah and her father Adam and a story of a rapist and a funeral.

PART 4

Savannah, Georgia

1938
"The night was dark and fearful
The blast swept wailing by;-
A watcher, pale and tearful
Looked forth with anxious eye."

"The Watcher"
Sarah J. Hale

The years would go back to another time and place. An old story had been handed down through generations by Lena Goolsby, Missy Mock, John Barr II and III.

Carrie Snow worked as a laundress from the age of 10. She was fourteen years old when she met Walter Grant II. He worked as a blacksmith and his work was much in demand by the plantations. The two had met at Lightwood Plantation; their views on slavery were similar. She was totally disenchanted with the violation of human rights, longing for the day she could leave it behind. Walter Grant was her ticket, so when he proposed marriage, she accepted. Through the years she had learned to love the gentleness and compassion of this thirty-five year old man. After two years of marriage she gave birth to Gale.

Gale decided to make her entrance into the world early during a windstorm, a gale from the Atlantic, when Carrie was eight months pregnant. On that morning she awoke to howling winds. Debris' flew through their mill house; unleashed doors and windows filled the yard. House tops sailed through the air. The screams of homeless people echoed through the streets as panic seized the city. Walter had been called to aid in the protection of the cotton mill, which had caught fire.

He was a man of conviction and honesty. Five years before he had become an abolitionist. His was a dangerous position as president of Friends against Slavery; the F.A.S. met weekly. Theirs was an organization who fed, clothed and helped to bring comfort to those who were oppressed. Walter became well known in Georgia. Slavery was in progress; however it had no written history before 1830. Many indentured servants and slaves filled the southern and some of the northern states. Their inability to speak English was problem number one; thought to be inferior, many were placed in manual labor positions. Their jobs were much in demand by the plantations, since King Cotton was Georgia's most precious commodity. Walter had worked on the plantations as a blacksmith, but the problems with slavery drove him to the cotton mills, so he had moved Carrie to the outskirts of the city.

Tonight fear clutched at the heart of Carrie Grant. She felt a tremendous pain in her lower back as the gale warnings were announced by the city police.

"What will I do if I am in labor? She murmured. "Walter may not get home tonight." Suddenly the pains grew closer together.

Carrie had delivered many babies alone and with the help of Dr. Steven Moore. They were the same age and he had hired her as his nurse. Dysentery, typhoid and malaria, along with yellow fever, were prevalent among the mill worker's families. Carrie was excellent in nursing these sick and destitute souls. Now, she needed a helping hand and there was no one available. Everybody was preoccupied just staying alive.

Getting up from the bed between labor pains she went to the trunk, took out a clean sheet and cut it into pieces. She was grateful the water bucket was full, the kettle filled. The stove had been stoked by Walter before he left. A sharp pain brought Carrie to her knees. As she crawled to her bed, a stream of bloody water gushed to the floor, as a gust of wind blew out the lamp.

"Oh! God! What will I do?" There was no time now for negative thoughts. She would be just as brave as the other women she had coerced while helping them deliver. Never in a million years did she think labor could be so traumatic. Focusing on her baby she began to encourage herself and in three hours her baby came.

"Oh! What a tiny, perfect little girl!" She wept. She took the scissors from under her pillow, cut the umbilical cord and tied it neatly.

"I have no name for her. I thought I would give Walter a son." Carrie wrapped her baby in a blanket she had made years ago.

The soft cry of her daughter awakened Carrie from a deep sleep. Her body was sore and she ached from the dampness of the room. Pulling the baby closer and the quilts higher, she fell asleep once again. She was grateful darkness and despair would not last forever and God was good, once more. Tonight she would be unable to hold the hand of the dying, as had been her reputation. Instead she held the tiny hand of her child that she had delivered alone. The gale stopped as suddenly as it started and it had brought devastation and pain to many. However, it had given her a child; a new lease on life. She would name her Gale.

The next few years passed rapidly and Walter left his cotton mill job to work fulltime with F.A.S., where dangerous situations were ever present. Members went missing, some murdered and maimed. The cost of freedom was high!

Carrie had found her place in the community working with Dr. Moore who was busy treating the many highly infectious diseases. Many dead bodies were sent to cremation in the Georgia Islands. The quarantine signs flagged many homes and businesses.

One early morning Carrie and Gale's lives would change forever. There was nothing unusual about this morning at five o'clock. Many times the destitute and needy neighbors would come to talk to Walter and leave with assurance. This particular morning was not one of those.

Walter was having a cup of chicory coffee as Carrie and Gale had not yet awakened and was sleeping soundly. A loud, rapid knock came and Walter answered the door. Suddenly, he staggered backwards, falling inside. An eighteen inch knife had been sunk deeply into his heart.

His murderer would never be captured.

Carrie Grant was in shock. She sat mute and stunned. Her mind ran on …."Why?" she asked. Walter's death had taken everyone at the cotton mill by surprise, but soon the scenario became clear. For years the F.A.S. had held secret meetings and Walter's involvement had many plantation owners riled. They no longer requested his blacksmithing services and there had been a price on his head for years. His had been a great work in the South.

Once, he had spoken. "If we do not help to free the slaves, then we become enslaved ourselves. None here can think themselves superior to these people who are suffering. They have no control over their lives. It is pathetic to see Negroes and Indians dropping like flies from the lack of care. Dysentery, cholera, typhoid and malaria are a scourge to us all. The graveyards and crematoriums of St. Helena Island are being filled with dead bodies every day. Eight kind souls have been burned or buried this week." Walter went on to admonished fellow F.A.S. members. "Gentlemen, our position is to educate, demonstrate and facilitate, so that the oppressed do not have to fight their battles singlehanded without counsel."

Carrie Grant, not being a cotton mill worker, no longer had a roof over her head and had agreed to move. Young Gale had turned twelve two weeks ago and was asking to meet her grandmother Sally. The gold coins Carrie kept in a fruit jar on the mantel were hardly enough to keep two people going and until she could find work they would have to stretch. Many women her age had a dozen children without husbands. There was no time for self pity and Carrie Grant was determined and strong and she would not cry. Her child deserved a good life and she had worked her fingers to the bone to keep alive and others needed her. She would find a good paying job and raise her daughter.

Three years later the wagon was packed. She had written her mother-in-law, Sally Ogen Grant. She announced the death of her son, Walter and asked permission to live with her. They could share Walter in death just as they had in life, with respect.

PART 5

Sally Ogen Grant's Home
Savannah, Georgia

1855
"I sing to him! I dream he hears
The story he used to love
And aft that blessed fancy cheers
And bears my thoughts above."

"I sing to him"
Sarah J. Hale

S ally Ogen Grant was now seventy years old. She was a handsome woman with a full cap of almost black hair. Her small features were a direct image of young Gale's. As was the custom of the times, she smoked a corn-cob pipe with great vigor. There were no frills, her apron hung to her ankles and her size three, high-buttoned shoes covered her feet.

Today, Sally's nose itched. The Rhode Island rooster crowed three times this morning before breakfast. Company was coming! She would make tarts from the apple tree at her backdoor. Taking the pipe from her taunt, wrinkled mouth she began to sing in her Irish brogue. *"My wild Irish rose, the sweetest flower that grows. You may search everywhere, but none will compare with my wild Irish rose."*

She would make chicken-n-dumplings, Walt's favorite. It had been nearly four years since Sally had seen Carrie and Gale. She was still grieving the death of her son, Walter. Mr. Rhett Baggs, a cotton mill worker drove Carrie and Gale, the fourteen miles from Savannah. He was keeping a promise to Carrie for assisting in the births of his twin sons. His ability to pay at the time had been impossible, but after today, the debt would be paid in full.

Around midmorning the horses needed a rest drink of water and would eat the sweet green grasses beside a creek. They passed the White Oak Plantation landmark and in a few miles their destination would be final. Carrie knew she could get work at one of the plantations. She had vowed to never work for anyone who had indentured servants or slaves. "Even if I starve to death," she had once told Walt.

The spring flowers were blooming on the roadside as Gale "oooed and ahhed" as they drove. Finally, Mr. Boggs stopped the wagon. "Black-eyed Susans! Oh, mums! Look! As far as you can see, millions of little black eyes staring out at the world. They look so happy!" She spoke excitedly.

Carrie's thoughts were of the gravesite they had left behind and a sudden chill grasped her bones. "If only I could place some of these on Walt's grave," she whispered lightly. "Walt deserves these and more."

Gale had filled her apron full of posies for Mama Sally; her generosity did not go unnoticed. Carrie was aware Mama Sally would need consolation, flowers and patience. She had not reconciled Walt's death and it would be tough getting through the next few months.

At last they drove down the front lane leading to the house, as Mama Sally came from the kitchen wiping her hands on her apron. "I knowed it! I knowed it! My nose has itched to death," she laughed with delight. Her eyes caught a glimpse of the dozen or so boxes that was included in with the baggage Mr. Boggs unloaded onto the porch, something was wrong!

Carrie, with Gale in tow, held her arms out to her mother-in-law, "I'm sorry," she said. "So sorry, Mama Sally. They don't know who did it. He died quickly. He didn't suffer." Carrie wept.

They waved good-bye to Rhett Boggs. Carrie called out, "Take care of the boys; good-bye old friend and thank you. Gale laid the flowers on the water-shelf on the back porch as they all walked inside. Sally Ogen sat, did not cry, and showed no overt sadness.

"I, I seen it clear as day, I did. I heard the death bell rattle in my right ear; it rung all night long. Where did you bury mah boy?" she asked Carrie.

"We buried him in Magnolia Cemetery. I though it fitting for a prestigious man to have the best funeral we could afford; we tried to send you word. The cotton mill had a burial insurance policy and we spent every cent and then some. I don't worry for myself, Mama Sally, but Gale must have a decent life and continue her schooling. I will look for a job; take almost anything, right now. I am willing to help out here, as much as I can. Gale is a good girl…smart as a whip. She will help by pulling her own weight. It's for sure I'm not afraid of hard work. I helped most of the cotton mill woman deliver their children. I sewed baby clothes, cooked and cleaned; I volunteered at the orphanages. We won't be a burden. We just need a chance to get on our feet," Carrie offered.

"Did you get my letter last week?" Carrie questioned. "Well, I don't know if I did or not. Can't read you know; I got two letters from somebody. I can't seem to get to the mailman afore he gets on down the road," she explained, handing them to Carrie. "No wonder she did not know Walt had died!" Carrie mused.

She opened the letter, and a newspaper clipping fluttered to the floor. She picked it up and read, "Wm. Walter Grant II; Murdered." As she read, Sally sat down in her rocking chair, laid her head onto its high back and closed her eyes. She rocked back and forth.

The floor creaked as her feet bounced up and down, keeping the rocker in motion. "The death bell was clear," she muttered under her breath.

Almost an hour passed, but there was no more discussion. The facts were laid out and final and she still had two people who needed her. Her best was all she had to give.

Gale placed the half-wilted flowers in Mama Sally's lap. "These are for you, we picked them down the road apiece," she said sadly. "Why thankee, Chile. Let's gettum in water and eat some tarts. I have chicken-n-dumplings, red-eye ham and gravy, and biscuits, too."

"It will be a good thing to have you here and you are welcome to stay forever. Hits the least I can do for my precious son. We'll help each other through this."

"Git off the porch, Rooster Red! Shoo, shoo," she hollered at the curious chicken. "You done spoke yore peace. Brought my family home, you did," she declared. Gale loved the dialect, and the quaint little woman she knew as Mama Sally.

The next morning Carrie met the mailman at the mailbox, a hewn out log nailed to a tree. Sally would tie a red ribbon around the tree to ensure her mail was picked up. Carrie thought it to be quaint. However, she chose to meet the mailman in person at the store a mile away.

His horse arrived around eleven o'clock. "Good morning sir. I am Carrie Grant and I am looking for work. If you'd be so kind to ask around, I'd be obliged," she explained timidly. "I don't know of anything right off," he responded. "But, I'll keep my eyes and ears open. I'll ask around, and leave you a note in Mrs. Sally's box if I hear of anything."

Three days passed and there was no note. Carrie walked four miles up the road to "White Oak Plantation." She was not prepared for what her eyes beheld. The big house was built on a square, surrounded by a labyrinth courtyard. The perfect upkeep of the house and property appeared to disguise its age. A large columned veranda was echoed by the balcony above. Basket-woven brick paved the courtyard, the perfect place for afternoon teas and evening parties. Countless silk curtains hung in every window.

As Carrie knocked on the front door, a new face peered through the window of the rotunda. She felt herself blushing, an intruder in an alien world. Had she been so young, or had she simply forgotten the commanding beauty of "White Oak?" She had attended Jesse Taylor's memorial service here seven years ago.

A yardman, busily hoeing the weeds from the freshly swept yard beckoned her to the stable. She could see John Barr long before she reached him. He was standing in one of the stables combing his dapple grey horses.

Their long, flowing tails and shiny manes were a sight to behold! "Such stately beauty should never be kept locked away," she murmured aghast.

John Barr turned and mounted his horse, glanced once in her direction, then rode away. His horse ignored her as well. Of all the arrogance she had ever witnessed, none could equal his! As they sped off, the horse's flowing tail appeared as silk shining in the sun. The stately horse carried a stately rider.

Carrie took the unspeakable cue; she had always believed, "What is to be will be." Today, she had made an attempt to find work and she would not let this one snub break her spirit! Starting her long walk home, she had barely walked outside the magnolia-lined dirt road toward home, when a horse-drawn carriage forced her into the wet ditch. "Whadda you want?" a commanding voice questioned. John Barr had pulled the carriage within a hairs length of her foot.

"I, I, I wanted to talk to you, but that's okay. I've changed my mind," she spoke sarcastically walking on down the road.

"Nobody changes a mind without giving an explanation," he said.

"Well, I… Well, I…" she stuttered.

"Come on. Get in the carriage. I'll give you a lift. Give me your hand," he stated firmly. Carrie was at a loss for words.

"Speak up woman! I don't have all day." Carrie held her hand to him. Then, sitting on the seat, she talked, telling him of her dilemma. "I need a job. I must be a working widow."

John Barr raised his eyebrows, looking straight ahead. Her blunt driven words captured his attention, and changed his demeanor. The conversation led to a job interview. "So do you have training in record keeping and managing workers?" he questioned. "If I decide to hire you, I will require you to live on my property. Your position will be one of trust. One thing you must understand, I value my privacy. My wife came from a totally different social standing than any of the women in these parts. She can be difficult to understand. Only an understanding individual can effectively work with her. She enjoys the theatre, reading Shakespeare, and poetry. How well do you read Carrie Grant?" he asked.

Lavania Stottard, Connecticut-born, Alabama-raised said,

"I said to Sorrow's awful storm'
That beat upon my breast.
Rage on thou mayst destroy this form,
And lay it low at rest:

But still the spirit that now brooks
Thy tempest raging high.
Undaunted on its furry looks
With steadfast eye."

"The Soul's Defiance was written when Lavania was suffering an injury much like me," she stated flatly.

John Barr was satisfied with this sassy woman, who demanded her place. Raising his voice to gain control, he grunted hastily, "One thing we need to get straight from the beginning, do not betray my trust! I make a powerful enemy."

Carrie had not given eye contact until this moment. Suddenly, she stared him directly in the eyes. "That goes both ways, sir," she retorted. There was no way this man was going to browbeat her! She attended too many F.A.S. meetings, learning in order to get respect, one must first give it. "Demanding respect is for fools with something to cover up," her voice rose. "I will not be bribed nor belittled by nobody. No job is worth my own self-respect."

John Barr was taken aback by this strong-willed woman. She was just what he needed to manage the "White Oak" staff. "When can you start?" he asked softly.

"Tomorrow," she retorted. "But, there is one thing you must hear first. I have a twelve-year old daughter. We can share a room, but it will need to be large enough to accommodate our comfort. Gale will attend school, thus, she will need transportation."

"Well," Mr. Barr answered quickly, "that won't be a problem. There are four children that attend already. One more won't overload the wagon. Your salary will be twenty dollars a month with room and board. Weekends are free." They shook hands. The verbal contract was sealed. "I'll send for you at nine o'clock sharp. Good day ma'am." He spoke emphatically, turning the elegant leather seated carriage around. What a day! Carrie's head was spinning.

Mama Sally and Gale listened intently as Carrie related the dialogue of the day. It became obvious Sally Ogen was not happy to have her family leave so soon. Carrie could not bear the thought of sponging off her mother-in-law. She must pay her way; Walt would want her to. Mama Sally sat in her rocking chair. Pouting had become her friend.

"You will have us every Saturday and Sunday. That's enough time to make you wish you'd never seen us."

Carrie laughed, "We won't have to unpack. The bags and boxes had been stacked neatly by Mr. Boggs. Gale was excited! She was going to live in a mansion; it was fairy dreams come true. She had opened the wooden shutter and spied as Mr. Barr drove away. The elegant horses and carriage were straight out of a story book and immediately, she felt like a princess. There was one thought she could not bear to remember. Her daddy would not be there; nor would he come to see them ever again. Her eyes filled with tears and her white apron caught their wetness. She would not cry in the presence of Mama Sally. After all, she'd lost her only child!

Carrie awakened to the strong smell of chicory coffee brewing in the blue and white pot. Mama Sally was busy making hoecake in her thin griddle on top of the wood stove. She opened the fig preserves she had made for Walter. He loved them best of all fruits and Gale had similar tastes.

After breakfast was over, and the tin plates washed, Mama Sally threw the dishwater out the open window onto her red-wiggler bait bed. Constantly, she fed the worms with potato peelings, meal, flour, and other scraps. Red wigglers were the best bait for pike, red-eye, brim, and catfish, that filled the creek and streams behind her house.

"I try to go a-fishin' at least twice a week. I spend my time this-a-way," Sally told them. "Sally's companion Cricket always accompanies her, wherever she goes. The red-tick hound is her protection. Once blazing the trails before her, he killed a rattlesnake, which lay sunning in the path," Carrie told Gale as they rocked.

Early the next morning, John Barr sent Bartus to load the buckboard and drive Carrie and Gale to "White Oak Plantation." Carrie left behind only a changing of clothes for each of them. They would be returning on weekends. Bartus, a freed slave, was a gentleman. He was taken with young Gale, seating her in the proper place to view the road.

Entering the grounds of "White Oak," Gale noticed the flowers trailing downward from the high balcony. On the veranda were pots, boxes, and tubs of flowers everywhere. The perfumed air was so noxious, she could barely breathe. A bronze water bird spewed sprays of water in all directions. At the base of the monstrous figurine were hundreds of silver and gold coins. She wanted, more than anything, to make a wish, but they had no coins to spare. There was no need anyhow; because her daddy was gone forever!

Bartus helped her from the wagon and she moved swiftly away from the inner courtyard. "My mommy must not see how I feel," she whispered.

The water from her eyes, mingled with the sprays from the fountain. Somehow, this was the release she needed. Now, she could give daddy to God!

With boxes and bags unpacked, Carrie and Gale settled in the Victorian room. The large fireplace housed the lightered logs needed to start a fire. Every area of the room was immaculate, even the toilet closet. Its enamel chamber had been shined. The heavy maroon velvet drapes had been dusted, and were hanging in perfect folds. The gold tieback tassels adorned the draperies and were seen again on the settee. A lovely bedspread tapestry was from the new looms in Macon. High above the bed frame was a mattress filled with goose down. "Oh, how soft!" Gale could hardly wait for night. Putting her arms around Carrie, "I love it here. Nothing could ever make me want to leave. Heaven couldn't be more beautiful," she spoke breathlessly.

Carrie smiled at her precious, innocent child. She deserved so much from life. She had seen her weeping at the fountain earlier today. "I swear I will give her the best life possible. Nothing will harm her," Carrie spoke vehemently.

Morning came and no amount of explanation could have prepared Carrie and Gale for the beautiful Eva Barr. "When God created her, he threw away the mold." Mr. Barr had said earlier today, while explaining her family history _ _ Carrie could hardly wait to meet her.

Evangeline Lyne was a direct descendant of aristocracy. "The Duke of Newberg," Mr. Barr went on…

In 1740, James Oglethorpe had settled in Georgia for several years. He had sailed along with dozens of families to America. King Charles II of England made grants to the Lord's proprietors. The Duke of Newberg corresponded with General Oglethorpe by direct means. His letter to the Duke was written from the fort and was dated 1740. In 1734, Oglethorpe took a visitor with him to England, "Tomachichi," a clever Indian chief. They would return with many ships loaded with guns, gunpowder, pottery and furniture.

Newberg was a parliamentary and municipal borough of Beckshire, England. This was the childhood birthplace of Lillith and Colin, who were married with their families blessing as were David and Agnes, a double wedding. Martha Tyne was sister to the Duke of Newberg. Together they arrived in Orange County, New York.

Later, Martha arranged for sons Colin, David, and their wives to settle in the United States. Only David and Agnes came. Lillith was pregnant, and Colin grew ill. There could be no leaving Berkshire. A few weeks passed, Colin grew weak and expired in late August. He never saw his beautiful daughter, Evangeline Tyne.

Colin was buried in the Chapel graveyard nearby. The mail took weeks and months to get from Berkshire to America. Martha would return to Berkshire five years later. She was getting feeble; arthritis did not agree with foggy, chilled Berkshire. She had arrangements to make. Above all, she wanted custody of Lillith's beautiful Evangeline Tyne. She would make her heiress of "White Oak Plantation." However, there was school in New York, the Opera, culture, and famous merchandising, actors and dozens of interesting venues to entertain her. She was thorough in conveying her wishes to Lillith when the door to the drawing room opened. Evangeline entered, bowed and spoke softly, "Grandmother, I have a picture of my father, Colin; I sleep with it each night. Mother says I may go to America with you for she is afraid I will have the problems father had."

Later, Martha would stand in proxy as Evangeline's mother. Little Eva was packed and ready for New York City. Afterwards, Martha would take her to Savannah, Georgia. She would pack the valuable antiques collected from around the world. Perhaps her granddaughter would enjoy her taste in opera, arts, and the exclusive things in life. Today, Martha would call Barrister Christian and they carefully made her will. She was slow and methodical to make her decision. They would leave for America tomorrow. Finally, she was packed and ready, as was Lillith packing for Eva. "What about your old wooden chest, Mother Martha?" Martha opened it and pulled a letter from the rotting leather lining and read aloud to Lillith and little Eva.

"Madam:
I convey greetings to you Martha dear.

I am given the understanding that many of our young soldiers are being stricken with malaria in Georgia.

In a few months, the Honorable Trustees of Georgia will send our resolutions to the tenure of land grants. You are required to clear and cultivate the property.

We are hereby allowed to give and devise our possessions to the lands in your province. You will receive some twenty-five hundred acres. A free title will be signed.

I apologize for entering upon so unpleasing a subject and the manner of my communicating my thoughts in writing.

I would to God that I could come to you in person, my sister.
At this time, I must take my leave; recommending you and yours
to the Divine Protector.

I am Sincerely Yours."

The Duke of Newberg had signed, and affixed his seal to the letter.

Martha re-read the letter from her brother. They had been happy children, but there were preparations to be made. Her land filled with virgin timber and rich soil would pass on. Hopefully, Lillith would protect and leave it as had she and later it would pass on to Evangeline. Lillith had married an Englishman from Liverpool. It was good to see Eva grow in the newly growing country – America when they visited twice yearly.

John Barr crossed his legs, yet leaned toward Carrie who sat upright. Her Regence chair faced his. "There are many things to talk about. I will get back with you this afternoon. I want to be the one to introduce you to Eva. Good day ma'am."

Carrie and Gale sat at the gate leg table with the servants. They had breakfast with Mama Sally earlier. Carrie knew from experience mealtime was the perfect time to get to know her staff. Their morning breakfast consisted of pancakes, bacon, eggs, grits, and cream-o-wheat. The coffee was perked in a coffee urn with round, glass drip. Pansy served Gale's plate with enough food to feed a railroad worker. Carrie quickly intervened, "We have already eaten. Do you always serve large portions?" she asked Pansy. Pansy became disgruntled, taking the act as a reprimand. "Ma'am, she need some flesh on dem bones. She skinny lak a starved slave. Ain't nobody live in dis house gon starve, long as I'se de cook! No Siree, I won't stans fo it!"

Carrie, taken by surprise at the anger of the obese woman said, "There will be no waste in this house any longer. Overeating is gluttony; gluttony is waste. If I must, I will plan the meals and ration the portions. Do you understand, Pansy?" she asked. "I will order and monitor all staples and other food for the entire plantation. Nobody will go hungry or lack for clothing or shelter. 'Waste not, want not,'" she retorted as she spun from the room.

Mr. Barr, who had been served breakfast alone in his nearby study, overheard Carrie's declaration. He was about to pick up his riding crop and hat when Carrie came speeding down the hallway. "Carrie, uh, uh, Mrs. Grant, will you come with me now? I will probably be late coming home;

I have to meet with the banker. A large part of your position is to oversee the comfort of my wife Evangeline," he instructed. "She has a helper, by the name of Oprah, with her most of each day. Oprah is twelve years old and as with most young girls, has a tendency to shirk their work. Your child must earn her keep, too," he went on. "She can help Oprah. 'Waste not, want not,' huh?" he said laughing. "It starts with you!" he stated leading the way upstairs. Secretly, he hated to start out strong with the gentle soul, while she was still in bereavement. However, it had always been best to start out heavy-handed.

The curved stairway was twelve feet wide, winding into a semi-circle. At the top of the stairway were dark green double doors. Each Windsor Castle door panel featured a family coat-of-arms medallion and was set in ivory. They had been repeated again on seats also front and back of the chariot she had ridden in yesterday.

Mr. Barr opened wide the doors, exposing Evangeline, his wife, sitting on a rosewood scrolled chaise lounge; a Biedemeier, one of great grandmother Martha's favorites. With the appearance of a bisque doll, a weak half smiled crossed her lips. She had refused breakfast. The broken Swatow plate lay in pieces against the fireplace; spatters of food covered the carpet and walls. Oprah was busy picking up the shards of glass and food and would clean the residue later. Her major task at hand was to serve Mrs. Eva in the Meissen European dishes depicting her great-grandfather, Lyne, loading barrels on the banks of an estuary.

"I see you've been at it again," Mr. Barr offered. He kissed the back of her hand.

"They never seem to teach these young, ignorant plineys how to care for aristocracy," Eva spoke.

"I have hired Mrs. Carrie Grant and her daughter Gale. They will take good care of you, darling," he spoke softly. "Gale will help Oprah. You will be responsible for both of them, Mrs. Grant. Now, Eva, if there is anything you need to talk about, I'm here. The dishes are running out!" he finished, patting her softly on the hand.

It would appear that Eva Barr had enjoyed every moment of the disaster she had created. She settled back on the chaise and exhaled loudly. A broad smile crossed her face. At last, he had come! He had come! Her eyes shined like liquid gold. Now she could sleep; the long nights had been so lonely, but they were over now that he had come! Once again, she had commanded his attention.

Floating like a vapor on the soft spring air, Evangeline slept soundly. She dreamed of her childhood in England. In Liverpool, heavy fog cast a blanket over the moss-covered oak trees. The cold drops of moisture gathered on her nose. Fierce, raging winds rushed whistling between the spokes of the carriage wheels. The station was in sight. Finally, horses were slowing down after a two-hour ride. An old, bent-over man came to relieve the carriage of her trunk. Evangeline alighted from the carriage. "This way; number four!" the man yelled. The train rested as tickets were punched, and passengers boarded. Five-year old Evangeline Tyne shoved her hands deeper into her muff, and turned up the fur collar against her neck as tears stung her eyes. She had never traveled alone before. Grandmother Martha had taken her to Orange County, New York. She remembered the times her father, Colin, would allow her on a fox hunt outside Liverpool. Hundreds of hounds ran across the woodlands and meadows, chasing the fox, a seasonal event, which she had loved.

Now, pulling her cape closer to her face, she sat outside on a long wooden bench, near a coal-burning stove. Its heat permeated her woolen coat and cape. Meanwhile, people ran to and fro outside the station platform, their voices blending into a hollow drone of nothingness. Eva was frightened until she saw him; Great Uncle Don Marshall. Grandmother Martha and Lillith had a picture of him on the bureau. He was wearing a military uniform. How regal he looked!

Walking straightway toward little Eva, he lifted her off the floor, into his arms, squeezing her with gusto! She stared straight ahead not understanding the overt act. She did not like the intimate greeting! Embarrassed, she fancied he could see her red face, and feels the look of rejection in his eyes from their shadows cast by the flickering platform stove. Taking her hand he explained, "We will be going on a long trip." Moving her quickly, they strode toward the man with her trunks.

They rode silently in a horse-driven carriage. The driver, dressed in black, reminded her of the undertaker who had driven her away to the graveyard. She shuttered with fear and sadness, but this was no time for tears. Eva took a deep breath and exhaled. They reached the loading docks, where the St. Frances was filled with people going to America.

Evening came and Evangeline Barr awoke from her dream. She never knew if it were real or the possibility of her overwrought mind playing tricks again. She was hungry so she rang for Oprah and in a few minutes, supper was served on European Meissen dinnerware and she ate heartily. "Opraaah," she cooed. "You did a lovely job cleaning my carpet. Ah don't understand what gets into me at times," she offered sweetly. "Mistah Barr nevah gets home before midnight. He nevah talks to me anymore," she said sadly.

Oprah said, "Yessum, yessum, I knows." "Oprah girl, I dreamed of my father Colin. It was so beautiful. He sang Barbara Allen and held me day and night, brought me back to life – his, this pipe. He smoked the most wonderful tobacco and always smelled sweet like honey and cherries. I am going to Prince George Hotel to meet him." She was enthused. "Yessum, yessum. I knows yo is ma'am," Oprah said, closing the door.

PART 6

White Oak Plantation
Savannah, Georgia

1845

*"Woman
That happy, wretched being
Of causeless smile, of nameless sigh.
So oft whose joys unbidden spring.
So oft who weeps, she knows not why"*

"Castles in the Air"
Eliza Townsend

In Georgia, cotton was king, Mr. Barr had told Carrie. Huge amounts of cotton were shipped from the seaport of Savannah to England and workers were needed. African slaves had landed in Jamestown as early as 1619. When Georgia was first settled, slaves were found in several other colonies; some were Indians. Settlers from the north brought Negro slaves with them to work the new land of the south and Plantations flourished. Owners became rich at the expense of suffering human flesh.

The Constitution, after 1808, forbade the import of slaves. However, slaves continued to be imported by smuggling until 1860. Many ship's captains from both north and south became exceptionally wealthy from illegal slave trade. Cotton mills were set up in cities along the Fall Line. By 1850, Georgia had over five hundred miles of railroads, which moved cotton, syrup, and other commodities swiftly to other states and countries. The Georgia Central connected Savannah to Macon. The Macon Western ran from Augusta to Atlanta, with branches leading off its main lines. Terminus had the state's largest switchyard in Georgia, and later became known as Atlanta. King Cotton reigned and ruled the south, and was in demand worldwide. Looms cropped up everywhere to weave fabrics for clothing and household commodities. The seed were crushed for oil and animal feeds.

John Alexander Barr II worked all day, and most of the night at Barr's Funeral Home. He had been given to insomnia since childhood. His mother had died of pneumonia when he was three. Guilt had plagued him most of his life. He had been raised by sister Mollie, ten years older than he, and a sometime father, who was away from home working for the railroad. "A man has to make a living," John A. Barr I had declared.

In 1824, by the age of three, young John had never learned to walk. He was taken to Atlanta by Brenda Miller, a distant relative and neighbor. Brenda had helped Mollie to arrange transportation to Atlanta where Dr. Henry Hartsfield splinted and bound Johnny's club foot. He'd learned to walk by age four; however, he walked with a limp. In grammar school, some of the children called him "Gimpy Johnny." He would blush and become furious with himself for being angry. He pressed forward determined to make up in intelligence the deficiency cruel nature had cursed him with. After graduation, John Barr entered New Orleans University. At twenty-five, he graduated head of his class, keeping the same momentum as in grammar and high school. He joined a law firm and continued to serve as a corporate attorney with Smith, Dalph, and Barr of New Orleans.

In 1848, Ezra Smith, John's partner, had lived in New York City most of his life. Ezra was a man about town and was connected in New York society. His mother was owner of The Bank of New York. Her family had developed a banking system used worldwide and she was president and overseer of her dynasty.

Ezra traveled home twice a year, while John Barr was a recluse; his head was always stuck in a book. Christmas was in two weeks and Ezra insisted John celebrate with his family and after much persuasion, John relented. A masquerade Ball took place on Christmas Eve, and John dressed in a tall white hat and tails, looking every bit the Southern gentleman.

The Ballroom of Martha Tynes' mansion gleamed vividly with gaslights. The spectrum of crystal prisms were reflected in the ceiling mirrors; the ambience was stunning to John Barr. As he looked toward the ceiling thinking he was looking at a picture, a lady, dressed in red velvet, moved steadily in his direction. Ezra Smith introduced them and John was careful to use his best Southern manners. The night appeared elusive to him, as did the gorgeous Evangeline Tyne. She was the bell of the ball, dancing every dance and still found the time to capture John's heart.

In Eva Tyne, he saw for the first time that inner life of an old, noble cultivated family, which he had so long hungered for. He never perceived any defects in Eva's way of life. John felt it to be the perfect one for an established lawyer.

The last night John was in New York, he escorted socialite Evangeline to the opera. The entourage of men wore silk suits and attended ladies wearing long flowing gowns with capes. The carriage drivers wore formal attire, including tall black hats. John was in awe of the proceedings, as they developed throughout the evening! This was the life dreams were made of. Eva was perfect in every way; she was a creature above all earthly imagination.

At first, John's shyness presented a problem. He felt a worthless match for this charming woman, for he had never had a membership in society. He could count on one hand his friends. Her family would think of him as a gold-digger and feelings of worthlessness plagued his nights. Basically, he thought himself a country gentleman lawyer. Raising horses, building stables, and helping neighbors with legal problems were his expertise. The major hindrance in the relationship with Eva was his self-deprecating thoughts. Although nobody had called him "Gimpy Johnny" in years, he felt it all too well. Evangeline could never love a man less than perfect. Carrying his feelings on his shoulder, John left New York for New Orleans without saying goodbye.

Two weeks later, Evangeline sent a rail gram to John, "Please explain your actions," it read. John responded with a long letter, pouring out his heart, his letter was definite, precise, and well formed. Summarized, "My mother died when I was three. My father worked with the railroad; I can only remember the hunger and poverty that my sister Molly and I suffered. Mama kept a light on in the windows, just in case Daddy came home. She kept his picture beside her bed, and kissed him goodnight often. I cannot remember him ever holding or touching me; he was not physically abusive. However, worse than that, he ignored me! He had treated me as though I was worthless, a nobody, and a cripple. When Mama became sick, the lack of food and care were obvious. Her grief and inability to cope with Daddy's absence cost her, her life. Luckily, I had Molly and at fourteen, she married a stranger who stopped by for directions to town. This act of compassion spared her life, and mine, for awhile. Then, she died in childbirth twelve years later. By then, I was grown, and no longer needed the church's Paupers fund. I took a job and moved to Savannah, finished school, and left for New Orleans Law School. I can in no way compete with your way of life. How could any man ask you to give up the elegance of your heritage to live in the 'slave driven' South?

Three months later, the bans were posted, and the wedding would take place in New York. John had heard stories of women who were attracted to ordinary men, but he never believed them, until today. After the reception, Morris Golden presented the bride with an envelope with Lillith's will, she opened it immediately. She had become heiress of Georgia Railroad stock and twenty-five hundred acres of land outside Savannah, Georgia. Grandmother Martha's will was enclosed, as well as a letter written by the Duke of Newburgh.

Four years passed before John and Evangeline would build their large plantation home, White Oak Manor. Laborers were hired to saw the wood from the woodland. In doing so, John installed the largest saw mill in southern Georgia. Builders were hired from both north and south to carry out the plan of architect Solan Daniels of New York. Excitement was around, hovering over the workers, as were John and Eva Barr as well. There was to be an heir or heiress to White Oak; Eva was pregnant; however, her euphoria lasted for only a month or so. In her fifth month,

Dr. Steven Moore ordered her to complete bed rest. Her complaints were heard throughout the house, evoking stress related problems. Months later, after a long and troubled labor, she became paralyzed. Despite Pansy, the cook, placing a knife under her pillow and an axe underneath the bed to cut the pain, Evangeline's baby was cut from her body. "Jist lak gutting a hog," Pansy had whispered throughout the cabins.

After an oil bath, the baby boy was taken to his mother. Eva pushed the delicate soft bundle away! "Get it out of here! Get it out of here!" she cried. Pansy continued to insist, "De baby bees hungry. Needs some tit from his Mommy," she pleaded. "No, No, No! Nevah, Nevah!" Eva spoke vehemently.

Later in the evening, Bartus brought in Zinnie the laundress to nurse the baby. Zinnie's baby was four months old. She would continue to nurse him until he was two years of age. This way she would not become pregnant again until the nursing ended. Pansy had spoken these words of wisdom before Zinnie gave birth to Billy. Zinnie was content with her new role as wet-nurse, since her breasts were engorged with milk; Billy never emptied them.

John Barr walked downstairs from Evangeline's room. He moved slowly, wiping the tears from his eyes. The smell of blood was still in his nostrils, he began to gag and heave. Thoughts of his new son did not enter his mind, as he walked without purpose to his office. Closing and locking the door behind, he flopped in his desk chair. Placing his face in both hands, he became silent. Suddenly, with clenched teeth, a groan rushed from his throat. Then, pulling a drawer open, taking pistol in hand, he loaded two cartridges into its barrel. His head lay back on the leather chair. Now, sad thoughts ran rapidly through his mind; he was motionless… stunned. One simple thought was coursing through his brain, "This would be too final."

At this time, he had not spoken, but thought of his wife's pain. He had not looked at his offspring, for his own pain was unbearable. Disappointment and humiliation filled his being. The beautiful woman he had met in New York had died to him! The wounded woman upstairs would forever be a stranger. Life was over for the both of them! John began to weep, he cried out, dropping the pistol onto the desk. The sounds of mumbling voices, creaking footsteps of the servants entered his office, their black eyes filled with fear brought him to his right mind. He left the room more ashamed than when he had entered.

Dr. Steven Moore came daily to dress the sutured wound. Eva responded to his tender care, and after two weeks, she was sitting up in bed. Pansy cooked gruel soup of boiled ham stock, mixed with overcooked meal. Carrie Grant had not left Eva's side since the birth of her child. Her womanly heart did not arouse a feeling of horror at times like these, for she was strong, caring, and wise. Many years she had walked side by side with disease, plagues, gunshot wounds, and similar births…worse even. Dr. Moore and she had co-existed for weeks at a time in the care of afflictions. Problems which sent others into a tailspin immediately engaged her attention. The sick room must be kept sterile! Carrie washed her hands thoroughly with soap, and dried them with hot towels from the oven. She expected no less from others who came and went from the patient's room!

The sick room was scrubbed down and washed daily. Fresh linens were brought and the patient's bed was stripped and cleaned with lye soap, and boiled for an hour in the cast-iron wash pot. The entire staff was on call twenty four hours per day; there would be no slacking! On a table beside the bed, medicines, decanters, and clean linens were stacked neatly.

Weekly, Carrie washed and pin-curled Eva Barr's hair, with a little powder and makeover. Eva was stunning and life was returning and she began to smile. Nightly, Eva sat as Carrie read the Bible, newspapers, and journals aloud until she fell asleep. Never once in the first few months did Eva ask for or mention her baby.

At times, Carrie pulled the bell cord for Oprah and Gale to carry the soiled linens for laundering. Many times there was a touch of fear in the girls as they walked softly in the presence of Eva Barr. Carrie could read them; knowing they were too young to understand the importance of their jobs but neither of them complained.

PART 7

"There towering with Imperial Pride
The rich Magnolia stands.
And here in softer loveliness
The White-bloomed bay expands."

"The Plantation"
Caroline Gilman

Two months later, Little John-John was a chubby baby, indicating Zinnie's milk was agreeing. He had begun to smile and coo and stared closely at his fingers. Strong and determined to hold hid head straight, he bobbled unsteadily. "What a sweet boy you are," Zinnie told him daily.

At times Zinnie fed both babies at once, first laying her six-month old son onto her right arm, then laying John on her left side. There was no coaxing at feeding time. Both boys sucked with great vigor. Only after the younger baby fell asleep would she allow the older to empty her paps.

Zinnie's workload had tripled. With the enormous amount of linens from the sick room, along with her own son to care for, she could hardly keep up with her work, and nurse John-John too. Health was of utmost importance for Zinnie and the babies. She was tired, however, but never complained; she needed help.

Bartus had watched the developing loss of energy Linnie experienced. He mentioned this to Carrie, who sent Oprah and Gale to help out. Neither of them could wash the heavy loads. However, they enjoyed hanging the clothes on the line. They had learned to make a game out of their work and would race to the clothesline, making bets on who could finish first; their giggles could be heard throughout the yard. Being able to get away from Mrs. Eva's sickness was like 'letting a pig out of the pen.' They were entranced with helping out during feeding time for the babies.

Zinnie was a natural as she sat in a cowhide rocker on the side porch, rocking and feeding her babies. The creaking chair evidenced the event and both Oprah and Gale sat close by crooning lullabies with Zinnie. Finally, they sang in whispers to the almost sleeping little ones.

One day, Mr. Barr stepped onto the porch. The scene was one he had never witnessed. One Negro baby and a light-skinned white one, both are nursing the same body. "Parasites!" he bellowed with disgust. He stood staring…invading the precious moment. His heart wanted to reach out to his son. However, somehow he could not forgive this small, delicate baby for destroying his life. Long strides pelted loudly as he crossed the porch. Opening the door, he left the scene as he had found it, slamming the door behind. Involuntarily, both babies jerked without awakening. Oprah and Gale stared until he was out of sight. "Well," Gale said hastily. "If I didn't know better, I would think a stranger passed by." "Yeah, he got no heart that's for sure. Just walked plumb by his own son. Don't even say thankee to Zinnie for saving his poor baby's life," Oprah said disgustedly.

Zinnie had not heard for she was fast asleep. Both babies lay limply in her arms, so Oprah took the younger baby as Gale removed the other. They lay down with them on the quilt pallet and hummed themselves to sleep. A cool wind blew throughout the porch for an hour or so as they slept in the shade of the screened porch.

Both Oprah and Gale had finished the sixth grade. In the fall, they would attend school in Savannah and they were excited; summer was almost here. They loved being together and this weekend, Carrie had given Gale permission to stay over the weekend at White Oak. Gale and Oprah had planned to pick wildflowers, violets, buttercups, and lilies with freckles at the creek, north of the plantation. Bartus had told them stories of a knoll overtaking the creek, and of the profusion of flowers growing there. "Dis be de bes times." His eyes lit up as he gestured with his hands.

Early Saturday morning, the girls arose, and ate a hearty breakfast. Pansy and Bartus made syrup cakes for the two to take along on their excursion. Bartus had work to do; each morning he would build the fire in the stove, draw the water from the well, and make the coffee before he went to milk the cows. By the time the milking was done, Pansy had breakfast ready. First, Mrs. Eva was served in her room. Next, Mr. Barr was served at his private table. Oprah and Gale had cleaned Mrs. Barr's quarters and asked Bartus for permission to spend the day at leisure.

Oprah and Gale ran through the courtyard into the freshly plowed ground. The broom straw patch led them into the deep woods and the sweet smell of clover filled the air. Chattering loudly, they crossed uncharted woods. After an hour of struggling through the over-growth of trees and shrubs, they saw the tin top of a building in the distance.

A house came into view that appeared to be abandoned. Hiding behind a large oak tree, they rested before carefully scouting out the area of the spooky house! There was no life in sight, so they slowly walked up to the old house with its front porch rotted down. However, its two by six underpinnings were sturdy. They peeked through the cracked window and saw a small kitchen littered with paper, cans, and burlap bags. Broken shards of glass gave the only color to the room. The sun shone through the window creating a multi-spectrum of reflection on the walls. In the front room, the fire hearth was falling through underneath the floor. An old barrel chair lay on its side, denoting an unoccupied status.

They heard noises! A busy squirrel dropped a chestnut onto the tin roof; it rolled down, hitting the ground with a thud and the girls were ready to run! There were aware of invading another's territory; with hearts beating rapidly, forgetting their mission, they ran toward the safety of home. They did not discuss their journey for fear of being laughed and poked fun at.

Two weeks later, Oprah offered, "Gale, if we don't pick the violets, they will be gone in a few days. Why don't we go tomorrow?" she asked. Gale had gone to see Mama Sally last weekend and Carrie had given her permission to stay at White Oak again. Friday afternoon, Gale waved goodbye to her mother and Carrie traveled home, alone. Saturday morning would not come soon enough for both girls. They were driven by curiosity and their excitement was exhibited as the night went by and neither of them slept well.

Saturday morning came at last! Breakfast was short for there was no time to eat. The fresh planted cotton fields filled their shoes with dirt. It hindered their speed. They would stop and empty the dirt before continuing. Once they had walked into the deep woods, they caught sight of an old wagon road. It led to a limestone mountain, high up on a knoll. Hurriedly, they climbed to the top. They were exhausted as they looked down at the clear blue stream below; their energy revived.

A reverent awesomeness filled them as if they were explorers of a new land. Holding hands, looking up into the sky with glorious wonder, tears filled their eyes. There was no need for words and both became quiet; this was a sacred moment!

They decided to play hide-n-seek, they would count to twenty-five, one would hide, and the other would seek. Drawing straws to see who would hide first was a custom they had learned in early years and Oprah won. She would hide as Gale counted, then began to seek. She walked for an hour without finding Oprah. The brush was high and broken trees lay throughout the area. After a while, Gale called out, "I give up. I give up, Oprah!" She screamed out. Then, Oprah, laughing, jumped from her hiding place. The hollowed trunk of a big oak stood majestic and massive. Its limbs hanged to the earth and pinned down. "I won, I won." She giggled wildly. They held each other, laughing all the way home. Violets and buttercups filled their apron pockets and arms; their day was filled with wonder and, they would make plans to return soon.

Two weeks later, the girls stood, once again, high upon the limestone mountain. Turning, running over the left side of the ridge where they could gain a clear view of their new world, both were euphoric. Gale stated emphatically, "This is our world. When we are here, we are the only people on earth." The wagon road was empty. There were no tracks in sight. The tired little girls moved slowly across the ridge; they were exhausted as neither had slept nor eaten well today. They came to the massive oak and huddled inside its hollow and fell asleep instantly.

Hours later, Oprah awoke. "Where is Gale?" She thought and began to panic. She called loudly over and over, but no answer came. She searched the ridge and Limestone Mountains. It was almost dark when she caught a glimpse of Gale in the distance, walking slowly toward home. Running to catch up with her, Oprah called out, "Where have you been? I called out to you over and over. I almost had a heart attack, Gale." She gasped. "I'm sick." Gale whispered, inaudibly. "We're gonna' gets in trouble," Oprah announced. "We're late! Bartus will be looking for us." Wearily, the two headed through the cotton patch toward home. Oprah held Gale close, helping her across the plowed field.

Luck was with them and nobody noticed the two come home or that Gale had taken a long bath. Anger and pain coursed through her small, wounded body, as she languished in the warm, cleansing bath. Pansy offered lye soap. "You must have ticks and redbugs," she quibbled. "Take 'dis lye soap, wash down, goot' now." She whispered with a concerned air.

Gale didn't know which hurt worse, the violation of her private body, or that she had not told her best friend the truth. They had never kept secrets from each other. Surely, she would die tonight! She wanted to be clean when the undertaker came for her body. Mr. Barr would know the truth; but, would he tell her mum? The pain in her body could, in no way, equal the agony in her heart. She lay still in mum's bed. Oh! How she wished her mother's arms were around her tonight! What would her mum say when she was told her that her child had died? Gale's mind ran rampant. "Jesus", she prayed. "I know you are up in heaven. You were watching when that man with hair all over his face dragged me into the woods and did all those terrible things to me! Why didn't you make him stop?" Gale asked, crying her first tears. She cried for the pain she felt and for the loss of her childhood. Finally, she wept for her immediate death. She prayed for everyone and mostly that her father would meet her soon. "I miss you, Daddy." She spoke as sleep came.

As Gale slept, a dream came. A thunderous nightmare, so vivid, it awakened her! It appeared she and Oprah was deep into the woods and she was hiding; Oprah was seeking. They were playing 'Hide and Seek,' but someone else had found her. A bearded figure loomed out of nowhere, clamping his hand over her mouth. There was a blunt strike to her head and she was paralyzed. She felt herself being dragged and time lapsed and her captor had ridden off on a white horse. She saw one black foot; it had almost stepped on her face as she lay dazed on a blanket of pine straw. Mumbling incoherently, she crawled on the ground where she had been dumped.

Gale had a strong conviction that she was dead and it was welcomed. At last, the long black buckboard had arrived; the two men on the front seat wore tall black hats. Everything seemed black; the horses, the clothing, and even the flowers lying on her coffin seemed black. She would be buried during the long black night, her Mum and Granma Sally had not come to say goodbye. She began to scream but nobody came. However, Eva Barr had heard the screams, sounding much like the owl's shriek. She had settled back in her comfortable Victorian bedroom and slept.

Carrie came in Sunday afternoon and found Gale lying in a fetal position, burning with fever. Immediately, Carrie began to sponge her with cool water until finally, the fever broke. She ministered to her daughter for the next two days and Gale responded to her mother's care. Not a word was spoken concerning her 'accident'. Oprah had come by Gale's room, but there was no eye contact. Gale grew stronger in the next two weeks; however, she was not her 'old self.' She asked her Mum if she could spend the summer with Granma Sally. Considering the poor health of her daughter, Carrie thought the idea to be a good one. Gale would continue to recover from this summer flu, and she would be lots of company for Mama Sally, too.

Oprah sat on the side porch listening to the metallic screams of a blue jay. Its cries were eerie! She stamped her feet on the porch, ordering its silence. It made a sound of sadness, death, and undoing. Cold chills ran up her spine as she watched the blue jay fly from limb to limb, refusing to fly away! "Yes, a bad omen was spoken!" Oprah told Pansy as she walked by.

School would start tomorrow and Gale would not be attending; Mrs. Carrie had told Oprah that Gale's illness continued. Oh, how she longed to see her friend; life was not the same without her and most of all; she missed the visits to the Limestone Mountain and stream. The sacred, secret place awaited their return; things were not the same anymore and Oprah was filled with sadness. There were too many losses to cope with and everything was in limbo.

Pansy had sent the message throughout the worker's quarters that Gale had been attacked with tick fever. "Dey drinks away yo blood and suck on yo till yo dies. Jist lak on a dog, ifen he gets ticks he be paralyzed and jist drag about," she contended. Oprah did not understand for she had been in all the same places with Gale and there were no ticks hitting and sucking all her blood. "Maybe it is the color of my skin," she thought.

Thoughts of horror crossed her mind; what if her friend died before she could see her again? She wondered if Gale would ever return to school. Maybe she would be crippled, blind, or never have a family of her own! In essence, what would she do without her? A rush of tears poured forth, much like the waterfalls at Limestone Mountain.

She had asked Pansy when she could go to see her friend. Pansy said, "No siree girl! You might ketch somefin. You might ketch da fevah iffin yo touches her."

Oprah sat on the veranda; the creaking of her rocking chair kept in time with her thought processes. Finally, she had made a decision! She would return to their secret place, it was the least she could do to honor her friend, Oprah thought as she left the rocker. With school starting, she would have to wait until Thanksgiving holidays to realize her dream. She would keep her decision to herself, for fear of rebuke. Bartus would be told of her plight later.

PART 8

The Rapes
White Oak Plantation

1850

"I shut mine eyes in grief and shame
Upon the dreary past.
My heart, my soul poured recklessly
On dreams that could not last."

"Aspirations"
Frances G. Osgood

S even months passed and Evangeline Tyne Barr was totally recuperated, despite her continuous complaints. Carrie, after long consideration and observation, made the decision to introduce Eva to John Alexander Barr, III. He was now seven months of age and had begun to pull up and crawl and had a ten word vocabulary. Carrie worked consistently, teaching him to say "mother" to a portrait hanging over the mantel in the parlor.

This afternoon, she had starched and pressed his white blouse, knickers and purchased new shoes and knee socks. A navy bow completed his ensemble. She powdered him down with loose starch and perfume from an atomizer borrowed from Mrs. Eva's dresser. Today would be debutant party time. "Eva Barr cannot continue to disown her son", Carrie offered. "He is a clone of her own baby pictures, littered upon the mantle shelf in the drawing room", she had explained to Pansy, as they prepared for the event.

Baby, John-John was almost too heavy to carry up the long winding staircase. Breathlessly, Carrie knocked on Mrs. Eva's door. "Entah", the soft British voice called out. Carrie opened the door carrying her precious bundle to the chaise lounge. Holding John-John with one arm, she pulled up a chair and sat with him on her lap. "John-John, who is this?" Carrie asked pointing to the lovely woman on the lounge. "Mula, Mula", he answered in a small voice pointing to his mother. Evangeline stared, speechless; then held her arms out to the son she had never seen. "He is so handsome", she cooed. "He is just like Lillith and Martha. May I keep him for a while?" Tears filled her eyes as she held her son close, smothering him with kisses. "You are so cute", she went on. "I love you, John Alexander." "Woce woo" he responded with a tiny peck on her cheek. As Carrie got up to leave, Mrs. Eva stated, "Look in the armoire, deah, there's a little box in the drawer, bring it to me." A silver rattle was extracted from the box by John-John, himself, giggling as he shook it wildly.

On her way downstairs Carrie saw Mr. Barr in the distance coming toward his office. As he entered the hallway, she spoke. "Mr. Barr, if you will go to your wife's room, you will find your bride. Your wife has come back to you. God had given us all a new chance." Hurriedly, John Barr galloped the stairs, taking two at a time. Two hours later the bell cord had been pulled. The Barr's were requesting dinner to be served on the Ming

Dynasty, Famile Rose porcelain dinnerware. A special request was for Zennie to dress in dinner attire and attend to the feeding of John-John in their quarters.

Carrie responded quickly to the request and loaned her best Sunday dress with the crochet collar, white cotton stockings and white shoes for the event, to Zinnie Coe. Zinnie pulled her hair back into a bun, walked up the stairway like an "African princess". Tonight she was not the laundress, a mother of an eleven month old son, nor the daughter of slave parents. She was somebody and walked proudly!

Mr. and Mrs. Barr were in the floor playing with their baby when Zennie entered the room. Evangeline took one look at her saying, "Ah clearly asked for Zennie. You may leave and fhind huh for me, if you please." John-John had crawled up to her, holding his arms up to be picked up by her. "Ze, Ze, Ze, Ze", he laughed. Zinnie reached down and picked him up. He began to unbutton her dress; it was time for his dinner, his caterer had arrived. Eva pulled the Victorian rocker up from the corner of the room as she fully intended to watch her son at dinner.

After his dinner, he fell asleep in Zinnie's arms. She got up and motioned Mrs. Eva to the rocker. Braham's Lullaby played on the player piano, as Eva rocked her son. John Barr sat in a state of disbelief. "This is an awesome sight!" he spoke. Zinnie closed the door behind her for she finished her mission; she had never felt so euphoric. A long, loud laugh found its way into the open porch as she laughed and danced, feeling like somebody!

Bartus brought the food cart and loaded the dumbwaiter. The beautiful china and silver were being used for the second time that he could remember. Pansy had made a beautiful meal of stuffed squab with orange sauce. "Hope dey wills bees happy. When dey ain't happy, nobody ain't happy!" Bartus elaborated. He continued to mumble as he walked back into the kitchen with a big grin covering his face. Pansy met him outside the kitchen with open arms. "I bees so happy. Dey family, sho nuff together." She caroled.

November came and Oprah was home from school for the Thanksgiving holidays vowing to keep her plan to spend some time at the 'secret place'. The afternoon brought perfect weather and she had enjoyed the Thanksgiving dinner that Pansy had prepared. She had roasted a turkey, made cornbread stuffing, potato salad, candied sweet potatoes, fresh collard greens, deviled eggs, and her favorite; pickled peaches and pecan pie.

Oprah had spoken to Bartus earlier and he had agreed she could be relieved from her duties the rest of the afternoon to pick wild flowers. "The goldenrod, wild daisies and black-eyed Susan's are blooming" he had told her. "Bring some home for Pansy; she was told to pick 'em when she had a chanst", he said. Picking the ax up from the woodpile, he began to split logs.

Oprah had walked in the direction of the tin top house. The flowers were tall, waving in the wind and the brown pine needles covered the branches on the ground below. The pathway was obscured by undergrowth; the broom straw was in profusion. "Pansy would like a new straw broom" she thought as she twisted and rung the cluster of straw. She would get Bartus to help her beat the blooms and weak straws off. Together, they would tie the round broom with twine.

She had completed her mission as the long last four straws were neatly bundled. She needed something to tie it together with in order to get it home without breaking the straws. Then she remembered… there was burlap, cotton picker's bags in the old house. She laid the straw in the path and headed there. She could barely see its top for the moss and tall growth of grasses and weeds. Finally, she reached the house. Her heart began to pound in her ears! She caught a glimpse of an owl sitting above the door stoop. "A bad omen" she thought. The whip-o-wills had begun their refrain. "Whip-around-the-white-oak" they screamed. The grass and dead limbs crackled underneath her feet as she moved onward. Suddenly, she fell into a sink hole which was hidden underneath the pine straw.

A tall dark figure, big and powerful, was bending over her, commanding and ruthless. She was powerless to stand or move. Her throat eked a smothered cry as the dark haired, bearded man started toward her with uplifted arms. He sprang like a cat, casting a blow to Oprah's face. The world became black. Swollen lips formed the words, "Help me!"

Bartus arose earlier than usual. Oprah had not come home last night. He spoke a few words to Pansy, took his musket from over the kitchen door and headed toward Limestone Mountain.

The wind had blown throughout the night. All pathways were guarded by the heavy brush and Bartus was not a young man. He could not hold out to search each animal trail; instead, he climbed up a big oak tree so that he could have a clearer view. He saw a white horse tethered to the front porch of the old house. He was somewhat familiar with the house because, Ben's family had lived here thirty or forty years ago. They had both hunted the turkey and had stayed over until the turkeys were on the roost. Bartus sat in the tree, speculating what to do next as a covey of quail flew in a flutter beside the house. Someone was coming! Bartus hid his musket behind the limb of the great oak and himself, as well.

The horseman rode past within a hundred yards of Bartus. The hoofs of the horse began to gallop, picking up speed as he headed past, but Bartus got a good look at him. The horseman was out of sight and Bartus climbed down from his perch. Taking his gun, he hurried towards the place Ben had once called home as the sun was coming up. It would be daylight in a few minutes. As he drew closer to the house, he felt a sudden rush to his brain. It seemed to obliterate all thoughts and sound associated with Oprah's being lost!

A drone of bees passed over head, looking for refuge from the coming winter, as he approached the old house. Pulling himself up by the rotted corner post, he stepped into the back door. Walking into the fire room, he called out, "Oprah, Oprah, where you is chile? Oh, deah Lawd makes me fine huh", he cried. He searched the house but she was not there. His heart was skipping beats and his chest felt as though it would explode. Continuing his search, he crossed the thicket near the stream running behind the house. He was exhausted and frustrated, so he sat down beside a poplar tree and rested for several minutes. He then picked up his musket and traveled on towards a growth of trees in the distance.

In a tall scrub of gall berry bushes on a hill, beside the old buggy trail, he saw a black mastiff dog, standing guard, near a bundle of burlap. As he approached, the mastiff located him and bristled, growling with teeth flashing in the early morning sun. Bartus was well acquainted with guard and search dogs. He backed up slowly and loaded the wadded powder balls into this gun. He was packing with speed, while he walked in a semi-circle to get the best angle. Protecting the burlap bundle was not easy. "If I could get the dog tuh move dis way, just a bit, it be good" he mumbled. Bartus aimed the musket carefully. "Jist one lead ball it'll bring 'em down." He continued to move slowly, and then suddenly stamped his right foot forward. The dog lunged at him and the musket went off just in the nick of time! The large dog lay at his feet; his heart was left hanging on the branch of a small sweet gum tree, while the liver lay in the briars.

Bartus rushed to the burlap clump and began to remove its contents. "Oh, Lawd, Oh, Lawd!" he cried. Blood had soaked through the wrappings and dried. Holding the precious child he had helped to raise, he prayed she was alive. Oprah lifted her little face with a grieved, astonished look in her big brown eyes. She pointed to her shiny, swollen leg with the bone protruding. The blow flies had found the blood soaked child. Bartus knew the pearly white eggs would soon hatch.

If Oprah heard anything Bartus said, she did not respond because her world became black, once again. Bartus must gain strength from the Lawd, for he would need it to get Oprah the long distance home. After carrying her half-way through the woods, he realized he could no longer carry her and his musket too. When he reached the big oak he shoved the musket, powder and lead balls high up into the rotten hollow. Now, he was free to carry Oprah in a more comfortable position as they headed home.

Stopping to rest, he checked to see if Oprah was still alive; her breath was slow and labored. They reached the 'big house' around noon. Bartus knew others were searching for him, as he stopped by the stables and filled the water trough with sweet hay and laid the girl's body there. Mr. Barr would be in Savannah today until about nine or ten tonight. People were dying daily from malaria and dysentery so his job was constant.

Pansy, overwrought with worry, was waiting for Bartus. Carrie had come looking for him before eight o'clock this morning and again at eleven. Pansy had told her "Bartus has a cow that's calving... he will be gone 'til de calf be boan". That seemed to satisfy Carrie. "She could always find a way to get things done." Pansy thought, smiling.

Thanksgiving had been a long festive treat. The table had remained filled, so tonight there would be no supper served. Mr. and Mrs. Barr would have pecan pie and coffee when they returned from Savannah. He had two funerals to conduct and dozens of loose ends to tie up before coming home. Pansy was free to attend to Oprah, but she was not prepared for what she saw.

Bartus carried a kettle filled with hot water, along with a galvanized tub. He would draw fresh water for Oprah's bath; Pansy had brought white rags and soap. They uncovered the mumbling, incoherent girl and placed her in the tub. They bathed her gently. "Lawd, Bartus, go gets Miz Carrie. We's got stichin' to do." Pansy cried, frantically. Bartus ran toward the house and found her walking toward him. He began blubbering to her as Carrie ran ahead of Bartus to the stables. "Oprah, darling, oh, my God! What happened? Who did this? Where?" she questioned, fiendishly. "We will have to tell Mr. Barr." "No!" said Pansy and Bartus in unison. "Promise, Miz Carrie, and promise you won't tell a soul." Carrie did not understand, but knew they had the right to make the decisions about Oprah's care. Bartus and Pansy was older and wiser concerning plantations and slavery matters, than she.

She dropped the subject for her concern was to clean the blow fly eggs out of the wounds, to stitch her flesh, set and tape her leg and encourage her to live. Two hours passed... The painstaking ordeal was over as Oprah floated in and out of consciousness. There were no screams, with the exception of Pansy's, who was sent out of the stables and, Bartus helped Carrie. He was faithful and kept his prayers going, too. After dark, Bartus brought Oprah into the house. As Pansy pulled the covers over the wounded body, she realized Oprah had not spoken a word.

Early morning came almost too soon and Bartus Reems had barely closed his eyes. Sweet Pansy's warm body was the only thing to comfort him now, for he had a job to do before the trail got cold. Skidding out of his warm bed, he put on his long johns, pulled a knit cap over his head and with great speed, traipsed softly into the deep woods. He climbed the big oak, retrieving his musket, loaded it and waited. Surely the assassin, rapist would return to the scene of the crime, or at least, look for his guard dog. "He was a slave hunter" he thought. "They's the only peoples tuh have red-ticks and mastiffs."

The price for a runaway slave was great, at least one half of the purchase price. On average, the hunter made from two to five hundred dollars a head for the capture. Bartus was a prime example of black suffrage. His mother and three brothers were separated at the New Orleans slave block and he had been sold to several different slave run plantations. 'White Oak' was the first place he had ever lived where he was free, because Mr. Barr had bought him and given him his freedom and encouraged his marriage to Pansy Monte, also a freed slave.

Pansy was proud, arrogant and sassy and had not taken to Bartus as first, thinking him to be coarse and demanding. He had not rushed her to become his wife and his gentleness and wisdom became most attractive to her. Within a year they had a ceremony in the parlor of the 'big house' with music and dancing in the courtyard. They never had children, but took Oprah as their own, almost twelve years ago, before her mother passed, begging Pansy to keep her child from becoming a slave. "She was just a 'lil baby" he thought as he waited in the big oak, blinking back tears.

Changing his position from the base of the tree, he climbed onto the same large limb he'd found yesterday, not visible from the ground. As soon as he had settled himself on the limb, two fox squirrels scampered to safety, sending out the message of an invasion of privacy.

The rhythm of horse hooves moved in his direction, as Bartus climbed down from the tree and crouched over, moving slowly to the area of the dead dog. A bearded rider on the white horse appeared and whistled once, twice and alighted from his horse; the dog did not answer the call. Bartus moved in closer as the stranger headed in his direction; his raven hair was full caped with a widows' peak. Bartus picked a broken limb from the ground and threw it, hitting the horse; the horse spurted off, running at great speed. Bartus stood behind a hickory tree, bracing his gun. His voice from behind the tree said "Gets over there a piece to yo right, varmint. Dere bes yo dog? He look lak de gal, don't he? All tore up an bloody-like, purty sight, ain't it?" He asked with disgust. "Now, I bes a fair man. I give ye a chance. Ye can run and I shoots ye in de back, else ye can stans still whilse I blows yo haid off. What it be?" He continued. "I counts tuh three. One...two...three" he hollered. The musket went off and the bearded man became faceless. The entire bottom of his face was gone! Bartus did not look back; instead he gave a big sigh of relief and spat upon the ground! He was thankful the man did not give him excuses; there were none!

Bartus turned and headed toward the turkey roost, thinking that if he were lucky, he could get one before the sun came up. He did not remember walking home; his head was full of thoughts much like 'word salad' in his brain. He could not wait to tell Pansy!

He had vindicated Oprah's abuse. "De rapis' be daid". He thought as he moved through the deep woods. His prayer was that Oprah would lead a normal life, go to school, and have a family. She must never know about his plight.

"Love'll take care of Oprah", Pansy had said as she took the warm bricks from the stove. She had placed them in a pillow case at Oprah's feet for warmth. Pansy had been sitting on pins and needles since Bartus had left this morning. She walked out on the porch and began to rock in the wicker chair, soon dozing off. She heard Bartus whistling as he walked across the cotton patch, dragging a big eight point buck behind him. Nobody, not even Carrie, had questioned his whereabouts today. The deer was the perfect excuse for using the musket, or so they thought. Pansy met Bartus at the edge of the yard and helped him pull the deer to the back yard. She gave him a recap of the mornings' events, telling him that Oprah had not spoken a word; yet, she did eat a bit of gruel, spoon-fed by Carrie.

Later, after Pansy had gone to bed, Bartus was restless; he wept to relieve his pain and Pansy had held him like a mother would a child.

PART 9

The Slave
New Orleans

1850

"Every day hath toil and trouble
Every heart hath care;
Meekly hear thine own full measure,
And thy brother's share."

"Duty and Reward"
Margaret L. Bailey

Bartus wanted to talk and weeping helped to relieve his despair, but some things a man can't bring himself to think of anymore. "What's past is past." His mother had once told him. "Don't look back, always go forward" She'd admonished. Tonight, he was not only tired, he was troubled, for all these years he had not brought himself to tell Pansy about his past life. Her kind soul had not allowed her to ask questions; she had taken him at face value, so he felt bound to tell her and soon he would. Pansy lay quietly beside her husband until she heard his breathing slow and she knew he was asleep; Pansy slept too.

Bartus was swept away to another time and place. He had been nine years old when he came to America with his family. In New Orleans, he, his mother and three brothers were put on the auction block and sold to a French family, outside the city of New Orleans. His job was to keep the wood cut and fires burning for twelve fireplaces and two stoves. The only spare time he had was in the summer. Even then, he spent much of his time gathering wood from the woods, cutting down trees and digging lightered stumps. As with all slaves, he was not allowed to read and write. After two years, his mother was sold to a South Carolina cotton planter. She had successfully pleaded with her master to release her young son as well, with his age being the main factor in the bargain. After fourteen years, he was separated from his mother again and had long since become a man. When he was sold this time, to a Mississippi indigo and cotton planter, he brought one thousand dollars. He was used for loading the heavy bales of cotton and hauling indigo and would remain in Mississippi until he was twenty-five years old. One day the cotton shed caught fire and Bartus was the only slave seen leaving the burning shed, however; Jake Stump, overseer had set the fire as a vendetta against the owner. Bartus was blamed and tied to a flagging post and Jake Stump used a rawhide, cat-o-nine-tails whip on him. The barbs struck him again and again until his flesh was ripped from the bone and his back was bathed in blood; Bartus passed out from the pain. At the first auction of the year in Charleston, he was sold again.

Bartus never knew why John A. Barr II, owner of White Oak Plantation, had paid so much for him. Bartus had heard stories of his kindness; John Barr was known to have never owned a slave, nor believed in slavery. John had been in South Carolina, conducting a funeral and on his way back from Dogwood Cemetery he decided to drive by the slave market after seeing the auction signs that had been posted from Savannah to Charleston.

Tethering his horse to the concrete hitching post, he walked the four blocks to the auction. As a 'man about town' he knew practically every plantation owner from Savannah to New Orleans, and Charleston, as well. Nearing the wharf, he saw dozens of slaves being taken on buckboards to their new destinations. Refusing to look at their faces, he walked on, head downward with his hat pulled down, covering his eyes. He was there to collect from General Hack Wainescott, for the burials he had performed last month. Wainescott owned Fiveash Plantation, seventy mile away.

The auctioneer's voices rang out. "What am I bid for this strong, twenty-five year old man. He's been broke to the whip, knows his place and can do about anything from blacksmithing to planting and…" Mr. Barr heard only the droning on and on of the auctioneer's voice because his eyes were locked into those of the young slave's. To break the spell, he walked around the slave block, looking for Wainescot, where finally, he located him near the docks. They settled their business and John took his money and placed it into the inside packet of his coat. Walking back the way he had come, he looked up at the young slave and once again, their eyes met as John's heart sank!

His own childhood flashed before his eyes, causing his brain to spin. The club foot of Gimpy Johnny and all the emotional pain associated with society's poor acceptance of him came like a flood and his imagination ran rampant! It was apparent a beating had caused the scars on the slaves' back and arms; large rope-like tissue was evident. Black and silver scales stood out like the 'cross ties of a railroad'. Some areas looked like a dried mud creek, cracked with plugs of black flesh missing from his upper arms. All of this reminded John of a poorly designed impression of injustice!

The auctioneer screamed, "going once, going twice, gone… for one-thousand dollars!" John Barr watched as other slaves ordered this young one on to the buckboard of James Thomas Taylor of 'Five Forks Plantation'. John Barr would not look back, for he had lost out. The Taylor buckboard passed his carriage and as it passed, the young slave looked straight into John's eyes again. "Hold it!" Mr. Barr called out loudly. The carriage behind the buckboard filled with newly purchased slaves, was driven by James T. Taylor, himself and it had stopped in the middle of the road. "How much will you take for the last slave you bought?" John asked. James Taylor, who had never had such an incident happen, said "John, you didn't make the first bid. I don't understand," he went on sarcastically. John Barr was quick to reply, "I need him. I'll pay you fourteen hundred dollars for him." He offered. "Sold" Mr. Taylor agreed. "What or where are you going to put him? You don't have a buckboard," he continued. "Don't need one, he will be riding with me," John replied, opening the door of the gold-crusted carriage for the foul smelling slave.

During the long ride home Bartus Reem told Mr. Barr in broken English about his past owner. "No man can own a soul." Mr. Barr spoke angrily. "I will have your Emancipation papers drawn up next week and you can leave when your want to and be your own man. But, when you start to leave I will need to know, for it is dangerous for you to travel alone in this area without a white person to accompany you," he went on. "I have connections in New York but you will have to go with an escort and have something waiting on the other end," John spoke deliberately. I have a former slave who was sent to me by my uncle and she refuses to be emancipated and go out on her own. "Too dangerous," she says. Pansy is about thirty-three or thirty-four years old and you may have her for a wife if she chooses," he offered.

"Why yo bees so goot tuh me, Massah?" Bartus asked.

"Well, I don't know Bartus, maybe it's because I like you. You remind me of someone I knew as a boy."

"Dis be mah lucky day, suh. I thanks my big Massah," Bartus said looking toward the sky; they rode the last ten mile in silence.

Mr. Barr stopped the horses and lit the lanterns on the sides of the carriage for it was getting dark. "The horses can see where they are going, but I want to see my own way." Mr. Barr explained. A big smile crossed Bartus' face and his unstilted belly laugh continued on for a few minutes. He had never had he been treated so well in his life and his "Ha, ha" echoed in the night air.

Most of the gossip ran rampant from one plantation to another... mostly horror stories. He felt special; he had never had a woman nor had he dreamed of being free, now he had been promised both and he vowed he would be good to his woman. He sniffled as he remembered his mother; it evoked a sweet nostalgia. He had worked hard and proven to be a good slave, as he promised her the day she coughed and hemorrhaged from the dust of the corn crib. She'd lived and worked in dust and yeast for years.

Alas, as they drove through the magnolias that lined dirt road, Bartus saw for the first time "White Oak Plantation". The courtyard was ablaze with lights, a large bronze water bird stood on its long legs with its head turned directly toward the sky and spewed water ten feet into the air. The lanterns from the carriage magnified the rainbow colored waters, filling the air as the wind carried the illuminating colors upward. "Yeah! Yeah!" Bartus responded to the sight his eyes beheld. Mr. Barr was pleased with Bartus' greeting to 'White Oak'; after all, his was merely a reiteration of everyone else who had come here.

Pansy was up and had kept supper warm for Mr. Barr. Alighting from the carriage was Bartus, who stood beside the carriage, staring at the emblazoned crest and shellacked wood, rubbing it gently. Pansy stared out from the porch. "Lawd, he be so ugly," she said, covering her face with a slap. "Dat young whipper-snapper better not bees no smart aleck," she mumbled. "Sho ain't goan boss me, no suh… sho ain't." She declared, with her hands placed firmly on her hips, she strutted from each end of the porch several times.

"Pansy, this is Bartus Reem and he lives here now, a free man. I will have him emancipated, next week", Mr. Barr said firmly. "He will be your helper; chopping wood, drawing water, boiling clothes, making lye soap and whatever you need him for, so don't you go and get so bossy; he will want to leave us." He said without cracking a smile.

"Yes suh ah hears you, suh." She responded turning her back to the both of them. Mr. Barr said finally, "You find him a place to sleep; he needs a good nights sleep." He added as he left the room.

Pansy did not want to hear anymore and stomped through the kitchen, showing indignation! She pulled the closet door open, pulled out the thickest quilt, laid it in the corner of the pantry, saying; "Here yo be, yo needs water all over, yo stinks! Have mussy, have mussy." She said, pointing to the quilt placed on the floor. "Yo come whenst ah calls for ya tuh mak de fire in de stove. Brefast be ready at six o'clock." She said, shaking her finger in his face.

Unable to sleep, Pansy tossed and turned throughout the night. The bright clear eyes of young Bartus haunted her and her imagination was running wild. She had taken great pleasure in knowing Mr. Barr had given her emancipation papers three years ago, for freedom for a slave was unheard of at that time. News had spread throughout slave quarters all over the South, evoking runaways to seek refuge at 'White Oak'. Pansy did not have a problem with others being freed, on a personal level, but she would no longer be held in the highest esteem among the Negroes, throughout the plantations of Georgia. After all, a certain amount of pride, admiration and sass was connected to the prestigious event. Another problem was, Mr.

Barr had not discussed the slave buying business with her and his failing to read her mind or ask her permission was akin to dishonor, so far as she was concerned. So she fussed; awhile.

Five o'clock came long before daylight and Pansy had a built-in alarm clock. She never waited for the chimes of the big clock, adorning the parlor; she arose, pulled her coarse feed-sack gown over her head and slipped into her homemade sack dress. She entered the kitchen, poured a pan full of cold water and washed her hands and arms, which ached all the way to her elbows, but "cleanliness is next to Godliness." She thought, as her teeth chattered.

Walking over to the pantry, she kicked the exposed black leg, lightly. "Up with Yo," she demanded. "Gits yoself tuh de woodpile and fetch some splinters. Brefast jist waiten tuh be cooked," she quipped. "Gets on now," she demanded impatiently. Then turning to open the stove door, Pansy rubbed her eyes again and again. The stove was stoked with fat-lighter and wood; all she needed was to strike the safety match. Behind the stove in the wood box was neatly piled wood and splinters, enough to cook breakfast, dinner and supper. "Lawd, lawd" she laughed under her breath; she then began a long hard belly laugh. Bartus joined in with her and the ice was broken. "Ha, ha" rang throughout the kitchen and without a word his bare feet left the kitchen, heading to the woodpile.

He did not come in for breakfast, because he had never eaten before dinner and even then, he ate the leftovers from several days; once in a while he would get corn pone and if he were lucky, there would be molasses.

Pansy finished the dishes, cleaned and swept the kitchen with her broom sage, which has been beaten and tied with twine. Sitting down at her work bench, she began to peel ten pounds of potatoes and there would be fresh venison, tenderized with a vinegar soak. She had her own herb garden connected to the back yard, outside the kitchen door. "Gots tuh be handy," she had said, strewing the seed beds last spring. Once in a while she would peer out the back kitchen door to see if they had sprouted; she was proud of her accomplishment.

She became concerned that Bartus had not come in to ask for food nor water. She stood at the window and watched him chopping wood, the muscles in his back stood out. Pansy was horrified! She'd seen something else; the sight of his back took her breath away! Her hand flew to her mouth in an effort to stifle a scream of ugly words. Indignation and hatred had claimed her thoughts, "Lawd, ah ben so wrong, duh po man"

While dinner was bubbling away in the large cast iron pot, Pansy went to the well and drew a tub of water, setting it in the sun to warm for Bartus. Next, she would find decent clothes for him and talk to Zinnie, the laundress, at dinner the two of them would resolve this need, today.

Bartus had split logs, hacked splinters and racked it all, in pig-pen style; enough wood for a month. Sitting on the big hack stump, he wiped the salty sweat from his face. He was proud of his craft and wanted Pansy to be proud of him, too. He had never been called lazy or good for nothing; he was a man of honor who worked for his keep. These thoughts evoked pride and his chest swelled.

Tonight he would ask Massah Barr for three milk cows so he could make butter. He would need a churn, but he could whittle a butter mold from a hickory stump; and this afternoon he would hunt for deer. Next spring, he would grow cabbages, rutabagas, carrots, peas and green beans. He had noticed the pitiful condition of the garden behind the stables and envisioned potatoes, garlic, onion, corn and greens growing there.

While Bartus ate dinner, Pansy was busy stringing haywire from the kitchen post to the clothesline and back to protect the privacy of Bartus Reem. With Zinnie's help, she would kill two birds with one stone by boxing off the tub of water and creating a place to hang sheets to dry.

"Dat bees perfek. 'Cain't nobody see him" she murmured. A fruit basket served as a shelf for the clean shirt, pants and drawers. Pansy dropped a large dollop of lye soap into the warming water. It would melt and soften the dried skin of Bartus, giving him a thorough cleaning from lice and vermin.

"The day ended just as it had begun- almost dark. It had raced through as a lightning bolt shoots through the heavens", Bartus thought as he stood in the tub, rubbing himself down with the coarse woven towel. Slipping into his pants and shirt, he left the drawers behind. "I ain't nevah wore no shoat pants" he said. He thought they were offering him a choice.

Finally he stepped onto the side porch and into the kitchen with filthy rags in tow. Zinnie met him, took the smelly rags from him and punched them into the wash pot to soak. She unmade the privacy curtain from around the tub; folding the sheets in a nice soft stack, moving quickly to the laundry closet. Bartus sat on the bench beside the gate-leg table, smiling from ear to ear; his white teeth glowing in the new darkness of the room. Taking a black gum branch, he pulverized the end and brushed his teeth, as his mother taught him. Its soft, sweet gum was cool to his gums and tongue; he had never felt better in his life. Pansy walked into the kitchen with his clean drawers in her hand.

"Yo cain't nevah bees a gentleman 'til you learns tuh ware de garb" she corrected.

"You means I puts dem on too?" he questioned.

"Dat be rite", Pansy answered. "Take offen dat shirt. I has sumpen fo you" she said softly.

Bartus did as he was ordered. He removed his shirt and turned his back to her. Soon, he felt her warm gentle hands moving with a rotating motion, covering his scars with pig lard, aloe and winter mint weed, mixed together. Her fingers massaged the railroad tracks of scar tissue. She could feel the cool permeating, relaxing ointment. Her hands were aglow with circulation, while her eyes filled with tears at the sight of whiplashes. Bartus had fallen asleep and his head drooped onto the eating table; he would stay there until the early morning. The stove that he had stoked earlier for the breakfast meal had become cold and dampness filled the room, rain was falling softly outside.

The quilt in the pantry closet welcomed him with its warmth and he slept until the music of the pots and pans awakened him. Pansy was in the dough trough making a type of milk biscuit from an age-old starter recipe given to her by her own Mammy. This morning she was humming a tune, for her world was right and she was happy because somebody needed her! A wide smile crossed her face as she gave her biscuits the final pat of pig lard. Shoving them into the hot oven, she opened the damper of the fire door sending the hot flames into the cast iron wall of the oven. The biscuits would be ready in a jiffy. Next Pansy forked the cooked, cured ham from the frying pan, poured water and a little brewed coffee into the left over ham grease. Stirring from the bottom of the cast iron fryer, the red-eye gravy was ready. Scrambled eggs and grits were taken from the warming closet, high above the cook top.

Hannah had set the table when she came to make breakfast trays for Mr. and Mrs. Barr. She waited as Pansy pulled the oven rack forward, exposing thirty beautiful, and brown biscuits. Hannah took three and wrapped them in the soft folds of a cloth napkin and completed her tray with coffee. She headed up the long stairway to the bedroom as the others ate heartily; even Bartus, who had not been accustomed to breakfast. "Mmmm", he grunted. Pansy glowed, refilling his plate a second time as she began to sing while clearing the table.

"Go down Moses, down to Egypt land. Go down Moses, down to Egypt land." "Hummmmm…" she went on.

"We's free Bartus, we's free; thanks dey Lawd we's free." She raised her hands, clapping loudly. Bartus smiled from ear to ear; he liked this free spirited woman with all her sass and would wait for her to invite him to be her man. "It wouldn't be long, now…" he thought.

A month after Bartus' arrival at White Oak, he awoke from a nightmare that had plagued him for most of his life. It was two o'clock and the quiet of the night was disturbing. Bartus was accustomed to the sounds of rats and coons in the corncrib as they'd crawled over his burlap bed, fighting for food. His fingers are scared from their bites and have long ago healed; however, the nightmares have not. The brutality of Jake Stump could not compare with the hardships and languishing death of his mother.

Bartus had suffered silently, waiting for a listening ear and he found it in Pansy. She heard his cries for the third time this week. Her coattail snapped as she hurried to him, again. After nights of feeling helpless, she made a decision to try her own treatment, entering his room in a flash. Bartus was sitting with both hands squeezing his head. "I's gots a hade ache", he groaned. Pansy took him in her arms, nuzzled his face and rubbed his head, kneading his shoulders as if he were a blob of biscuit dough, bringing relief. She stood with her hands moving methodically on his face, cheeks and mouth.

"Youse ain't gots no mo hade ache. I's dun cured yo." She moved directly in front of him, whispering words only they understood.

"Woman, I sho loves yo sassy ways! Yo be's perfek. It be's de power of a goot man tuh makes a goot woman." She stayed with Bartus on the closet floor that night and, they decided to be married. Pansy would discuss her wedding with Mr. Barr in the morning; she had always longed to be a bride and this was just the man she had waited for all of her life.

PART 10

The Burial
White Oak Plantation

1850

"I carried my musket, as one that must be,
But loosed from the hold of the dead or the free,
And fearless, I lifted my good trusty sword.
In the hand of the mortal, the strength of the Lord."

"The Veteran and the Child"
Hannah Gould

Pansy had become bewildered, because Oprah had not spoken a word in over a week now. Today Pansy had made venison stew, so she borrowed a plate from Mrs. Eva's antique stock that she knew Oprah had always loved to look at it through the bow-front glass china cabinet. The child had only left her bed to use the chamber and no matter what was asked in conversation, she showed no sign of trying to speak.

"Lawd, mah baby be def and dum" Pansy said to Carrie, who was dressing the fractured leg. Dr. Moore said, "You've done a good job, Carrie. It's as good as I could have done" he added. "She's healing nicely but, it will probably be six more months before it will be completely healed and she is due a routine check-up."

Outside in the early morning a mocking bird sang, its melody was haunting. The moon was full, spring had come, and grass and green weeds grew around the magnolias. Massive clusters of dandelion burst through the weeds. Peach blossoms filled the enormous fruit orchard with fragrance. The pear and apple trees were pregnant with buds, dogwoods and red maples adorned the fences and woods outside Sally Ogens log cabin. She watched the sound of spring from her kitchen window. The redbirds and thrashers were mating in the air, every bush and tree rang with their melodious courting music. The red-headed epilated woodpecker had chosen the top of Sally's great yellow pine to drill several holes. She did not notice because she was busy scrubbing the porches.

Ordinarily, Sally was a happy-go-lucky soul; singing most of the day, however, this was not one of those days because today she was frustrated. She had made a new dress for Gale again yesterday, using the same pattern she had cut from newspapers. She was not able to fit the pattern to the child, and thinking she was losing her touch, she resigned herself to get help from Carrie. "Carrie, could sew most anything, without a pattern" she said with confidence to Gale, Gale said nothing.

The weekend was a beautiful time to relax and do nothing, Carrie thought as she headed out the Magnolia lined road of White Oak Plantation after asking Mr. Barr to drive her to Sally's. Carrie knew she had been needed to care for the sick, however, many 'sick' situations, along with her financial management position, had become too much of a burden.

"I don't think I can take anymore problems," Carrie told Mr. Barr, before leaving the plantation. "Oprah doesn't seem to be mentally sound; however, her leg is much improved and with both Oprah and Gale out, there is so much to be done," Carrie said quietly. She sounded tired, thought John Barr.

"I will take your request for help into consideration." He said. "I know things have been hard on you. I need to thank you for your generosity toward my wife and son; I failed to do so before now. They would both have died, had it not been for you." He remarked, turning away from her. John stuttered, looking for the appropriate sentence; "How could I have been so foolish and selfish, thinking only of my own pain, that I could not see yours? I ... I ... I want to make it up to you," he went on. "Women like you can never be bought; you live by your integrity."

Reaching his hand inside his breast coat pocket, he pulled out two fifty dollar bills and handed them to her saying, "You will receive forty dollars per month starting Monday." Shaking hands with Carrie; the verbal agreement was sealed.

Sally Ogen sat silently on her front porch awaiting the arrival of Carrie. As she pondered over the past few months, one thing came to mind. The scrawny little girl who had come to live with her no longer existed, for she had grown up in a short amount of time.

There had been no discussion with Carrie involving Gale's need for properly fitting clothes. She had let the seams out as far as she could, then pieced some of them, but they were not attractive. "Gale needs to get back to the plantation before school starts," Carrie has said when she first brought her home for the summer. Knowing the hectic goings on at the plantation Sally did not want to put anymore pressure on her daughter-in-law, but "Today we must have a reckoning," she planned.

The beautiful chariot blazed in the sun as it moved gracefully along. Its magnificent shellacked wood, designed with the family coat-of-arms, was the finest in all of Georgia. Stopping in front of Sally Ogen's house; Carrie alighted from the carriage with the grace of a noble woman. Mr. Barr was cordial to Mrs. Ogen and tipped his hat as he removed Carrie's tapestry valise from the back seat. After saying goodbye to Carrie, he turned the horses around and headed to Savannah; he had a body to bury today.

John Barr had not been prepared for what he had seen this morning. The body of an unidentified man had been found by beaver trappers around the 'Old Limestone Mountain'. There was no identification on his body and a large part of his lower head had been blown away; a black

Mastiff dog had been shot a few steps away. The authorities had been notified and a search had begun for the killer.

Mr. Barr was astounded; the land belonged to him! A man had been killed on his plantation! There had been no rumblings of information from any of the farm workers as to anyone being missing; nor any reports of sightings of strangers on the land.

The puzzle began to perplex him as the day wore on. He drove his horse a little faster than usual as he headed home, for he needed to get home before dark. His land had always been private and nobody had ever been given permission to hunt or trap there except for the field hands. He drove into the livery stable, unhitched the carriage, and took the gear and trace chains loose from his horses, locking them into their stalls for the night. Ben Samuels, one of the farm hands, had placed fresh hay in each horse's trough. He was ready to saddle Eagle, for his ride home, when he noticed a strange horse outside the corral gate. "Whew, what a handsome animal!" he declared. The saddle and saddlebags were still attached and the only thing missing was the rider, which was nowhere in sight.

It appeared the horse had not been fed for sometime as he had pawed holes in the ground near the gate. Ben had filled the water trough so John decided, "the horse can stay here until the owner comes for him." He opened the gate, took the saddle from the horse and slung it over the fence along with the saddlebags.

The sun was going down and the day was almost over. John had not planned on this extra work he was doing now that he had reached home. It was too late to scout the ridge or brush the carriage horses so he rode Eagle to the house and went to bed.

The night had been restless for John Barr; questions had plagues him and, he had not the slightest idea as to how to solve the mystery he was now facing. He was up at the crack of dawn; "I must get going," he declared. He walked to the corral and looked at the strange, new horse.

"He has excellent breeding," he thought to himself.

"With a little washing and brushing, he could be a remarkable animal!" he mumbled.

He walked around the horse, picking up each hoof for inspection; the mane was trimmed and groomed. John shook his head, "Astounding!" he declared, "A solid white horse, with one black hoof." He saddled his horse, mounted and rode toward the limestone ridge.

As his ride took him down an old wagon trail, past the long forgotten sawmill, he began to smell putrid, rotting flesh. He rode near and could hear the blow flies singing a tune to their banquet on the ground. It was a large black dog with brown markings that had been reduced to skin and bones. Thousands of maggots would be feasting for the next few days. What appeared to be the heart and part of a liver, was hanging from a nearby bush. The stench almost provoked regurgitation of his breakfast.

As he moved on, he observed burlap bags, for the purpose of picking cotton, in the tall brush. He assumed that they had been taken from the old house where they had been stored for safe keeping until the cotton harvest began. He moved away from the area and noticed several hoof marks in the dirt as he rode around a nearby stream. "Probably the Constable and his men," he guessed. As he approached the old house, he noticed that there were more horse tracks, but they were wind-worn. "When tracks get cold they are hard to read." He thought.

Sliding down from Eagle, he squatted on the ground for a closer view and on the right front hoof print; there were two missing nails from the horseshoe. "The Constable sure has his work cut out for him," he said, scratching his head. He climbed back on his horse and headed home.

The sun was coming up and he dreaded going into town. He had breakfast with Eva, left a work schedule for the stable workers and checked the new horse again. As he lifted the horse's hooves once more; he noticed there were two nails missing from one of the horseshoes!

Ben had groomed the horses and had them ready to pull the carriage for the burial of the murdered stranger. "The casket would be light weight, not very durable, but free of charge," John thought, as he drove into Savannah. He would be buried along side of the hundreds of typhoid and malaria victims on the Island.

The grave had been dug and he and four of Barr's Funeral Home workers would bury the body. Preacher Robert Rayburn would take care of the eulogy and prayer. Neither a pauper nor stranger could ask for more. Inquiries had been made prior to the burial but nothing was forthcoming. "There was no one to claim the body. No wife, children, nor family to mourn for him," John Barr thought, wiping away the tears with his sleeve and hoped that his helpers had not seen his weakness. Preacher Rayburn's voice rang in his ears the rest of the afternoon and during the long drive home.

"He has preached his gospel, 'This stranger in our land; rode to his death in a strange land', he quoted loud enough for a whole congregation of mourners to hear. Too bad only a half dozen people heard," he quipped. John Barr thought, "If they were not deaf, they soon would be."

"The stream he was found near could not wash away his sins; nor could the cries of his voice keep him from his maker." The preacher continued. "God above heard and will make the final decision. All we can do is to give him a resting place. That is why we are here today. 'Go and sin no more; lest a worse thing come upon you'," he quoted from his bible.

The six men left the cemetery; each had other work to do back in Savannah.

"Who was this man and what was he doing on my land?" John questioned himself.

"Why wasn't he buried?"

"Why was an expensive dog, such as a Mastiff, killed?"

"Why was the horse allowed to go free?"

"It seemed that one would never have left such a handsome, well-bred horse behind." These questions bombarded John's mind as he rested in the parlor, later that evening. Evangeline had come downstairs for dinner and to play with their son, John-John, instead tonight she would become a listening ear. John had always respected Evangeline's opinion; once she was drawn out of her world. Her judgments had become clear and concise, for hers was breeding, an Aristocratic view, her family had laughingly credited to themselves years ago.

"John deah, mah heaht cries for you, mah dahlin'." She said, patting his arm, consolingly. "White Oak has fohevah posted lands. We cahnot be at fault foh this atrocious act," she quipped softly. "I'm prowhed of you mah husband, you are the joy of mah life," she murmured, kissing his neck.

"Lord, what did I do to deserve such a beautiful wife," he crooned. "I think it's time to thank you; Mrs. Barr, for such a handsome son," he retorted, hugging her close. She smiled up at him and together they walked up the stairway to the bedroom. All was well, even in the dark, troubled night.

"Although, Carrie was worn out, a mother can never be too tired for her children; to hug, kiss and, hold them," Carrie thought as she walked up the front steps of Mama Sally's house. It seemed as though years had passed since she had been home. "Home," she said in a kind voice, as tears of joy filled her eyes. She called out, "Gale, where are you, baby?" The figure coming from their bedroom could not be the same little girl she had left just three short months ago. Mama Sally had joked about putting weight on Gale's bones and, she appeared to have gained ten or twelve pounds in the time Carrie had been away. Her breasts were enormous and having had many years of training in nursing care, Carrie could not believe what her eyes were telling her. Something was very much amiss with her daughter's condition. She and Mama Sally sat close beside Gale's bed as the terrible truth unfolded. Three hours passed and, there was not a dry eye; nor the possibility of a tearless night among the three weeping females.

Gale could not look at the two people she loved more than any other on earth. Never in life, would she have brought such shame and sorrow to those two courageous and caring women. Almost six months had passed since she had seen her friend Oprah. "What will I do if the same thing happens to her," she wondered? "I should have told her and Mum when it first happened," she repented. "Oprah has to know! She must not go near the woods or Limestone Ridge," she cried, as her little heart was breaking with remorse.

Mama Sally sniffed loudly, blowing her nose on the rag from the pocket of her feed-sack apron. "I'm sorry I let you down, Carrie; Gale came to me seeking safety and I have not done much to help her. I should have knowed; Lord help me... not our little Gale," she wept.

"I'm an old woman now, but as a young'un I was able to help dozens of women-folk with being in the 'family way'. "I feel so stupid," she continued on with disdain.

"I'm just an old, foolish, worn-out woman; a good-for-nothing Granma," she babbled, as tears poured from her swollen eyes.

"Hush it, neither of you is to blame," Carrie lamented. Her face had swollen and her voice was barely audible. "Any court in the world would put the blame squarely on me. That is where it belongs, on me," she cried! "I am her mother, I am responsible; I let White Oak Plantation manipulate and command my every move," she replied, vehemently! "What good mother would help the whole world when her daughter's life was going to hell in-a-hand-basket," she quipped, hoarsely?

"Everybody wants a piece of Carrie."

"Carrie do this, Carrie do that, I have no life of my own, nor time for my precious, raped and pregnant, twelve-year-old daughter," she sobbed! "As God is my witness, I will find that low-life scoundrel and he will die," she exploded! "Oh God, please help me, help us all," Carrie begged. "Forgive me Gale, if you can and, please find it in your heart to keep me in your life and I will prove to you that I can be a good mother and grandmother," she said. Her small voice was hoarse and lifeless.

"You know, Carrie," Sally said, not looking up from her trembling hands, "you had Gale, I had Walter, and now Gale will have us a little Walter or Carrie," she said, placing her arms around Carrie's shoulders. "There is a great possibility, we could have a little Sally," Carrie whispered softly. The wrinkled, little old lady laughed.

Gale sat in bed holding the two, kind and understanding mamas in her arms, when suddenly, the room filled with laughter. "*Laughter maketh a heart merry.*" She quoted from the Bible, which she had been reading a lot lately. They all knew, in their hearts that this tragedy would strengthen their bond, for after all; '*Love will conquer all*'.

Morning came and Gale had lain in her mother's arms throughout the night; at times she had snubbed so loudly, it had awakened Carrie. Mama Sally had chosen to bring a cot into their bedroom, "Just in case ya'll need me," she had said. The plain truth was, she was not ready to break the bond of friendship that had been established last night.

Sally in her old age, was beginning to understand her own feelings and even more about love. She had slept soundly throughout the night; for she had her family with her and a faint smile expressed her inner feelings. Today, she would bask in the feelings which had willed her to sleep last night; in fact, she felt just like cooking pancakes and sausages for breakfast, Gale's favorite! The Scuppernongs growing on the creek bank had served to produce a rich purple jelly and there was pear marmalade and blackberry jam ready to be enjoyed. She would bake a celebration cake, with chocolate layers an inch thick. Granma Sally was euphoric this morning for the cloud had passed over and it was time to live and enjoy what was left of her little time on earth.

Carrie awakened to the pungent fragrance of frying sausage. She had never been able to sleep when this wonderful smell permeated the world of Mama Sally's kitchen. "Mama Sally knew just how to spoil her two girls," Carrie thought.

The night had been long and drawn out; her arm and shoulder had frozen with Gale's weight as she slept. Carrie had not been aware of the pain until she tried to turn over. Each move she had made throughout the night had caused Gale to stir about; therefore, she was content to lie still until morning when, memories of the night before started to plague her.

How would she break the news of the pregnancy to the people on White Oak, she wondered? Oprah would feel betrayed by Gale's secret. Both girls were raped at the limestone ridge and if Gale had told Oprah, perhaps she could have been saved. Would John Barr understand that Gale needed to stay in school and support her in this effort? Also, arrangements would be needed for the baby. "There is plenty of room in our bedroom," she thought. "The baby can share our room." A smile crossed her lips; she would take this proposition to the Barr's as soon as she returned to work. Her decision was to forgo the extra money Mr. Barr had promised yesterday in lieu of his allowing Gale to come, with her baby and, live with her at 'White Oak'. It would be months before Gale would give birth; recover and return to work as Eva's maid. This was the only alternative Carrie could muster because it was for sure; she would no longer be separated from Gale. Taking a chance, she would 'throw herself on the mercy of Barr's court', so to speak. If all else failed, she would find work elsewhere, although she had some basic limitations to do so. She hated slavery almost as much as she hated the man who had violated her daughter. This very thought sent Carrie into a dither and she needed a plan. First, she must see John and Evangeline Barr. "The farm workers are not safe," she thought. "There can be no peace at 'White Oak' until this vile man is caught!"

The weekend rushed by and Carrie had a business to run. Personal concerns would have to take a backseat to the pressing needs of the plantation. She promised herself that she would wait for the opportune time to break the crushing news to John Barr and it could, perhaps; change all their lives.

Bartus picked Carrie up late Sunday afternoon and, acting totally out of character; she felt a strange need to question him about the general area of the limestone mountain. He would certainly know; if anybody would, about that area since he had hunted deer, turkey and coon there. Some enlightenment on the subject was needed before she went to see the Barr's. Another thing she needed was to know what Oprah knew concerning Gale's pregnancy. She may very well know the identification of the perpetrator, even though she was still unable to speak.

The only regret Carrie had concerning her time with Gale this weekend; was that she had not told her of Oprah's rape. She had been sworn to secrecy by Pansy and Bartus and she must ask their permission before any discussions with Gale could take place. Her best approach was to take the people at the plantation into her confidence; since they had taken her into theirs. "No matter what happened; Oprah will be cared for the same as Gale," Carrie mused. With that thought, she settled herself on the buckboard seat and enjoyed the pungent, sweet smell of spring filling her nostrils. The banks of the dirt road were filled with a myriad of spring flowers; wild plum trees were like lace dressed fairies blowing in the wind and, it rejuvenated her.

"Bartus, I have to talk to you and Pansy tonight," she said without thinking. "We will wait until after chores are done and lights are out throughout the house, I have much to say." Bartus had a whimsical look on his face; as though he were embarrassed or did not quite comprehend her request. She reached over and patted his hand and said, "Don't worry; this is nothing to do with you personally." His countenance changed for he still had a problem understanding the straightforward way in which Mrs. Carrie presented herself.

The early night was plagued with a strong, ill wind. Unlike the day; it tossed small whirls of dirt and debris' into the water barrels and troughs. Pansy was restless, "Doze ill wins gone blow in fate," she declared. She stood on the side porch and her gown filled with air like a balloon. "Lawd, evathing's gone blows away," she cried. "Bartus come quick, gets yo pants offen de barb-wire fenst, else dey be in Atlanta by mawning," she bossed. Bartus acted hastily; as he had always done, for this was his woman. All of her needs came before any of his. *'His mother smiled down from heaven,'* as he ran to the barbed-wire fence.

Carrie had settled down after all the windows and doors were closed and locked to the house. It was now a safe place to be during a dust storm. As she walked toward the kitchen; where all conferences were usually held, a chill ran up her spine. A sudden dread attacked her with a fierceness; paralyzing her throat. "These people can only stand so much," she thought, as she sat in her usual eating place.

"What da fuss is," Pansy asked? "I knowed sumpin' be wrong; dat ole ill wind done gone and dirtied up evvathing," she spoke deliberately. "Ah makes a pot-o-coffee fo yo ma'am," she went on. Bartus said nothing; he had been told there would be a meeting, which told him that something was going on with Carrie. He sensed that something was amiss on his buggy ride home with her this morning. "Yeah, sumpins up, fo sho," he thought. He grabbed a splinter from the wood box and whittled without rhyme or reason.

Carrie cleared her voice and began as Pansy started pulling the cups and saucers from the cupboard; making enough noise to wake the dead!

"I want to tell yo sumpin' first, ma'am," Pansy said nervously.

"I thinks Oprah dun gots sprung-up. She ain't had no woman-thing in three months now. She pukin' evvah mawnin'; yestidy, she ruint evva sheet in da house," she lamented.

"A, an, an" --- she stuttered, "She jist too young; she be jist a baby. Lawd knows, I hates it fo her, I sho does, yes, ma'am," she said deliberately. She had worked hard on her sentences for weeks; she had tried to get up enough courage to tell somebody.

Carrie felt the blood drain from her cheeks; her suspicion had been right! She wanted to get up and run, but her legs would not cooperate. She took several long, deep breaths and exhaled slowly; she had learned how to quiet down her rapidly beating heart. Pansy poured the coffee, while Carrie poured her tears. She cried out, "Oh no; God help us"! A large reservoir of tears sprang its leak from within her soul. She howled like a lost kitten in a snowstorm. She wiped her face with her hands; her eyes had become red and swollen.

Bartus handed her a clean kitchen towel so that she could blow her nose and wipe her eyes. As he spoke, his voice sounded five decibels lower than usual; he reached out and drew fragile Carrie into his arms. "Ummmm," he hummed. Pansy, with outstretched arms, needed comfort too. The three stood in the middle of the kitchen floor and wept for the times ahead and for those past.

An eternity later; Carrie cleared her voice once again, "Too much has happened here that I don't understand," she said, holding back more tears.

"Sit down," she said to Pansy; taking her by the arm.

"I went home this weekend to find my daughter in the s-s-same situation," she sobbed. "She is about six months pregnant and has felt her baby moving inside her two months ago." She went on, "She was raped by a man over by Limestone Falls. Apparently, she and Oprah had lain down to take a nap. She cannot remember much of what happened; but, she awoke to see the bearded face of a man standing over her. The horse he had been riding was solid white with the exception of one black foot. He knocked her almost out, dragged her away from Oprah and, proceeded to put his filthy hands on my child," she said through clenched teeth.

The gleam in Bartus Rheems eyes came straight from 'the pits of hell'! He felt powerful and good, for justice had been done! He had exonerated the crimes committed against the children all by him self.

"Da Massah in heban be glad," he laughed aloud.

No more little girls would suffer at this maniac's hands. It had been taken care of forever; throughout eternity! A small wan smile crossed Pansy's face; yet her eyes rolled, almost giving her away. She was finding it hard to stifle the giggles creeping into her throat. Lifting her hands; she looked toward the kitchen ceiling, "Praise be de Lawd," she prayed in earnest. "De Lawd be praised," she repeated; as Carrie looked on quizzically.

"I know the two of you well enough to know you have a secret you haven't told me," Carrie said. "What is it?" She demanded.

"Da man what rap' our chillums be daid," Bartus said. "I knows, I pulled da ole musket from ovah da doah, puts da big ball in, powdered it up heavy like, pulled ba'k da ole flintlock and blowed his haid slap offen his body," Bartus smiled. "He got a fair chanst; better'n he gived ahr babyz," he said with pride.

"Dat be da man Massa Barr bury on da islan'; didn' deserbe no buryn, shoulda jist lets de buzzarts hav'im." He went on, "Po' lil' babyz; dey be havin' babyz dey selves," shaking his head as he spoke.

His eyes grew large and shining, giving way to the large stream of rolling tears coursing down his face. The broken man wept for the loss of Oprah's and Gale's childhood innocence. They would both drop out of school, never to return. "Oh, mah Lawd, what fate," he mumbled. They had been forced into an adult world and their pain would never be resolved.

Pansy and Carrie added their tears to Bartus'. Sadly, Carrie said, "The storm blew in a wet night." Suddenly, they all began to laugh. Their laughter was as healing as their tears had been cleansing and each of them knew that they and the children would make it. Somehow, with God's help and each others support they would overcome this tragedy. Now, Carrie knew her next step would not be as difficult as before. The Barr's were intelligent people; surely, they were understanding people as well. She would call a meeting.

The meeting in the formal parlor took place the following evening. The gorgeous fireplace mantle was alive with a pair of Lustre candles. Each end of the mantle board held Swedish Neo-classical Ormolu vases of cobalt blue. A large painting of young Evangeline Lyne Barr completed the ensemble. Two majestic Wainscot chairs sat in a conversation setting; their backs held the crest double scrolled, of winged cherubs above their panels, pulled together with stylish griffins.

A French carved gilt wood fire screen depicted a needlepoint Neo-classical vase, resembling the ones on the mantle. On the right wall, an eight foot fluted walnut and poplar table sat. Its only ornament was Martha Tyne's, continental oak and iron mounted, marriage chest. Its top was adorned with foliate iron straps on an open plinth base, incorporating four wooden wheels. This had been a gift to Great Grandmother Martha on her wedding day, by her brother, The Duke of Newberg. Eva Tyne had acquired it on the day of her marriage to John Alexander Barr, II.

The grandfather clock in the parlor struck three and John and Eva had not yet arrived at the assigned destination of their choice. Carrie was enveloped in the tranquility of the massive room. Many of the furnishings were from periods Carrie had never seen; even in books. She had never paid full attention to the detailed portrait of Eva Barr; even when she'd brought John-John here. The young woman looking down from the enamel and pearl picture frame could not have been more than eighteen years old. Her countenance gave command to its viewer; its Madonna innocence compelled one's total attention. Even from the height above the fireplace, Eva stared out in a condescending manner; evoking a disdain in Carrie's psyche.

John Barr entered the room with his wife holding on to his arm. Tightening her grip, Eva appeared only to emphasis her need for his attention or perhaps to imply the depth of their relationship. They took their seats in the Wainscot chairs and Carrie chose the settee, a few feet away and safely out of their circle. Mr. Barr cleared his voice then spoke deliberately. "We have much to communicate; as I have studied over the lack of help we currently have at the plantation. The same problems exist with the farm laborers, as well," he offered. "Mrs. Barr and I have made plans to build four more houses for our workers. Each house will have its own well of fresh water and, a small garden spot," he added.

"We will cut timbers from our woods, reactivate the saw mill and become self-sufficient as much as we can. Every room will be sealed with yellow pine, a fireplace and, outside toilets, which will cut down on sickness. We are also prepared to build furniture and furnish each room," John spoke decisively.

"We have a special surprise for you, Carrie," John stated. Interrupting her husband, Mrs. Barr said, "Yes Carrie, ah have been busy drawing up the plans fo'ah yhour new home, you will have only the best. I am going to New Yo'ark, to buy yhour furnishings," she exclaimed happily. "Afteh all, deah; you dheserve it," she added.

Carrie was bewildered and had no idea what this was all about. However, she knew that all their plans would change after they heard what she had to say. "We may be able to pay a little more than I quoted you the other day," Mr. Barr went on. Carrie couldn't take it anymore; she screamed, "Stop it, you don't understand; you don't know what you are saying! After you hear what I have to say, you may not want me here."

She gasped for breath and began again; knowing the lovely lady above the mantle and the still beautiful woman in front of her, swathed in silk with a bit of lace at the collar, was sitting in judgment of her. Carrie had never witnessed a woman with such excess pride. Her primadonna look could never fit into her own world, she thought.

Her story was finished after two hours and she had left nothing out; the rapes of both children and their pregnancies. Stunned, Eva Barr's tears flooded her cheeks, soiling the lace collar of her beautiful dress; she was speechless.

Mr. Barr's mind was working overtime and he could not process all he had just heard; even with all the loose ends, he could not connect them to the man he had just buried. "Who killed him?" The answer came as soon as he asked himself this question. There was only one type of gun that could have caused so much damage, a flintlock; its lead ball had been imbedded in this man's brain. His thoughts ran rampant; "who could have pulled the trigger?" only a person, who used an old musket, was the obvious answer and this narrowed that field considerably. "But what was the motive?" he asked himself; the answer was on the tip of his tongue.

"Bartus!" "Bartus was protecting White Oak from a born killer" he said angrily! "Mrs. Carrie, go get Bartus and Pansy, I have a few words they need to hear."

Carrie left the room in haste knowing Pansy and Bartus were waiting for the outcome of her meeting with the Barr's. She took a seat at the table with them and reassured them that they would be treated with dignity when meeting with the Barr's. As was his nature, John had conferred with Eva in Carrie's absence and when Carrie, Bartus and Pansy entered the room, everything became quiet. Bartus, with hat-in-hand, had opened the door for the ladies, as he was always a gentleman. Carrie entered first with Pansy following close behind; who was shaking like a leaf in a windstorm. Bartus stood with the veins standing out on his neck. The muscles in his body and face quivered with fright. The three of them were ready for whatever was to come their way.

He and Pansy had decided that they would use their Emancipation papers and get Mrs. Eva to take them to New York. "How cans ah axe Massa fo enough money tuh stahts oveah", he thought? "He been goot tuh me", he continued. "Ah sho hopes he don' sells me tuh ah bad Massa", he mumbled.

John Barr stood from his seat and walked directly toward Bartus; his hand flew forward and Bartus backed up in surprise. John's hand was too close to him now and Bartus could not escape. "Congratulations, Bartus Reem", he said, smiling. "The world has one less vile man to contend with", he offered. "I buried him into the ground; it was a paupers funeral after all. We have all done the right thing and I want us to put it behind us now and get on with our lives. I am presently prepared to build four more houses and will furnish them according to the needs and preferences of each family", he stated grandly. "Bartus, you and Pansy will have your house built within the next six months. White Oak Plantation is a twenty-five hundred acre Province and we need to expand and improve production."

"We have proven to the South that we can make profits without resorting to slavery. Ours is a unified farm", he smiled. "We are self-supportive; we grind our own grains, grow our own vegetables, process our own meat, weave and sew most of our own clothing." John Barr went on proudly; "Now, we are going to saw our own logs, rip our own boards and build houses and furniture for our own people. We will help to make the State of Georgia the greatest state in the Union," Mr. Barr spoke with authority.

Evangeline Barr stood and slowly walked toward her husband, speaking as she walked. "Both Gale and Oprah shall have their own rooms. We will put a nuhesery in both houses. We might as well put three bedrooms in all houses, othah wookahs have babies and need more room, don't you think so, dahlin'?" She spoke sweetly to her husband.

"Mah very own house, ah'd loves to hafe mah own cabin," Pansy giggled.

"No, not a cabin, only homes, sealed walls, glass windows, two porches; one Noath and the other Saoth," Eva said.

"No ma'am, cain't live in no Noath and Souath house; gots t'be looken East when de Lawd comes!" Pansy looked horrified.

"Whatevah." Eva stated.

Carrie exhaled and breathed a sigh of relief. This weekend she would tell Gale the good news, but right now, she needed a place for Gale and the baby. She would deliver in three months or less. She talked with Mr. Barr who said, "I'll get right on your house, Carrie, tomorrow I will get the sawmill going. I'll bring a new blade, bands and grease to get it moving. I'll send Ben Samuels in to Savannah tomorrow, with a list; we will order windows and furnishings later. He added, "You will have your house, lady, sooner than you think." He guaranteed.

Oprah sat coloring in books and wrote her needs out on paper. She was weak from vomiting in spite of Pansy's herbal tea and buttermilk. Her basic memory gave way to nightmares:

She had fallen into a hole and broken her leg. She was excited to return to Limestone Mountain, but can't remember whether or not she saw it. Where is Gale, Carrie had asked her? "Why can't I remember Gale," she questioned on her tablet? Her brain held a secret that refused to come forth from her lips. One day, she wrote, White horse; bad man. She had never answered Gale's letters.

Mama Sally sewed through the week for Gale, the pink and blue Chambray dresses were gathered under the breast, with flowing skirts. These were not the pretty ruffled dresses she had worn before and it made her feel old. She cried, "I want to go to school and become somebody." Her baby stirred within her and she calmed herself; afraid her baby would hear her. "Baby, I don't hate you, I just don't understand why you chose to make me your mother. Didn't you know that I am too young? I'm just a little girl and I love to play with Oprah and our dollies, pick flowers in the woods and play hop-scotch. I can never tell ghost stories again because they will frighten you," she said; rubbing the large, dark purple stretch marks on her hard belly. She would show her mother when she came home this weekend the marks of discomfort, as her belly stretched.

Carrie came home early Saturday morning. She had good news to tell Gale and the two of them talked for more than an hour. Mama Sally had said not one word and when she couldn't hold it back any longer she burst out, "What about me," she questioned? "I will be losing my whole family again." Carrie had been so carried away in her telling to Gale, she had forgotten Mama Sally. They would need her help with Gale and the baby while Gale went back to her job. It would take a lot of effort to bring this to fruition; 'a place for Mama Sally at White Oak.'

Before Carrie left them Gale asked if she could see Oprah. "I miss her so much, Mum," she said. "Could I please go with you to see her next week," she asked? Carrie had never told Gale about Oprah's pregnancy and there was no way to tell whether or not her visit would help or hinder. She also knew her daughter was lonely for her friend.

Workers were busy breaking ground, planting crops and cutting trees into timbers; in addition to maintaining their other duties on the plantation. Getting everything ready to build houses was not easy task; much planning and expertise had gone into this development.

Mr. Barr had brought in two new families and the women folk would help in the big house and, the men would work at the saw mill and construct the houses. Workers were excited and willing to press forward for a better lifestyle, so the entire plantation was buzzing with excitement. Ben would take over Bartus' job; he had cut enough cord wood for a year and racked it, but he would no longer build the morning fires, since spring had arrived and fires were unnecessary. Ben would also do the yard work.

Ben was willing to work hard in order for his family to live in one of the new houses. He had learned to build cabinets; chairs with split rawhide, buffalo, cow and deer skins. He used straw, corn shucks and cane bottoms in some styles and he loved being creative. He used his expertise to help the other workers learn. His skills were excellent as was his personality. For most of his life he had worked with horses and he knew them well; even the new one he had found outside the corral!

Ben Samuels had checked the new horse; cleaned, brushed and groomed him. He discovered that even though the horse was wearing practically new shoes, there were two nails missing from the horse's right foot. This small task would require permission from Bartus before a replacement could be done. He placed the excellently tooled leather saddle on the horse he had named "Buck" and, rode over to the saw mill to talk with Bartus. He needed guidance on the horseshoes and planting the vegetable garden. Ben knew Bartus would be too busy with the houses to plant and his help would be needed, which he was willing to do, but needed ideas and supervision.

Mr. Barr watched Ben as he rode down the wagon road. He was impressed with the way Ben had cared for his horses and this horse was special! The only place he had ever seen this particular breed had been among his father's stock horses, many years ago. The saddle was one of a kind; hand tooled for a special person; a man who was strong, flamboyant, charismatic and, wealthy. John would see the Constable tomorrow; the strange death needed closure. There was a possibility that this stranger, found on his plantation and, the horse was connected. Violations of both Gale Grant and Oprah Ward could have been perpetrated by this man.

"How could it ever be proven; since neither of the girls saw the body he had buried," he thought. "Both of them had been knocked out and Oprah still had not given a description of her attacker," he pondered. "Bartus was the only person who could vouch for the man who had been riding 'Buck', but he did not see the violation of either child," Mr. Barr concluded, as he rode into Savannah.

The sun was high as the moss shaded the road and blew gently in the wind of the canopied road. It was hanging freely and looked for all intents and purposes like 'an old man's beard'. John Barr was lost in thought as he traveled on alone. The clop-clop of the horse's hooves kept the same rhythm; the Cicada's serenaded with their songs ringing loudly, declaring life and the reproduction of spring.

John arrived at Constable Ezra Carnes office as Ezra was on his way to the mailbox. "Good morning, Ezra," John offered. "I would like to talk to you." Ezra motioned him into his home. As they sat in deep conversation, Lillian, the kitchen maid brought hot biscuits, fresh churned butter and two large glasses of cold buttermilk, pulled from the deep well. "What a treat," John Barr acknowledged as he took his second sip. "This beats Mint Julep any day; it really quenches a mans thirst," as he continued to smack his lips approvingly.

"As I was saying," Ezra offered, "I have circulated bans throughout the south for almost two months. The law will drop this investigation so far as I know, John," he said. "I am back where I started as I have been over and over the same concerns and questions you asked. The case will always stay open, but I don't have the help, time or energy to work on the case anymore. Unless some accident or further abuse of a female is called to your attention, we will have to assume that the man you buried was the villain," he spoke decisively. "John, I don't think our conversation should be made public; women can cause quite a stir. There is no need to bring about fear in our county and the less said the better."

"Then I'll continue to keep the horse for another month and if you hear of anyone who's missing the animal, they can contact me," John stated. It was apparent that his law degree evoked the ultimate respect from Ezra Carnes. "By-the-way, Ezra, I will have a marker made for the grave; what name would you suggest," he asked? "John Doe will do," the Constable said shaking hands with John as he opened the door.

July came and a rush was put on the saw mill workers to produce quickly. Trees were cut and hauled to other plantations to be ripped and sanded for the interior walls of the houses. The fear of the approaching winter urged the workers onward and they worked nightly until dark. The rotation of housing would begin as soon as the third house was built; Carrie Grant's being first. Bartus and Pansy were second and Ben Samuels third. Ben's present cabin would be the first in rotation and it was a prize.

He had his own furniture designs built into his cabin with washstand and toilet closet on the back porch.

Finally, Carrie's house was completed and Evangeline Barr wanted it to be special for her companion. She and Carrie were busily going through the attic picking all the pieces that had once overrun the mansions rooms. She wanted Carrie to have her choice of furniture. Mama Sally had been working on the dozens of yards of material, goose downs, piping, tulle, satin and velvet that Mrs. Barr had ordered from New York. Sally Ogen had finished the window draperies, chair cushions and covered a French settee for the front room. Mrs. Barr had suggested that Sally set up a sewing room in one of the empty houses so that she would have plenty of room to work. She and Ben would work together designing, building and decorating furniture for the new houses.

In a few weeks, Ben Samuels had finished the long oak table, two benches and two chairs along with a full standing hutch for Hack and Lula Frame. The Frame's would take his house during rotation with their six children and special attention would be needed for their sleeping quarters. Ben would leave all the furniture he had built during his stay there. Later, the workers would build outside toilets and dig new wells for each of the new houses. The toilets would be at least on hundred yards away from the houses for health purposes.

Carrie's furniture was brought from the 'big house' on moving day and she discovered that her bedroom would barely hold the four poster bed, dresser and chest of drawers. There was not room for the beautiful chair Eva Barr had picked for her so Carrie placed it in Gale's room along with a rocking chair. Ben Samuels had made a canopy bed for Gale attaching netting to protect the baby. Carrie's furnishings were like those that she was forced to sell after Walt's death. This thought stung her eyes, evoking great sadness for several moments. Through the years, she had shed many tears over her losses and today they were reborn.

Mama Sally's contribution was appreciated by Mrs. Eva as she had dozens of chairs and cushions that she wanted recovered and made up; but she would wait until the workers were settled and their primary needs were met. Sally had never been happier; she had her family and her Red Tic hound by her side. She would share Carrie's bedroom during the time she was needed to keep the baby. Sally Ogen was a natural decorator, seamstress and designer. Her dog, Cricket, had earned his way by catching rabbits and would bring them directly to Sally unmarked by his teeth. In times past, Cricket would scratch on the kitchen door where Bartus would receive and clean tomorrow's rabbit stew.

Gale had been brought back to 'White Oak' along with Sally, a couple of months ago and her baby was due in two weeks. "The trip from Sally's was a rough four miles," Carrie had confided in Eva. "I can't be too far away from Mama Sally. She is getting tired of Gale anymore," she said. "What do you think of Gale visiting Oprah?" Carrie asked. She felt that she should ask for permission lest there be repercussions, in that Oprah's condition could be exacerbated by the large pregnant Gale. "Ah think it is a puhfect ideah," Eva Barr responded. "They have to find out soonah or lateah."

Gale was excited, for tomorrow she would see her friend, Oprah; it had been almost a year since they were together. Carrie and Pansy would go along with her. She had done very little sleeping but, lots of resting for the past two months. She was heavy and her baby had been carried high and begun to drop. The nerves in her legs were almost paralyzed from the pressure. Pansy had taken one look at her and spoke decisively, "Hit's a gal you's got her up high-lak." Gale had not told her mother or mama Sally of her choices to name her baby. If it was a boy; she would name him Walter Grant May and a girl would be named Lena Mae May. "My baby does not have a father, so it 'may' be God's child," she thought. "I will never be able to go back to school because the law forbids girls with babies to attend. My baby will not know the problems I have and I will never let anyone hurt it."

Carrie, being so caught up with administration, had very little time to be with Gale, although she checked on her constantly. Mama Sally had made the baby's diapers and little gowns with drawstring necks and cuffs. She had doubled the feed sacks and covered them with soft, old blankets, taken from her trunk, for the crib bedding. She had knitted booties, caps and blankets in light green, white and yellow. She had the rest of baby-hood to sew for her great grandchild and she loved being an important part of her family's life.

PART 11

Lena's and Missy's Births
White Oak Plantation

1851

*"They saw delighted
from the inland rocks.
O'er the broad deep,
poured out Pandora's box"*

"The squabble of the Sea Nymphs"
Mercy Warren

The midsummer daybreak ushered in a strong chill and dew covered the ground, dripping softly from the roof outside Gale and Carrie's bedroom. A chatter of gray squirrels fought over the large chestnuts that had fallen to the ground during the night. At a distance, Gale could see the goldenrod, wild purple and white Asters, bending in the breeze. She had felt, all night, a deep pressing in the bottom of her abdomen. Her ribs were sore from the baby's moving, pressing and kicking its way out of its tiny incubator. Gale knew absolutely nothing about birthing babies! She did not want to know; but she would find out soon enough.

Carrie entered her room around ten o'clock. "Are you ready to see Oprah," Carrie asked, smiling? "Oh yes," Gale cried. Pansy led the way to Oprah's room and Gale stared, questioning, at the bulging, bloated Oprah who had gained weight in the three months she had been pregnant. Oprah's large brown eyes lit up as Gale entered the room. She screamed, "Gale, Gale, Gale!"

Carrie and Pansy were shocked; it was a miracle! "Gale was just what Oprah needed to bring her back to us," Carrie laughed. "Thanks you, Lawd," Pansy chimed in. "I cain't wait tuh tells Bartus." She ran through the house, disturbing the sleep of John-John and Billy in the breezeway. Soon, the building filled with every available worker on the plantation. If the girls noticed the room full of visitors they did not let on. Running her fingers over the leg that had been broke, Oprah spoke; "Dey say dat Mrs. Carrie, Pansy and Bartus made a clay and vinegar poultice and wrapped it up." She placed her hand on Gale's stomach and felt the baby moving inside her. Looking around about her, she was embarrassed. "Yo baby want git outta there, it' kickin' like crazy," she said, clamping her hand over her mouth to shush herself. There was no talk of the violations, as they were caught up in the moment; having eight months to recant.

Carrie agreed that Oprah would come over and sleep with Gale and the two talked until the early hours of the morning. They slept late the next morning and Pansy had kept their breakfast warm. The two pregnant 12 year olds drank their milk and ate a light meal. Pansy had told Bartus about Oprah's delight at the sight of Gale. "Spoke her best words, she did," Pansy giggled. She and Bartus had watched as Oprah walked toward Gale's new house with hardly any limp. She had not complained of pain and it was good to see the change in the little girl they thought they had lost three months ago. Oprah and Gale were inseparable for the next several days.

Carrie knew Gale's time had come and alerted Ben, who rode to Savannah for Dr. Moore. After a long and restless night, a flood of water seeped through the pad Carrie had placed under Gale's side of the bed. Hurriedly, Carrie assisted Gale in bathing and dressing; readying her for the birth of her baby. All was ready when Dr. Moore arrived. He had planned to see Mrs. Eva tomorrow and would stay over if necessary. He did not discuss the fear that filled him, but prepared for the worst. Gale was a child and was not large enough to have a big baby. All along, he had tried to control her food intake so that her baby would be small. "A baby can grow once it gets here," he had stated.

Gale was a Trojan and did as she was told. She cried out at times; but, having her mother by her side every moment, mopping her face, cooing, directing each breath and assisting the doctor, brought comfort. Pansy was frantic; bringing her butcher knife, which she placed under Gale's pillow and Bartus' ax, under her bed. "Gots to cut da pain, she be jist a baby herself," she said. "Mah baby, mah baby," she crooned. "Shhhhh," the doctor admonished. Pansy clamped her hand over her mouth, unloaded the stack of clean towels and made her exit. Feeling faint, she called for Zinnie to take her place in the birthing room and promptly opened the bottle of ammonia and sniffed heavily. Needing something stronger for her nerves, she headed for the pantry and took the cooking wine from the shelf, opened it and emptied the bottle.

What seemed like hours later, the loud cries of baby Lena Mae were heard throughout the 'big house'; that is, everywhere except the kitchen. Pansy was sleeping so soundly, her snores could be heard from the birthing room.

Zinnie had been excellent help. She was self-assured, confident and willing to oblige, having become proficient in birthing babies from helping with the workers families. She had learned the hard way that, many times these babies were born to twelve year olds as this was the way on slave plantations. "Rape is rape!" she mumbled angrily as she bathed, oiled, diapered and dressed the baby. She had never before seen a baby that weighed four pounds! The perfect little girl was strong, healthy and beautiful; her jet black hair was full. "She is marked with a widows peak; destined for a hard life, but will be strong, courageous and fearless," Zinnie had said, at the moment of birth. The young mother had been given a little laudanum to kill the pain and help her rest; tomorrow, Zinnie would help her learn to breast-feed.

Dr. Moore ordered nine days of bed rest, without raising her head from the flat pillow. "There's a danger of hemorrhage; I will be staying overnight in the guest room, if you need me," he admonished. "Both children are doing well," he said. "Rarely, do we use sutures, but when one is so young they need to give birth without tearing. It helps them to heal faster and children do not know proper cleanliness measures after childbirth," he reminded Carrie. Pulling his stethoscope and medications together, he left the room and walked down the hallway to the guestroom; he was tired and needed sleep.

The thought of babies having babies made him sick. In all his years of service to the community, he had not prepared himself mentally, for the next case. "Carrie Grant is the absolute, best help," he thought as he entered the guest room. He would see Evangeline Barr tomorrow, check back with Gale and examine the pregnancy of another twelve year old named Oprah. "Only dedicated doctors would work under the duress of typhoid, yellow fever, dysentery and gun shot wounds, not to mention what he had just gone through," he mused as he finally fell asleep.

Gale held tiny Lena Mae May, but she was unable to feed her, as she had no milk and, her delicate baby had a voracious appetite. Zinnie took her from Gale and sat in the rocker beside her and fed her from her own breast. Her Billy would soon wean himself since he was months older than Lena. Her little man was walking and making sentences; his favorite toy was a little horse and buggy that Bartus had whittled from birch wood. Bartus had replace the wheels twice already from Billy's excessive use.

John-John was seven months old and was very near weaning himself. He had become interested in the little wagon Billy played with and had almost abandoned his rocking horse that had been sent to him from New York. They loved each other; 'Bee-wee and John-John', they called themselves. Together they had a box full of toys Bartus and Ben had made. The large chest sat on the back porch where the two spent most of their day playing. The more delicately made pieces were put away until the boys got older. There were wagons and horses with trace chains made from braided haywire, plaited twine tied to a small leather gear and saddles, handcrafted by Ben Samuels. John-John was a meticulous little guy while Billy played hard and fast, leaving the toys scattered around the porch and yard. Bartus had a job replacing lost saddles, ropes and other plantation needs for the two young farmers. "Boys, Boys", he laughed as he whittled away on the soon-to-be-lost or broken toy.

Oprah came to see Gale's baby; her curiosity was growing. Her mother had told her that she had come from a cabbage patch. Lately, she had learned some pretty cold facts of life, realizing there were many more she would be confronted with in the next few months. As she walked into the room, she could see that Gale was lying very still. Oprah approached at the foot of the bed, speaking softly she said, "Gale, can I see yo baby?" "Yes", Gale responded sleepily, pulling the covers back to expose the tiny bundle. Oprah sat on the edge of the bed, uncovering the baby and counted her fingers and toes, one by one. "She be so purty, Gale; I loves her. She is a real live baby doll," she sighed. "Remember, we always wanted one, now we don't have tuh pretend anymo," she smiled, happily.

Gale smiled wanly as she was not yet awake; her world was not real at the present time. The medication made her sleepy and she was tired of the big bulge between her legs. When Mum had given her a bath this morning, she had seen the one her mother had removed that was filled with blood, before it was replaced by a clean one. The old folded bleached white sheet had been torn and used to pad her 'private parts', much like the 'woman thing' that had come on monthly before she became pregnant.

Gale had returned to her work as chamber maid and Lena Mae May was not six months old. She was beginning to crawl, could sit alone and say "Momma", as she lifted her arms, commanding attention. Gale, reaching over to pick her up from the floor was suddenly filled with a rush of love and tenderness. Her child would not be unloved; she had sworn that oath long before Lena was born. In fact, the first time she felt a life was growing inside her was the day she made her sacred vow. There were times when she felt as though her heart would burst with excitement and love. One small, direct look from beautiful, dark eyed Lena pressed all disturbing thoughts from her mind and melting her heart. Gale had no bad thoughts today and right now her greatest joy needed a clean diaper. Since her milk had never come down, Zinnie continued to feed Lena every two hours during the day. The major problem persisted when Zinnie came into Lena's sight; she would cry for 'Ze, Ze, Ze'. "This is not fair," Gale declared. "I want to be her mother in every way and, sometimes I think Lena loves Zinnie more than me," she complained to Carrie.

Ben Samuels traveled at breakneck speed to notify Dr. Moore; Oprah was in labor. He had made this same trip only six months earlier for Gale. Dr. Moore heard the sound of loud banging on the door; the dreaded day had arrived. He hastened to 'White Oak' with Ben Samuels in close proximity. Oprah lay speechless during the examination, suddenly, her screams filled the room. Dr. Moore rushed to her, kneeling and taking her face in his hands, giving her directions. Within the hour, her five pound daughter arrived, squalling loudly, into the world as twelve year old Oprah, held her gently.

Missy was sturdy, beautiful and endowed with jet black hair and the same widows peak as was Lena Mae May. Carrie and Zinnie gasped, simultaneously, as they stared at the child in disbelief.

"Who, Oh God, who?" Carrie spoke first.

"Both babies have the same father," Zinnie remarked.

Dr. Moore gave speculative looks; no other words were spoken. He gave final orders to the women, closed the door and left the room.

Pansy, who had been barred from the room, sat outside listening to Oprah, cooing and making promises to her small bundle of joy. She watched, as the doctor rode out of sight, before entering. Tiptoeing, she moved toward her daughter. Oprah's eyes opened wide! "I made dis baby all by mysef, I did," she smiled. "I loves her." Pansy smiled from ear to ear, careful not to speak. If truth be known, she had brought the ax and butcher knife, to help out the pain, but remembering how they had acted when she tried to help Gale, she kept it to herself. She laughed, unconsciously; the joke was on them as both were wrapped in a flour sack underneath the bed. Pansy laughed aloud, now; Bartus would be proud of her, she had saved Oprah!

Carrie's new home was not very high or imposing; it was however, comfortable and warm. She had planted magnolias along the entire roadway. Eva Barr had given her an antique, ornate organ, tapestry settee, two stuffed, matching chairs and a commode table. Mama Sally had made pink and white chambray curtains for Gale and baby Lena's room. There were damask drapes for the parlor and Georgia Cotton Mill curtains from the looms of Columbus Textiles, were an addition to the present beauty of the house. The small kitchen had one window topped with a small swag held in place by two large nails. A Hamilton wood stove of porcelain and cast iron, blue in color, matching the swag above the window. Pots and pans were sent up from Thomasville Ironworks, as were the fire dogs, depicting two young slave girls.

In the dusk of evening, the gray bird with the red breast, sang in the newly planted magnolia. Mama Sally was pleased with the birds and animals living at 'White Oak'. It was as if they knew how much she loved them and hated to leave. They had decided to follow her and were quiet down in the brush across the lane. The workers were building fires in the yard; this was their time to meet around the great fires in the middle of the rows of cabins. As a nightly event, they would share the news, gossip and make decisions, as one big family. Eva Barr was responsible for keeping accord at 'White Oak'.

Carrie and Gale's cottage was separate from the old cabins as were the other three and they had not been a part of the 'goings on'. With Gale and the baby asleep, Sally and Carrie talked about the new homes celebration as they walked down the lane to the rhythm of hand clapping.

"Go down Moses, down to Egypt land."

"Tell ole Pharaoh, to let my people go."

Some danced repetitively around the fires while others sat in deep conversation.

"Sho is gots tuh gits shelter outten de win an rains," one said.

"I likes comin' home tuh de fire hearth, yes I sho does," said another.

"Betta git back chile outta dat blak conah else ole 'Bloody-Bones' gone git cha," someone said.

"Yeah, Ole 'Bloody-Bones come fo chillums what don't mind day Pappy and Mammy. Yes suh, Bloody-Bones gon git cha, go-o-o-on git cha," his voice excelled loudly! The children ran screaming to safety, with back doors slamming, echoing one after the other.

Bloody-Bones came most every night, for it was the only way the grown-ups could relax, smoke their pipes, dip their snuff and, discuss stories that the children didn't need to hear. Hambo, Bartus' dog knew about ole Bloody-Bones; he would tuck his tail between his legs and hide underneath the house with only his eyes being visible. He always recognized the story and the workers all laughed at him; he was funnier than Bloody-Bones.

Ben Samuels told the story of the mule that would point quail.

"De ole mule would walk wit his nose tuh da groun' til' he foun' da birds, den he throw da tail up, an jist stands der wit one foot in da air." The crowd hooted loudly. The workers stayed until the fires burned out; around eleven o'clock the relaxed bunch, found their way home.

They were well into harvest time and the half-picked fields of cotton, as far as a man's eyes could see, beckoned to them. They would be picking cotton until after Christmas this year. Eight workers had been sent to the sugarcane mill. It was run by two syrup makers, two grinders to feed the mill, two to cut, top and clean the cane and two to pile the wagons and haul.

Blind Ginny was the best mule for pulling the leverage pole that fitted into the grinder which manipulated the grinding wheels. She would walk round and round sideways, all day long, keeping the grinder in action. The sweet juice would pour into a barrel to be dumped into the hot syrup vats. One man at the grinder would feed the mill, while the other controlled the full barrels and replaced them when they were full. These were the only times Ginny was allowed to stop, drink water and eat a small bucket of an oats and corn mixture. Another mule would take her place tomorrow.

Metal cookers were used to boil the sweet juice. The syrup cook had the most important job of all because; overcooking would turn the juice to sugar, undercooking would sour in the jars and become good only with the skimming and debris' for cane buck. Buck was well known in Georgia as a poor man's drink, after fermenting a few weeks. This potent alcoholic beverage was sold on the black market by many plantations. Mr. Barr allowed his workers to consume the entire supply of buck from 'White Oak'. The high spirits of the workers, night fires, singing and dancing, were largely a part of their recreation and family outings. Corn whisky and cane buck had their places and buck was sought after throughout the South, there was not yet a stamp tax.

John Barr was pleased with the progress of 'White Oak Plantation', for production in lumber had a 99% increase, cotton had doubled, as had syrup, corn and indigo. Bonuses paid to workers had an approval rate bypassing most 'Southern States Mutual' reports. More than a completed day dream and years of management, he was competitive in industry and his name had become known worldwide as a slave less plantation, icon. Tonight was one of his rewards.

The party went on......

PART 12

White Oak Plantation

1853 – 1855

"For every heart hath some fair dream;
Some object unattained,
And far off in the distance lies
Some Mecca to be gained."

"Bones in the Desert"
Anne C Lynch

C amp meeting time came to White Oak Plantation each year after the harvest was over. In preparation, hundreds of candles and kerosene lamps were being suspended among the trees. Numerous torches flashing to and fro in the soft winds cast a shadow from the large trees, giving an appearance of an indefinite depth to the area. The solemn chanting of hymns, by the workers, swelling and falling, blew with the wind and was stored in the hearts of its listeners.

Carrie and Mama Sally sat, mesmerized by the impassioned exhortations, earnest prayers, loud cries and promises made to God. Camp meeting was well on the way and would last for two weeks or more, descending on the hearts and minds of those who were open to receive and would continue as long as the crowds came. Many states now held camp meetings and as they spread had reached Georgia. The blazing campfires falling on the assembly of worshipers was comprised of the sensible, weak-minded, rich and poor alike and all had come with one common goal; to worship God. John Barr was an exclusive donor; White Oak workers were cooks and food servants.

The large oak stump in the middle of the camp was the focal point for the Reverend Haskell Bell, of White Oak Plantation. He claimed the Lord came to him in the night ten years ago; saying,

"I want you to carry my gospel to the world." Although he had very little education, his wife, Lou read for him. He was a very dynamic speaker and most every listener was moved by his exhortations.

Area plantation owners allowed their slaves to attend these services; reckoning they were more subdued and willing to work for their masters if they were allowed religious practices, but only the trustee slaves were given this privilege. Most of the plantation owners nearby could allow their workers to stay late into the night and they could still get home at a decent hour in order to rest before their work began the next day. None of them were given the opportunity to spend the night, even at an all night event. As the crowds waned, the revivalists moved on, but not before each soul was baptized in the same creek they had cooked and drank from.

The plantations were solemn for weeks as the workers and slaves returned to their homes. All energy had been expended; just as the fires had burned out in the campground. They had learned to cooperate, help each other, share food, clothing, have quilting parties and other essentials in their lives. Largely, they had become part of 'The family of God.'

White Oak Plantation was among the first to build a church on its grounds and welcomed whites and coloreds alike with its small, open, double wide front doors. Gale and Oprah, with their baby daughters would occupy the same pew. Their seats were spaced wide enough to accommodate quilt pallets at their feet so that Lena Mae and Missy could sleep during the long two hour services. Linnie, baby Lena's wet-nurse, had weaned her two months before as she was now almost two years old; Oprah had been able to breast feed Missy. Both babies were marked with a widow's peak in their front hairlines, but, Missy commanded attention from viewers, with her straight black hair and soft bronze/gold skin; her beauty was enchanting!

Pansy, sitting behind them in church, said, "Yeah, boffum gone has a hard life, yessum, sho is now; marked by da Widow's Peak." Her sad disappointment was more than either Oprah or Gale would understand. They had both sworn that just the opposite would happen; both were tired of her rhetoric.

FIVE YEARS LATER.......................................

It was obvious the revivals had started at White Oak Plantation and the third revival, since the new church was built, had started. The Church of all Faiths was holding meetings once each week and sometimes twice as there were lax times and the workers and field hands had free time. The Reverend Charlie Bob Mock had been invited by Reverend Haskell Bell to officiate. Reverend Mock had brought his eighteen year old son, David Adam Mock, with him to the Plantation. It had been love at first sight for both Oprah and Missy Ward. Adam was drawn to Oprah's astounding beauty and her ability to care for her three and a half year old daughter. His heart palpitated rapidly just watching the two interact, in the church services, the world and each other. Pansy and Bartus were delighted with Adam Mock's sincerity and grown up ways. "Goot breedin'," Bartus said, "gist plain goot breedin'." Pansy agreed and if Oprah chose this young man; they would not stand in her way. Adam worked at the loading docks in Savannah and was concerned; maybe worried, about his financial position. He could not offer Oprah the life in which she was accustomed and he had an aversion to having his woman work. Admiring her womanhood and motherhood, the decision was final; these two things would take precedence in their marriage. If they were to be married, she would continue to teach and develop young Missy's social skills, while he made the living. He believed that a man should be the head of his household. He had been raised in a proud family; his heritage was that of a man's pride; self-identification demanded control of the purse strings. No female in the Mock family had ever worked; Oprah would not be the first! "With hard work and God's help, they would make it." he smiled and whistled; as he walked toward the Savannah docks, the next day.

The wedding would take place in the spring with all the plantation workers present. Although, she loved Bartus, Oprah had requested that Mr. Barr give her away, for she knew that even he was supported by Mr. John Barr II. "If it weren't for him; me an Adam wouldn't evah be tuh-getha," she rationalized. "It was da church, Mistah Barr built da church, an even otha plantation came and brings dey slaves to da services." Bartus was in full agreement, "He sho been goot tuh me, sho has." Pansy's lips held a pout until Bartus reached over and patted her gently. Then as suddenly as a summer storm, she changed her course of thinking. "He sho has, he builded me a cottage, taked me away froms de cabin life, maked me a free woman too, ah gots papahs tuh proven it," she giggled. She had pointed to the two frames Ben had made for their anniversary three years ago. The wall came alive with one word *"EMANCIPATION"*. It was the only one visible from Oprah's bed.

Evangeline Barr planned the wedding and reception; John Barr had agreed to give Oprah away. Gale would be her Maid of Honor and her very own chile, Missy, along with Lena Mae, would be her flower girls and John-John would be the ring bearer. The wedding would take place after the announcements were made.

The date of the wedding was posted and Eva and Carrie began the hectic creation of 'a wedding fit for a queen'. Linnie and Billy Coe decorated the church balcony and pews with streamers of white bows of satin and net. The workers had swept the church and yards. Clean and white benches Ben had made for the church were placed in angled rows beneath the big live oak trees in front of the courtyard. The waterfall was cleaned and running and each flower pot was filled with colorful bouquets. The front balcony was a profusion of flowers, laden with Ivy and mixed flowers, their runners filled with plumes of draping buds. Workers had placed dozens of fence posts into upside down triangles and wire was strung around each post, on to the next. Green and variegated English Ivy, taken from the oak trees in the backyard, was twisted around each pole and three foot wide panels of white lace were draped over the wires. Yards and yards of lace had been purchased from New York for the event. Beginning at the Alter; white carpet had been laid down the aisle and onward to the place where the carriage would stop.

Sally Ogen had sewn the bridal gown and head-dress; the bodice of the gown was adorned with lace inserts around the neckline. Yards and yards of soft white tulle and net were sewn into the skirt; her veil would trail five feet behind her. She would wear beaded white satin boots, of the latest fashion, that buttoned past her ankles. No detail had been spared for this day.

The courtyard had been set, for today was 'Oprah's Wedding Day'. A banqueting table was adorned with damask table cloths made in Damascus, Syria, and containers of deer fern sat in clusters on the sides of the basket woven, brick courtyard. Tubs of flowers and bows of white satin flanked the serving tables and magnolia blossoms centered the long banquet table from one end to the other. Each invited guest had a calligraphy written card at their place at the table. Pansy, Zinnie and Lou had baked cakes, pies, candies and made gallons of lemonade. There would be Mint Juleps, served from the Veranda of the 'big house', for those who chose to, have a 'toddy', a toast to the couple.

The almost impossible task was computed; it was nine o'clock and the wedding was scheduled for eleven am. "We must hurry," Eva Barr said; exhausted. "We have to bathe and dress quickly." Carrie agreed, turning swiftly toward her cottage.

John Alexander Barr, III had, a month or so ago; studied under his Mother, as to how to become a gentleman. His Mom had told him of the dignified manner in which he would conduct himself at the wedding of Oprah Ward. Today was the day and he would prove to his Mother what a big boy he was and how well he had learned his lessons from her. The little pillow he would carry was four inches by four inches and gold wedding bands were attached in the middle by pink ribbons. He was especially proud of his new knickers, cropped jacket and his excitement was evident as he showed off his black leather boots.

Gale and Lena looked like sisters instead of Mother and daughter. Young Lena was smaller than Missy, despite the six months difference in their ages. This demure, petite beauty had been classified by Eva as that of a Dresden China Doll. Her skin resembled alabaster and her coal black hair and dark eyes were a contrast to that of her mother's. Gale was much like her father, Walter. Today, a twinge of jealousy arose when she saw Adam and Oprah's interaction. She felt as though she was losing her sister to an unidentified stranger.

"Could this be what marriage should be", she wondered? There was no man who would be as perfect as her own father. A touch of nostalgia flitted through her mind. At times, she could still see him as he staggered with the long knife in his heart. "His heart had been broken by a knife and hers had been broken when he died", she thought miserably. "This was no place for tears, this day was the most important one in Oprah's life," she mumbled.

She had been brought back to reality by her mother's soft knock on her door. Lena was dressed except for slipping on her dress. The soft, pink taffeta dress was caught up at the bodice and tail by rosettes of the finest French lace; her jet black ringlets hung in clusters around her small shoulders. As the day wore on many people spoke of the rare beauty of both flower girls. "Are they twins?" someone asked. Eva Barr called them, 'My little girls'; her attachment was obvious. Lena, at age four, had become precocious; quite able to count, print many names and read from picture books; her imagination was vivid. She had taken command of Missy and taught her how to count and read by pictures. Before the wedding today, they would practice their walk as flower girls.

Today was Oprah's wedding day.

The workers were dressed in their finest; Eva Barr had seen to it. The elegant coach, used by Barr's Funeral Home, was enclosed in glass and decorated with lace and flowers, its elegance stunning. Bartus, dressed in a tall black hat, tails and white gloves, sat as a dignified gentleman. The horses wore pomes attached to their bridles. Bartus sat proudly on the front seat, looking neither left nor right, as Pansy sat beside Oprah in the glass enclosed coach.

"He was taking his Cinderella to the ball. This is a day to remember," he thought as a tear touched his eye. Blinking it away, being careful not to soil his white shirt. "If they could only see my back, they would know I'm only a slave." His memory ran rampant. Then, "What a day for a slave," he thought, and gave a controlled laugh. Today, his heart was fuller than his eyes as he thought of his mother and brothers. Pansy noticed Bartus' emotional state and signaled him, "Shhhhh," she said. He had heard her and composed himself. "She knows me so well," he thought as he drove past the throng of people carrying two of the three women he loved most in the world. His heart yearned for his mother; "She would have been so proud!"

Ben rang the church bell promptly at eleven o'clock and the organ began to play. The glass coach had stopped and the seated guests stared at the most astounding sight they had ever seen! Mr. John Alexander Barr, II, walked to the coach door, which had been opened by Bartus; he extended his hand for the beautiful Oprah to alight from the coach. He was serious in his role as though Oprah was his own daughter. As she stepped onto the steps of the coach, she took Mr. Barr's arm and stood confident and smiling, looking straight ahead at the Reverend Charlie Bob Mock. Adam Mock and his best man, Remus Hoyt, took their places beside the Reverend as Oprah caught the eye of her husband to be.

Bartus brought Pansy from the carriage, in the same fashion as Mr. Barr had taken Oprah's hand and fitted it neatly at his elbow. Slowly, the procession began down the beautifully decorated isle. Carrie, behind the lace covered curtain, softly played the organ and sang;

"Drink to me only with thine eyes,
And I will pledge with mine.
Or leave a kiss, within the cup
And I'll not ask for wine."

The end of her song was a cue for Lena and Missy to strew the flower petals. She continued to play softly as the two angelic children moved toward the front. They moved forward, with cheeks as pink as the dresses they wore; their faces were aglow as their excitement arose. John Alexander Barr, III, was moving slowly behind them about ten steps away, staring straight ahead; he had the appearance of an 'Adonis'. Evangeline Barr was focused on the young Barr heir. He had inherited her gracious flare for cultural activities. "Yes, young John Barr is certainly a direct descendant of English aristocracy. Today, culture has been introduced to Georgia and they will never be the same in these parts again." She said, smiling broadly. "If only Martha was here." The thought floated and fleeted quickly as Eva daubed her eyes.

Gale's, Maid of Honor's, bouquet of roses and greenery was tied with a satin ribbon; its streamers flowed gently from her lace gloved hand. Ben had been careful to remove the thorns before both hers and Oprah's bouquets were made up.

Reverend Mock began the service......

"Dearly beloved, we are gathered together..."

The quietness of the church was deafening; not even the wind dared to interrupt this solemn occasion. The couple completed the wedding ritual, exchanged rings and knelt before the church's alter where, Reverend Charlie Bob Mock, blessed the sanctity of their marriage.

Oprah and Adam were driven by Mr. Bartus Reem to the reception being given in their honor. The tables were ready with a roasted pig sitting in the middle of the serving table; a red apple fitted tightly into its mouth. Curly collard greens, pickled apricots and peaches, along with oranges and grapes, embellished the long silver trays. Those who could not read their place cards were guided by Evangeline Barr and had been told ahead of time, to watch the host and hostess and emulate their body language. For this reason, Carrie knew full well that Eva would be careful not to scratch her nose!

John and Eva Barr gave a toast to the couple, with lemonade.

"Ladies and gentlemen, White Oak Plantation is honored to give you Mr. and Mrs. David Adam Mock; May they be blessed with many years together."

The reception began and at some point Eva Barr accidentally dropped her fork onto her plate; the plates rang out like Christmas bells, one at a time. Laughter could be heard from the next plantation; they had emulated Eva Barr's gestures! The party lasted late into the afternoon and was enjoyed by all.

Cleanup was not completed hours later and would take weeks to put things in order again. Each family took enough food home for tomorrow's meals and most of them had been given the next day off to rest and recuperate. There was lots of work left to be done putting things back in order after the extravaganza.

Mr. Barr sent and envelope to the guest room and had insisted Bartus take a pitcher of Mint Julep to the bridal suite as well. Oprah, nervously opened the small envelope; squealing with delight as two crisp one hundred dollar bills floated to the floor. Adam, had never in his life, seen this much money at one time!

"I will buy us a house on the Row," Oprah said. "Then we will be close by wher' yo works. I nevah lived wher' dey didn't be's people." She explained, in a frightened voice. "Missy will need yo when yo comes home fo dinnah."

Oprah drank two glasses of the Mint Julep, Adam poured for her, when her world began to spin, and her tongue became stiff and non-compliant with her brain, so she rambled on and on. Adam would make sure she rested, but; he had no idea of how to unleash the seemingly hundreds of buttons on the back of her dress. He was still fully dressed, so he went for help from Pansy Reem; who was ready for bed, her head tied up and wearing only a long flowing gown. Not listening to Adam's request, she ran to the bridal suite, having no idea why; fear clutching her heart. Oprah was sound asleep on the velvet chair, still dressed in her bridal gown! Adam, panting from Pansy's pace, was exhausted. "I, I, I didn't knows how to get her dress off. I, it's all dem buttons." Pansy laughed, as she gently unbuttoned the dress and with Adam's help, removed it. She placed it on a silk covered hanger from the armoire and hung it on the back of the door. After Adam removed her shoes; Pansy, removed her white silk hose and readied her for bed. She pulled back the covers and watched intently as Adam picked up the gowned body of the lovely Oprah and put her into the bed; she quietly left the room.

Adam blew out the candles from the wall sconces and undressed in the dark; slowly hanging his formal wear in the wardrobe. He took a deep breath and exhaled; then slid between the cool cotton sheets. Oprah was breathing softly beside him as he snuggled close to her warm body; holding her gently, he slept too. The exhaustion of the day had become obvious.

While all of White Oak Plantation slept, Oprah awakened to the warm breath of her husband, on her neck. She was startled at first, and then began to kiss his shoulder, his neck and his cheek. "Mah husband," she cooed; like a Turtle Dove singing to her mate. Adam began to stir; his eyes flew open, "Where am I?" He questioned as his eyes focused on the portrait, above the mantel, of St. Michael, the Arch-Angel.

"I'm in heaven," he whispered.

"Yo sho is, dahlin'," Oprah mumbled softly, kissing him for the first time, ever, on his lips.

"Mah dahlin', my wife," he declared, pulling her close.

There were no more words or need for any. Outside the brush birds were stirring about at dawn; the hoot owl screeched, "Oh, oh, whoo," the world had not affected this moment. The only sounds heard were the sounds of their own breathing and the rhythm of their heartbeats; exhausted they slept again.

Adam opened the door, hours later and, stared down the hallway as the Grandfather clock struck nine. He retrieved the silver tray, perfectly arranged and placed near the door; loaded with hot biscuits, fresh butter, bacon, grits, peach jam and coffee. The newlyweds ate heartily and stayed in the bridal suite until mid-afternoon; talking for hours before making the long move to Savannah. Both were ready to embark on their new life and held hands as they went in search of Missy.

As they stepped from the hallway to the side porch; a voice cried out, "Muh, Muh." Adam reached down and lifted her up, "Haw yo been, girl?" He asked. "I had brefas with Me-Maw Pansy," she stated. Then, placing her hands on her hips said, "I sept wif Lena and we played games, jes lak yo and Miss Gale, Muh."

Earlier that morning, Mr. Barr had taken the glass-enclosed coach back to the funeral home. He had a wonderful feeling today because he had given young Oprah a wedding to be talked about for years to come. Evangeline had enjoyed it more than anyone, making him realize how much she missed the parties, plays and Opera until yesterday. "I will take her to New York." He vowed. "She needs to look up her Uncle Don Marshall; I will surprise her with train tickets on her birthday, next month."

The horses galloped into the tree-lined city of Savannah, pulling the fine coach, which would be polished and put away for some other great occasion. John smiled broadly; his day had been complete, the world loved him and he returned the emotion. He regained his composure as he walked into his office.

Ben and Bartus had been dispatched by Mr. Barr to hitch up the buckboard and move Oprah and Adam to The Row, in Savannah. Tomorrow, Adam would return to work at the docks and he had arranged with John Barr to move Oprah and Missy's belongings. The two beds Ben had built for them, was loaded onto the wagon, along with other household goods Pansy sent to help Oprah start keeping house.

There were no tears as Pansy hugged the child she and Bartus had raised. They had watched her grow up, felt her pain during her pregnancy and were now ready to give her to Adam Mock. "Least-wise she doan be no slave." She whispered to Bartus when his eyes filled with tears.

Adam rode on the back of the buckboard with the boxes of clothes and household articles; arriving at The Row, around three o'clock. Once they arrived, Oprah was given her choice of three empty houses. She chose the one with the large stoop on the front, a back porch, a good well of water, a front parlor and two bedrooms. This house would do until Adam had the time to build on. It was close enough to the school for Missy and the docks for Adam. Oprah wanted to be close to her new husband as she had never been alone before and Missy needed him.

Missy was busy walking through the empty rooms. "Dis one is mine." She called out. "Move my bed in here!" She ordered Bartus. He loved a bossy woman and was entertained by her little hands on her hips. "She goan be some woman," he said to Ben. "Yes, Suh, sho ain't goan let nobodys push huh 'round," he laughed.

Adam, Ben and Bartus unloaded and placed the furniture in the rooms, while Oprah set up her kitchen, placing the dining table and chairs in one end of the kitchen. Oprah took one look at the scantily filled rooms and was sad for only a moment. Then she remembered, "I have Adam and he has me, we both have Missy and we are a family, a real family!"

The rest of the day went smoothly. Pansy had loaded her up with staples and a few groceries in cans and boxes. She had sent a coffee pot, frying pan, kettle and biscuit baker. She sent something else… Oprah recognized the dishes immediately. They had been the only thing salvaged when Pansy's mother's home had burned years ago. Her mother, now Missy's grandmother, had survived the fire that was believed to have been set by radicals, fighting the emancipation of slaves. Oprah began to cry, the large tears dripping onto the collar of her dress. "She gave me da bes' she had, I cain't nevah repay huh." She declared.

Ben and Bartus left after unloading the furniture and emptying the buckboard. Pansy had sent her only toilet chamber and washstand along with Oprah. Her little girl would have what she needed even if she had to do without, she had said.

Ben went by the hardware store to purchase materials for tomorrow's work where he purchased a glass cutter, a keg of small nails, two hand saws, two cross-cut saws, an anvil, a hammer and a hack-saw. Bartus also bought for himself, a mirror and an enameled chamber pot with pink painted roses. "Don't tell Pansy, she be so wired up; no suh, she gits all ovah huhself." He said to Ben, as they headed home; it was late and they wanted to get home before dark. Ben turned the horses in the direction of the plantation. He was considered highly educated with a fifth grade education. He prided himself on being able to travel and read signs. In fact; he stopped at a sign leading out of town; a "wanted poster" was tacked to the side of a mile post. Reading aloud to Bartus, he spoke clearly;

"James, last name unknown; runaway slave.
Five hundred dollars reward
Contact: Ambrose Sullivan, Owner
Five Forks Plantation,
Savannah, Georgia"

As Ben re-read the poster, a wagon sped by; Bartus stared at the flying wagon, feeling the wind as it moved past. "Lawd, theys in a mity big hurry, jist 'bout runs us offen de road," he told Ben. Up the road a ways, the wagon had hit a soft sand pocket, turning it over into a deep ditch. The passengers were thrown clear but the horse's leg was broken. Ben and Bartus were in a hurry to get home, however they could not leave without checking the condition of the passengers. Ben checked the driver while Bartus looked at the man who had been in the back of the wagon. "This one's alright, the driver is alright, jist shook up, kinda knocked out, is all," Ben said. Bartus was unable to answer; he grabbed the man from the sandy ditch and hurriedly threw him into the back of the wagon.

"Drive Ben, fas' as yo can. Gits us home now," he ordered!

"Yes sir," Ben responded. He had never questioned Bartus before and was not about to start now.

It was almost dark and they could make it if he drove fast but, he turned to Bartus and said, "We don't want to end up like those poor fellas back there." Bartus replied, "Lawd, hep us, oh, goot Lawd, hep us." He begged.

Ben was careful to drive down the middle of the road, since the buckboard had no lights, no lanterns and the horse was night blind!

"Either, I have to drive at breakneck speed or we could pull over until Mr. Barr comes by and follow his lighted carriage." Ben explained.

"No," Bartus demanded. "Hits gonna be a little bit o' moon tonight, we goes on."

"Yes, sir," Ben agreed reluctantly, since they needed at least thirty minutes more of daylight to make it home before dark.

"Bartus, what do we do now?" Ben questioned as darkness settled around them.

"We's gon' git strait in de middle of de road, is what we gon' do. Hoss got a God-given instinct; she will git us home." He said.

Luckily, Ben could not know the real situation of Bartus' thoughts, because the real truth of the matter was that Bartus was scared to death. Ben had not seen the chains on the slave's legs or that he was even was a slave, because he had been covered by a tarpaulin. Ben had been so preoccupied with the other man, he was not aware that Bartus had loaded one into the wagon.

"Thanks, Massa, fer de dark," he mumbled, looking upward; to which Ben replied, "You're right, man, it is a good time to pray."

Ginny, the night blind horse slowed almost to a complete stop. Bartus said. "Ben youse git on her back and guide her and I take de reigns." They were still ten minutes from White Oak when Ben mounted Ginny's back, urging her on. He stroked her softly, talking to her constantly. "Come on girl, you know you can make it. Be a good girl now, don't let me down!"

Ginny did as she was told and soon they were onto the magnolia lane and only a few yards from the courtyard. She could now see her way to the back porch, because the 'big house' was all lit up.

"Yo kin gits off to you house, I kin take care ob de wagon." Bartus said when they were in front of Ben's cabin.

"What about the man?" He asked. Bartus was shocked; Ben knew that he was hiding something.

"I'se gits Pansy tuh bandage him up and sends him on his way."

Ben did not question him for he had a long day ahead of him and was glad to get home.

Bartus ran to the house and was grateful for the darkness. Having heard Bartus drive up, Pansy opened the door and returned to her bed. Bartus lifted the unconscious man from the wagon, taking him into the kitchen. He woke Pansy, bringing her into the kitchen pantry, where he had hid the slave; opening the door slowly so that he would not frighten her.

"Lawd hav' mussey, he be a mess! Bartus, yo'se gone and dunnit now! He be a slave, Yo'se gonna gits boffus kilt and I'se ain't gone mess with dis mess 'uv a man!" She argued.

"Pansy, I ain't knowed yo'se tu be's dis way wif peoples. I agrees wif you, he be's dirty, he be's stankin, he be's a mess, but he be's mah bruthur, James!" He cried, tears coursing down his cheeks.

"I'se be sorry, Bartus; ah nevah knowed. I'se gon heats de wattah now," she said gently.

"He sho do stank."

The night was a long one and Bartus watched Ben as he went into the house and his lamp went out. Slipping out the back door of the house, he headed for the wagon to get a hacksaw. He could finish the job more expediently with an anvil and ax, however, he was not able to use anything that would create noise. He could not take a chance that anyone would find out James was at 'White Oak'.

For hours, Bartus cut the shackles; sawing, then resting for a time, until they were completely loose. James was free; if he lived, he was only partially conscious. Bartus' hands were bleeding from the broken blisters.

Pansy had cleaned the cut on the back of James' neck and his upper right arm. She had left to go back to the cottage after more than three hours of working with the slave. Bartus stoked the stove for the breakfast meal and crammed the shackles through the fire door, covering them with wood and a lightered knot. He would remove them when he took the ashes out tomorrow and, bury them with the dirty clothes.

He walked over to James and wiped his face with a wet cloth. "Peebo," he said gently. James' eyes began to open, close and blink.

"Don' talk, Peebo, saves yo energy, ah's heah, Yo be's alrite nih, brotha. We needs to shave yo haid, youse lousey," Bartus said. "Us'll burn yo rags 'n hides yo. Ain't a sole know who yo be, 'ceptin Pansy." He said mater-of-fact. "Yo hungry, I gits yo sumpin." The warming closet held baked sweet potatoes, ham and a couple of biscuits and James ate every crumb.

"Bartus, yo lives heah?" The statement was a question.

"Yeah," Bartus answered.

He was busy cleaning and shaving the long braided hair, until at last James was clean and shaved. His perfectly round, smooth head was without spot or blemish except for the new bruises had recently acquired.

Bartus packed the filthy clothes into the stove and gave James the clean clothes Pansy had laid out on the chair for him. He dressed hastily and felt cleaner than he had since the day he was born. Bartus had made him shave his private parts, too. "Youse git lice on one place, yo gits em all obah." He had said, extending the straight razor to James. "Peebo keeps yo hand steady-like. Yo sho don' wanna cut yosef on yo tallywhacker." He laughed. "Yo'd make a ugly gal." James grinned and a loud giggle was stifled by Bartus' hand.

It was almost daylight now and in a couple of hours Pansy would light the stove for breakfast. Bartus gave James a quilt, the same quilt he had been offered by his Pansy years ago, and put him in the same closet. Taking another quilt, he rolled up on the kitchen floor and although he closed his eyes he was unable to sleep.

The door opened at six and Pansy entered as Bartus sprang from the floor as Pansy's foot hit the back porch. Bartus hit the stove saying, "Gots tuh tak de ashes out, afta hit cooks down dis mawning," he offered.

"Goot, it sho' needs it." She replied.

James was brought from the closet and told he would have to continue to hide for an indefinite period of time. Today, the pantry closet was the only place Pansy had to make sure no one entered and she placed her chair in front to assure James safety. When she had a good look at him later in the morning, she had to laugh. This could not be the same man she had seen last night as she cleaned his wounds. He now appeared much older with the shaved head. If he grew a mustache, he would look distinguished and could easily become incognito.

The day was sunny, bright and clear and the stables were in need of cleaning. Since Ben had been busy working in the furniture business, they had not been kept up, so Bartus had joined Ben at the stables for that purpose. Buck was frisky and needed a good rider to work him out.

"A man can always tell what a horse is saying, if he understands horse language," Ben quipped. "I'll take the saws and hammers to the mill and be gone most of the morning."

As Ben rode out toward the woods, Bartus dug a large hole in one of the stables and buried the shackles and covered them with straw. "Whew," he exhaled. For the rest of the morning, he cleaned the stables, loading the compost into the wheel barrow and strewed it over the ground in the garden. "Goot fertilizer," he mumbled. Tomorrow, he would return to the sawmill, but today he would plant the fall garden and just think, rest and relive the past weeks.

Pansy helped Carrie prepare Evangeline Barr and young John-John's breakfast, because Carrie had been busy with last minute details of putting away the trappings of the wedding; she would need to get into the pantry. Pansy was quick to say, "Jist puts 'em on duh table, ah'l hep yo wif it." She said, as she peeled potatoes. Carrie placed the linens on the table and walked out; she would use all the help she could get. If anyone needed help, it was she.

"I'm tired, tired, tired," she lamented. "I need a rest, I think I will go home and take Mama Sally, Lena and Gale with me." She told Eva Barr later that afternoon, "We all need a break; I must have a rest and when I come back, I will train Lou Haskell to help out with the household chores." She offered.

"You desuhve it deah." Eva had agreed.

After a month of being shifted from the pantry to Bartus and Pansy's cottage, James had become weary. "Ah needs tuh wook." He thought, rubbing the stubble on his freshly shaved head and had grown a mustache at Pansy's insistence. Soon, she would introduce him as her cousin from Cairo, Georgia and would tell everyone that he had worked at her Uncle Charlie's Syrup works. This had been his primary job at Five-Forks Plantation; Pansy had sprinkled red pepper on his pant legs every day to keep the slave dogs from detecting him. "Jist in case they comes," Pansy said.

Dog Days of late summer had already come, three weeks ago. The slave, James, had been tracked to the outskirts of Savannah. The driver for Mr. Ambrose's plantation had stated that he had passed a buckboard loaded with supplies carrying two Negroes; one was young with a slender build and the other was slightly older, with graying hair. Bartus had seen them talking to Mr. Barr as he was cutting cord wood and did not look up from his task.

A large Mastiff dog and a red tick hound were being held on a leash by the bounty hunters. Mr. Barr was talking in a barely audible voice, "No, there's nobody here that fits that description. If I have any news, I'll contact Ambrose Sullivan," he assured them. Apparently, the evidence had not been discovered, even after passing the stables. Bartus knew that burning the shackles in the stove would eliminate any trace of odor and since he had buried them over three feet deep, even the horses would not paw that deep.

Mr. Barr checked with Constable Ezra Carnes on Monday morning because he was concerned about the bounty hunters going out to 'White Oak'.

"Ambrose Sullivan just won't give up, John," he said. "Somehow, he's got it in his mind that the buckboard the driver saw was yours."

"Ezra, do you think it possible for a night-blind horse to start out from the General Mercantile store at six-thirty and reach my plantation before dark?" He questioned, growling. "How would they have time to stop, pick up a slave, help out the injured driver and get to the house?" He asked again. Ezra Carnes was no fool and he knew that under regular circumstances it could not have been done. "When horses fly, that's when, John." He chuckled.

Bartus had to start making plans for James' 'formal' arrival to 'White Oak'. Somehow, a way had to be found to make it look as if Pansy's cousin had arrived to see her, so Bartus and Pansy had cooked up a scheme. In order for it to work, Bartus would have to get James off of the plantation so that he could make his grand entrance to 'White Oak'; and the plan would begin tomorrow morning.

Mr. Barr had told Bartus a couple of weeks prior, "The old fence on the east end of my property, needs replacing, and it's long over due," he had said wryly. "You can borrow one or two men from the saw mill to help." He continued.

"Ise'll tak care ob de problum, myself." Bartus replied, keeping his back to Mr. Barr.

The plan called for James to be placed under a tarpaulin and taken away. At the crack of dawn, Bartus got up, to put the plan into action. The squirrels were scampering around on the ground, jumping from tree to tree, frolicking, mating and searching for food. The fog occluded the pathway as Bartus rushed to the stables to hitch up the wagon. Fence posts, wire stretchers, wire, nails, posthole diggers and James, were loaded on to the flat bed wagon. A tarpaulin covered part of the wagon load as it rolled through the lane of cabins and cottages, passing Ben Samuels house; both men signaled 'Good Morning'.

"No wonder Mr. Barr likes him so much, he's always up and about his work early." Ben thought. Lacing up his work boots just a little bit faster than usual, he was in a hurry, for his desire was to be dedicated to 'White Oak', much like Bartus; his mentor.

The wagon came to a halt in a large grove of scrub oaks which was obscured from the road. Raising the tarpaulin from the load, James alighted from the wagon.

"Peebo, yose gon hafta makes yo own tent, youse'll bes here fo awhil'. Pansy bake yo some biscuits and plenty ob ham." "I brung yo a jug o water and Ise'll be bak fo yo soons I can." He said, turning his back and walking back to the wagon. The supplies were unloaded and he began his work day.

The long rolled out wire was stretched and nailed onto the posts that Bartus had busily stabilized, in the dozens of holes he had dug into the ground. After the fence was hammered to the post, Bartus left for home. It was almost dark and Bartus had not eaten breakfast nor lunch and was hungry. His heart was heavy for he had to leave his brother in the woods, with no protection! His plan was working, thus far and, tomorrow he would bring James some fancy clothes from the clothes pantry. The pantry held mostly clothing others had left at the plantation throughout the years.

Next, Bartus would need a letter to Pansy from Peebo, her cousin, announcing his visit; but who would write the letter? Neither he nor Pansy could write. "Whew," Bartus said. "I'se don know who tuh trust." He stood shaking his head. "Mabee we hafta ax Ben." He spoke indecisively. "No!" Pansy said. "Ah knows de one , Gale." She said, snapping her fingers. "She be perfect." Bartus knew he could not approach Gale, but Pansy could.

Gale was up and about as Pansy knocked on their cottage door; Lena was still sleeping.

"Come in," a voice called out.

Turning the glass knob to the door, she entered and had not been there but minutes until she had her letter. Gale had printed it as Pansy requested; wondering what was going on, but never asking. She trusted Pansy, yet; she had not heard of Peebo, a cousin of Pansy's.

Gale missed Oprah so much and she needed to be with somebody her own age. Lena cried for Missy; her playtime had been limited since she had moved to Savannah. Tonight, Gale would ask her mother if she and Lena could move closer to Savannah. She had lived there for twelve years and it would not be like starting over. She would be eighteen in a couple of months and her child would need to go to school soon. Also, she would like to have a husband like Oprah.

Supper was over and Gale's pot of Irish stew had been consumed. Carrie and Mama Sally were tired; cleaning and wrapping the equipment used in Oprah's wedding had been more than they had bargained for. Sally would be through with her sewing soon; as every new cottage down the lane had custom made curtains and seat cushions and she was ready to return to her own home.

After breakfast the three women sat in the front porch rockers. "Let's go home, Carrie said quietly. "I'm tired; I yearn for the cottage and creek." Mama Sally and Gale both agreed, so Bartus drove the four females to Sally's; they would stay until four o'clock on Sunday, when he would pick them up.

As the wagon rolled toward Sally's house, Lena sat in Bartus' lap, holding the reigns, squealing; "Gitty yap." The horses responded to the small shrill voice and it was apparent that she was the only one to enjoy the four mile trip. They arrived to housework; the yard was littered and the front porch was covered in leaves. Sally opened the back door, flipped the thumb bolt lock from the front door and pulled it open. The dank, musty odor, along with dead rats rotting on the floor was overpowering; Sally had put out arsenic pellets before leaving for 'White Oak'. She and Gale opened the windows and doors to let the stink out and to let in the fresh air.

Carrie had become sick, heaving and throwing up; it was apparent she was not well. Unlike her normal personality, the 'I can' lady was becoming withdrawn and had lost fifteen pounds in the last six weeks. Her pale face told the story of a woman suffering. Mama Sally had not noticed the change in Carrie until a couple of weeks ago because her work demands had been so stringent. The weeks of planning and carrying out for Oprah's wedding, months of sewing, designing and recovering furniture had left her little time to be concerned with anyone, even Carrie.

One thing she was sure of; Carrie having worked closely with Evangeline Barr, a testy, arrogant, perfectionist could have contributed to Carrie's weight loss. Also, Mr. Barr had promised to get help for her, but had never done so and she refused to beg; it went against her Irish grain. If Mr. Barr had forgotten his promise to Carrie, surely, Carrie would not remind him; she was too proud!

Getting out of the house was the only thing on Carrie's mind, for the smell of rotting flesh permeated the house; inside and out. Finding the path toward the creek; she walked alone, needing time to think, regroup and to contemplate her life and where it was going. She had now worked for the Barr's for over five years and though she was not financially sound; she had saved twenty-five hundred dollars and Gale had another five hundred and fifty saved. Carrie had kept it all rolled together and placed in a small leather purse, crammed in the back of the wardrobe at 'White Oak'. She had tied it to the coat rack and covered it with hanging clothes.

Lately, she was tired and thirsty most of the time and blotches covered her face and hands. There were times she felt that her brain would explode, if only for a moment. Working in crisis situations had taught her to distance herself between stressful events and sanity. The numbness she felt in her fingers and legs would pass, however; the chest pains she was experiencing had not been reduced by baking soda and water that Pansy had made for her most every night. Denial too, could cost her, her life; she knew this from serving others.

Carrie began to unwind as she tossed pebbles at the turtles, asleep in the sun. They clung to the rotting logs lying in the creek and as the pebbles hit, they dislodged and swam downward. She was caught up in the sounds of the rolling creek, filling the caverns below. The hollow sounds made by the falling water were no less than the empty, hollow feelings she carried inside.

"Perhaps, this is how I got my name, could I have been born to 'carry' the burdens of others," she asked quietly, as she walked toward the house. She promised herself that she would see Dr. Moore, the next time he came to see Eva.

Gale had been unable to talk to Mama Sally and Mum last night. "Maybe, tonight will be a better time." She hoped; the rest of the day would be busy.

Granma Sally had purchased a quarter of beef from a neighbor last year and had canned it. Tonight, she would cook tripe along with syrup and corn pone, to satisfy her craving; they ate without conversation. Lena ate heavily, chattering and jabbering away about a rabbit she had chased down the buggy trail.

After supper, Granma Sally repaired her chicken house and restobbed the wire fence around the pen. The chickens had been turned out to fend for themselves while the house was closed. They had a better chance against weasels and foxes, which could not climb trees.

"The ole foxes shore has been hard on mah chickens," Mama Sally said.

"Foxes, huh" Gale said. "That sly old fox living down the road is more likely; I betcha," she laughed.

"They never got to Rooster Red," Mama Sally sounded pleased. Looking over her spectacles, she went on. "Shame on you girl, they's mah friends." A crease appeared across her forehead as she cleared her voice, and then looked down; not meeting Gale's eyes.

Lying in the red velvet chair, winged chair in the corner, Gale read fairy tales to young Lena; then tiptoeing softly, she carried her sleeping little girl to bed. Carrie sat alone, isolated from the others; somehow, her separation brought peace and rest and she should thank them for this privilege. Sunday morning Carrie had begun to feel a little better. The dread of her commanding job filled her mind and the only stimulation of the weekend, was Lena, who had managed to entertain herself, despite the sad faces surrounding her.

Pansy packed fried chicken, biscuits and gingerbread from last night's supper and covered the top of the box with a cloth. With the letter in his pocket, Bartus would mail from the Barr plantation. The mailbox was outside the lane on the road. He knew he must not place it in the box until Mr. Barr went past on his way to work.

He headed east on the property, parking the horse and wagon near the fence and walked to the patch of scrub oaks. James jumped, ran a little way then turned and came back. Bartus had awakened him.

"Broughts yo sump tin teet," Bartus spoke first. "Gotcha some clothes, too. Hit'll bees 'bout foah mo daze afore we gits de lettah an' I comes fo yo den, dis be da las' time I comes an' dis is all de sump tin teet ah gots fuh yo."

Bartus finished the fence, climbed aboard the wagon and patted the letter in his pocket. Fear began to seize him; "what if the postman was suspicious? Why would anyone mail a letter from the same box it was addressed to? He thought, "Lawd, ah almos mess up, ah sho nuf did," he corrected himself.

Speedily, he drove the wagon past the three mile crossroad and onto Miles Plantation. A full row of mailboxes were in sight and some of the flags were up. He placed the letter under the outgoing envelopes; then keeping the wagon in the same direction, he headed home. He had made a full circle traveling almost eight miles to mail the letter. The second part of the plan was finished and now he would wait for it to return. Pansy had dinner ready when he reached home; there was ham pie along with sweet English peas filled with dumplings hoecake bread and left over gingerbread.

Three days passed; Pansy went to the mailbox and it was empty, not a scrap of a letter had arrived! On the fourth day, a small dirty envelope arrived and a small disgusted utterance came from Pansy. "Hopes dis be mine." She said, it certainly looked like the one she and Gale had addressed. Her name looked strange to her but, she was proud. Even if it held a false message, today she could be somebody.

She stopped back by the wash tubs where Zinnie was going about her daily routine. "I have a letter; could you read it to me?" She wanted to practice her speech so that it would sound real. "Whats yo needs, Pansy?" Zinnie asked. "See if dis lettah be mines." Pansy said. Zinnie took the envelope from her hand. "Yes it be's youse." She responded. After hearing the message Pansy ran into and throughout the house with joy. "Mah cousin coming." "Peebo, be comin'." She called loudly.

The message was out and the third part of the plan was complete; there should be no problem now. Word had spread throughout the plantation 'like wildfire'. Pansy would be the honoree; her cousin from Cairo Georgia would visit her. If all had been told, Pansy's family was all dead. Apparently, she has forgotten she had a 'cousin Peebo'?

By nightfall the fires were lit at the cabins and music rang throughout the yards and lanes.

"Swing low, sweet chariot, coming for to carry me home."

The banjos played, voices reached a crescendo and settled, time and time again; dancing and preaching went on until late into the night. The fourth part of the plan was about to spin into action. Bartus would ask Mr. Barr for the buckboard to pick up Peebo from the train. The letter had said the train would arrive at three, however; it had not disclosed what day. Mr. Barr asked Bartus when the train would arrive and he could not answer. "You don't expect me to give you the time and horses to go to the station and spend the day or a week waiting, do you?" He questioned. Bartus, Pansy and Gale had made a mistake! The only thing he could do now was to let James walk; but, how would he contact him?

"Oh, Lawd, how's I gon gits tuh de propety tuh picks up James?" He wondered.

It was true, however; Bartus had left the wire stretchers where he had replaced the old fence. Taking the wagon, he went to the east property, there he found James; dressed in a suit, white shirt and shiny black and white spectator shoes. Bartus folded the tarpaulin and loaded the wagon. James lay flat in the moving wagon with his head under the seat to diffuse the sun. Bartus drove him past the three mile crossroad; put him out and came home from the easterly direction.

Later that afternoon, James was walking to "White Oak'. Mr. Barr had come upon 'Peebo Gamble', walking barefoot down the road with white and black spectator shoes in his hand and a coat thrown over his shoulder. There was no baggage-----?

Mr. Barr stopped his carriage.

"Need a ride?" He asked.

"Yes, suh," Peebo answered.

"Going far?" Mr. Barr asked.

"Goin' tuh mah cousin Pansy's." He answered.

"That would be the Barr Plantation, I'm John Barr." He said, extending his hand. Peebo moved his hand out, as he had seen others do.

"New shoes," Mr. Barr questioned.

"Yes, Suh," he responded.

"I had some like that one time." Mr. Barr said, matter-of-factly.

That statement made James squirm and if the carriage had not been rolling so fast; he would have run, especially when he saw John Barr glancing downward at his feet and legs. His pant legs had ridden up and the scars from the shackles were fresh. The bottoms of the shoes had a monogram inside which read: *Made especially for J. A. Barr!*

As they approached the magnolia lane, Mr. Barr looked directly at him;

"You are the runaway slave from the Ambrose Sullivan Plantation, aren't you?"

"Yes, Suh" James responded.

"How do you know Pansy, Bartus or anybody else at 'White Oak'? He asked.

"Bartus, be mah brutha." He said, looking downward.

"You can stay 'til they catch you; I'll try to find a way to help, but you must promise not to tell a soul, not Bartus even, that I know about you," He directed.

"Ah Promises," James vowed. "Mistah Sullivan kilt mah Ma and 'lil brutha, too. Two more bruthas ova't his place." James went on.

"What did you do over at Five Forks?" John Barr questioned.

"Ah runs de surp wuks." He said.

John Barr was interested in the production of syrup. They talked about how they assembled syrup for the market and ship cross-country. James knew the works from A to Z.

"I makes yo a goot man." He promised.

They had reached 'White Oak' and Peebo was smiling.

John Barr was never surprised at what he might be confronted with. There was one thing for certain; there was no boring moments at 'White Oak'. He remembered a conversation of long ago when he and Bartus rode into 'White Oak'. Much of the words James had told him; he had heard before.

"I think I ought to ride over to Five Forks and talk with Mr. Ambrose Sullivan." He decided.

Three O'clock struck the grandfather clock in the parlor and a tired Carrie was slumped in the overstuffed Wainscot chair. Dr. Stephen Moore, Sr., made his monthly visit to see Evangeline Barr. He trudged up the long stairway; after all these years, he had become accustomed to this long flight of stairs. He would make the visit short as possible; Eva Barr was doing well as was evidenced by her busily cleaning her own closet. "My, her disposition surely has changed," he thought.

John had purchased tickets to New York where she would buy a new wardrobe, even after buying one here before leaving. Unable to keep her feet on the ground; she danced and pirouetted around the room. In one week, she would see Uncle Don Marshall, classmates and friends. She was going home to New York!

Dr. Moore had seen a troubled Carrie Grant, as he came up the veranda steps. She had been walking ahead toward the rotunda and her gait had slowed considerably, since he had last seen her. Now as she was walking toward him, he could see the dark circles under her eyes and the pallor of her skin. "She is suffering." He said inaudibly.

Carrie called out to him before he could exit the porch. "I need to talk to you." They sat on the veranda as the overhead wind-propelled fan blew softly in the breeze. She emptied her problems on the ears of a tired old man and friend. They walked into the parlor where he drew a vial of blood. She was barely capable of working; sheer determination was her only motivation.

"No matter what; Eva Barr is stress enough to drive her crazy." Dr Moore thought. "I'll return in two weeks with a report for you," he said. Turning his buggy around and holding the reins with one hand, he waved goodbye.

"He has been a teacher and dear friend," Carrie thought as he turned out of the plantation and onto the dirt road.

'Five forks Plantation', was a sight to behold! John Barr surmised as the plantation came into view. Angle iron, hanging above the entrance of the gates was bent into large four foot letters; A. S., signifying; Ambrose Sullivan. The long straight roadway, led to a large columned white house, but there was nothing special about it except to the people who lived there.

The cotton fields on both sides of the road leading to the yard were filled with field slaves. The huge, split, black-jack oak baskets, running over with cotton, were set on the long wagons. Four of the slaves were replacing a wagon wheel with a jack. Three slaves were hunched underneath the wagon, holding it up, while the other one pushed the wheel into place. Revulsion brought a chill to John Barr. The hair on his arms stood up; as did his blood pressure!

"This is a sick, depraved place!" He mumbled. "Certainly it is one that I could never live in; and be able to live with myself. A man must have dignity and I don't see any here!" He said disgustedly. "Nobody could blame a body for leaving, running away or dying, if necessary, to escape this woeful lifestyle." The thought of Bartus and James' mother crossed his mind. If, Ambrose worked to death; how did the brother die?" He wondered.

The sun was high overhead, yet a chill was in the air. It was as if he was in the presence of evil! John pulled his coat together and buttoned the front. It had been several years since he had seen Ambrose Sullivan and he had forgotten what he looked like. Then, his eyes focused on the foreman, with whip in hand, walking up and down the cotton rows cracking it loudly.

Ambrose Sullivan was a powerful man, even in his early sixties. The long black hair, hung from his nose and ears into his mustache and the eyebrows covered most of his forehead; his gruff voice was almost as bad as his 'bite'. "He would never receive the Humanitarian award from the ladies at the Orphanage in Savannah," John laughed at his own analogy.

Sullivan's buggy had been coming at a break-neck speed; its driver had been none other than Ambrose Sullivan, himself. It had taken a few minutes for him to get out of the buggy. The three hundred pound man had never been known to smile; his manners were even worse than is gross looks.

"Good morning," John Barr said, extending his hand.

Ambrose Sullivan growled, "Whadda ya want? Cain't you see I'm busy? I've been busy looking for a slave named James Reem. He musta disappeared from the face of the earth. If he's alive he'll come back. I've got his two bruthas; Rolf and Scamp but they ain't no good. Troublemakers; both of 'em. All they do is keep an uprising amongst the other slaves. I'm gonna sell them next month. I'd sell them today if I got an offer." The exasperated man ran on and on.

"You've got an offer; I'll give you five hundred apiece for each of them." John spoke hastily.

"You can take 'em today, and if their sorry brutha, James, shows up, you can have him for nothing. You can have his papers too."

Ambrose Sullivan smiled for the first time.

John Barr took the ownership papers and wrote a check, while the two slaves were being loaded onto his buggy. They were heading home; Bartus would be so excited to have his brothers free. John Barr exhaled quickly; else his heart would beat out of his body. He had begun to whistle without a tune. He was happy!

The cane mill would double production and 'White Oak Plantation' syrup was on the map! Cairo, Georgia would have some competition. The three bedroom house of Bartus and Pansy would accommodate James, Rolf and Scamp without a problem. The buggy pulled into the magnolia lane as both Rolf and Scamp sang out "Praises De Lawd."

The lane was filled with workers again tonight. Fires had been lit and a banjo's twang, twang, and alerted the cabins and cottages the festivities would begin. A roasting pig was turning slowly on the skewer spit and 'slave stew' filled the large black wash pot. Every garden vegetable, from their home grown garden, had found its way into the pot as Ben and Bartus had prepared the stew.

Bloody Bones would come again tonight and the children were excited.

Rolf and Scamp would have their baths, heads and bodies shaved; as had James a few days ago. Bartus had been utterly surprised; he fell on his knees, clasping his hands together.

"Thanks be tuh de big Massah in Hebn. Yo brought my bruthas safe." He cried, babbling and wiping tears on his arm sleeve.

"Mistah Barr, bes de bes man dat evah lived." He shouted to the crowd and the crowd went wild with applause. The anvil and ax were brought out and both men were cut from their shackles; as they fell away, the small children sang, "Let Freedom Ring". Now that Rolf and Scamp were free, it was time to take a bath. Bartus sat alone as Rolf and Scamp were shaved by James and the lye soap for the bath would kill any germ.

Bartus started to moan; he was overcome with emotions. This act set off a pandemonium of moans, akin to crickets in a snuff can.

The last thing Mr. Barr had to complete was to apply for Emancipation papers for James, Rolf and Scamp. He had been a lucky man to get James for free; throwing his head back, he laughed a deep belly laugh. "Ole Ambrose got the nasty end of this stick!" He whooped.

Next week, the syrup mill would be put into high gear as James, Rolf and Scamp implemented the new plan to become more productive. The markets in the north were begging for syrup made from cane; they had an abundance of maple syrup and molasses.

Barr plantation now had enough workers to open its own stores; syrup would be put into gallon, half-gallon and quart cans. The syrup would be hauled into town and sold at the vacant building he had acquired five years ago. It was just inside the city limits of Savannah; Mr. Barr would hire help to run the store.

"When the stores get on their feet; I will throw a shindig the likes of which Georgia has never seen." He told Eva.

"Yoah ahr so clevah, mah dahling." She retorted.

"There will be bonuses for production and a profit sharing plan, as well. The way to keep good help is money." He speculated.

Eva smiled her demure soft smile. "John, I think yoah have lost yoah everlasting mind." She crooned.

Rolf was never asked and because slaves did not talk to their masters about personal things; he did not tell John Barr that he had a wife and two sons. Both sons were too small to be tagged.

John Barr watched him closely and discovered his work was excellent. He had first been sent with James and Scamp to the sawmill. The order had come in from Massachusetts for 'Georgia yellow pine' lumber. The complexity of the sawmill needed a man who could figure board feet, cut the six by six foundation timbers, post, tongue and groove and wall boarding; Rolf was just that man! He enjoyed his work, his freedom and his brothers; but he missed, beyond word, Persimmon and his two sons.

Persimmon, a beautiful Creole, had lived in New Orleans. She had been raised in the French Custoe LeBlanc family, since the age of four. Her biological mother, Sophia, had been a governess for Sharri Le Blanc when she disappeared on her way to the market. Young Persimmon had been raised along with their own daughter, Sharri. Both children were the same age, studied together and were accepted into debutante society. They traveled, went to the opera, picnicked in the park and had graduated high school together in June. The graduation had been held for thirteen young adults in the courthouse basement. Then Persimmon had disappeared.

The Riverwalk was the last place Persimmon had been seen. The two young women had strolled down Bourbon Street onto Royal and over to the Riverboat, docked at the wharf. They had hob-nobbed with friends and acquaintances and it was late when, with their parasols open, they turned to go home. Sharri's account of the incident was verified by spectators who recapped to the Constable.

Known slave traders had accosted the girls; they had run through the alley from the waterfront to Royal Street. The shortcut back to the LeBlanc house was Persimmons undoing. She was captured, abducted and taken to a boat waiting in the harbor. Later, since she had been rendered unconscious during this ordeal, she could not remember who she was or how she had come to live at 'Three Winds'. By this time, she weighed seventy-eight pounds; a skeleton of a woman. She had been purchased for a Mississippi plantation owned by Hansel Peck whose acreage was primarily located in the rich delta region.

The depressed mood of Persimmon caused her to be sold within the year. Her inability to work was a result of her upbringing for she had had her own maids and absolutely no training in housekeeping. Her time had been occupied with the large volumes of Macbeth, Hamlet and Shakespearian plays. In South Carolina, Persimmon was sold again to Ambrose Sullivan, of Georgia.

Ambrose Sullivan had never been known to keep a housemaid for any length of time, especially, if they resisted his groping and other sexual advances. Persimmon, intimidate him with her education, knowledge and wisdom. He had forbidden her to read, even locked the library to keep her out.

"No slave of Ambrose Sullivan will ever read." He swore. "Makes them act high and mighty." He went on to his wife. Later, after catching her with his newspaper; a decision was made to send her to the fields.

It was love at first sight, for Rolf Reem. He could not bear to see the heavy cotton straps wearing into the tender skin of Persimmon's shoulders. He always chose the row beside her, so that he could help to fill her cotton bag and keep her up with the other cotton pickers; a double workload for himself. If he were caught, it would mean a rawhide whip for him. Their love grew, even though they had almost never been alone. The second year together, their first son was born and yet another in the third year of knowing each other.

After Mr. Barr heard Rolf's story; he knew that he would have to try to purchase Persimmon and her children. There was a major problem though; he did not have a house for them. Bartus and Pansy's house could accommodate four people, but not eight! "I promised Carrie some help months ago and Persimmon should fit the bill." He pondered.

Two weeks had passed as Carrie had awaited the results of her blood test. She had felt worse, for the last two weeks than ever in her life. Dark circles surrounded her sunken eyes and she had lost another three or four pounds. Last Saturday, Mama Sally had taken her red tick hound, personal belongings, sewing machine and had gone home. Carrie's impatience had hurt her feelings almost daily, over the last few days. She did not feel useful anymore; her life had always been based on helping her neighbors, friends and family, she needed more stimulation.

The wedding and house furnishings were completed and today, she would go home to her chickens; they needed her. Her little cabin needed patching in places and some new door jambs, as well. She wanted to go fishing; she missed that most of all. This conversation had been held with Carrie and Gale at breakfast this morning; Carrie did not have the energy to respond.

It was late when Dr. Moore came and Eva saw him drive up; as he approached the house, he heard her call out to him. He spared no time in getting up to her room; perhaps Carrie had been taken for the worse. Instead, Evangeline was overcome with anxiety because John-John had skinned his knee. He bandaged it quickly and soothed the mother and son. "Days like this is why I want to rip up my shingle and go fishing," he said angrily.

Carrie was waiting as the doctor stood at the parlor door. "Carrie," he said, without looking at her. "I need to take your blood pressure," he coaxed. "How have you been eating, have you been sleeping well, do you have problems urinating, what about your bowels?" He asked, listening closely to her irregular heartbeats. She had worked with him long enough to recognize when a condition was serious, even though, he would never tell her if she was terminal.

"Ole Bessie Nalls had the same problem years ago, had diabetes, high blood sugar; back then we had very little medication to help. Now we do." he went on. "Brights disease is a bad one." He said. "Never rely on your own diagnosis." He had once told her. "Even we doctors need a doctor sometimes."

Carrie was asked to lie back on the settee while he listened carefully to her heart and lungs. Eventually, Dr. Moore placed the stethoscope and blood pressure cuff into his leather bag.

"Carrie," he said, almost in a whisper.

"You know, long ago you and I had a talk about death and dying?"

"We both agreed the truth should always prevail, didn't we?"

"Yes," Carrie said lamely. "I am aware of my condition," she spoke softly. "There is one thing I need from you," she went on. "I want you to promise me, the only person you will tell is John Barr," she finished.

"It is not necessary for Eva to know, she would be frantic! It would serve no purpose to tell my family," she said sadly.

There were no tears, no regrets; she would die as she had lived; courageously!

Carrie's world had stopped; her thoughts ran rampant.

"Gale has asked to move to Savannah, I have friends there and would like to get reacquainted with my childhood playmates," she pleaded. "We will move back to Savannah so I will be close to the hospital. I have many friends there, you know." Smiling through her tears was difficult.

With a pat on the shoulder, he gave her a small vial of medication, along with a bag of sulfur; reminding her, once again, how to take it.

"Keep your kidneys flushed; drink plenty of water and remember you can have no sweets."

"Make your move to Savannah as soon as you can, I will see John Barr when I get into town." He said, tipping his hat to her.

Carrie was not stunned because the diagnosis was the same as she had guessed; her family was all that mattered now. She had given the sick and needy among the mill families her attention and they had depended on her expertise. 'White Oak Plantation' had required her best. Now, her family, who had always taken second best, would get the rest. She must make plans quickly, for time was running out and, she must move her family to Savannah as soon as possible.

The next morning John A. Barr called for Carrie. Sitting in one of the Windsor chairs, as she walked in, he smiled as he blew circles of smoke into the air; Gale was on his mind, as was Carrie. John Barr had lost his own mother at an early age and he had very little actual memory of her and what he did remember was not pleasant. Molly, his sister died with the same disease Carrie has and she was carrying a child. But, his own personal tragedies passed and he was living proof 'one must go on'.

He had been struck with the realization of Carrie's natural beauty, the first time he saw her and many were the times he wished Eva were more like her. He had noticed lately, the hardness in her face, her eyes no longer sparkling; even her gait had slowed. At first, he had attributed it to the death of her husband; later, to Gales tragedy. Feeling guilty, he blamed himself for Carrie's disposition. "She was overworked." He admitted. He had not protected Oprah, Gale or the plantation from villains, rapists and slave hunters. Lost in thought, he had not heard Carrie enter the room.

"Good morning, Mr. Barr." Carrie addressed him as she had always done.

"Sit down," he said. "Pansy is making us some chocolate milk."

"Thank you sir, I am aware of the content of this meeting; first I'd like to reiterate the conversation I had with Dr. Moore, yesterday," she spoke firmly. "Your confidentiality is of utmost importance to me," she went on. "I need a few favors from you. Bartus and Pansy are my confidants so; I will talk to them about packing and hauling. Finding a house will be a problem; I would like for Gale to be close enough to Oprah and Adam, so that Missy and Lena can grow up and attend school together."

"I will be close to Dr. Moore and the hospital." She stated, clearing her voice.

"It has been a pleasure living at 'White Oak'; I have gained new friends and experienced cultural differences. Most of all I have learned that plantations can survive without slavery. If my Walt had taken your route, he would be alive today," she went on, looking downward.

"You, Mr. Barr, will one day be rewarded for the modest way you have fought slavery. You will go down in Georgia history as being a 'brother of the brother-less', 'father to the father-less' and a present help in that time of need." She had paraphrased scriptures, mixed with heartfelt thoughts. She went on, "I am giving you two weeks to find my replacement and in that time I will have trained her." She declared, laying her head back in the wainscot chair.

Knowing Carrie's serious illness was in the last stages, he was astonished at her performance. "She is some woman; the world could do with a few more like her." He thought as she spoke. To alleviate the pressure of Carrie's responsible actions, John explained the future plans of 'White Oak'.

"Rolf has a wife, a Mulatto, educated in New Orleans." He stated. "From my understanding, she is left at the Sullivan Plantation with their two children and I plan to make a substantial offer for her, if need be. She has experience as a housemaid; is educated and capable of attending Eva's needs."

Carrie listened intently as he talked.

"After thinking long and hard; I am prepared to give you and your family a place to live, food and medical help for the rest of your lives. Gale will eventually marry and until then, I will see that she and Lena are cared for."

"Since it is necessary to make the move to Savannah, you deserve severance pay and some extra to assure your financial comfort," he offered.

"Go, with my blessings, to your destiny and remember you are not alone." His voice shook.

"You may call on me, day or night," he said, pulling on his coat. Wrestling in the inside pocket, he handed her five hundred dollars.

He stood up, Carrie followed suit, and they shook hands. John Barr exited the parlor and from the hallway, he called back to her; "Bartus and Pansy will be available at your convenience."

Exiting in haste; his eyes were wet.

Carrie continued to sit before the lighted fireplace. The once red embers began to die; the flame was gone, long ago, as was the story of her life. She had remained professional throughout the course of conversation. There had been no pity in his eyes; she would have hated that, for she refused to become an albatross around anyone's neck. Self-pity was not in her; she would continue with her present plans to move to Savannah. Gale and Lena were her priorities and she would write to Mama Sally telling her of their plans.

The next morning, Pansy couldn't get breakfast soon enough! Somehow, the birds sang sweeter and longer than she had ever heard before. Oprah would have Gale again; Missy and Lena would start school together, a few years from now. Washing out the dishrags; she hung them over the front of the still warm stove, to dry, singing as she flapped them in the air.

She walked down the lane toward Carrie's, swinging her arms in the rhythm of her song.

"Steal away, steal away, Steal away to Jesus"

"I ain't got long to stay here."

"Ah sho bes glad I'se don' hafta steals nothin' from nobody. I'se gotta husbun, a cotege." She repeated with delight.

The front door was open and Carrie was waiting; she had taken boxes from the shed to pack in. "Careful, roaches live in empty boxes." She said. "I don't want to take them with me." She and Pansy packed her best dresses. "I only want to pack today what I won't be using for the next two weeks." Carrie spoke matter-of-factly.

"Betta saves outten a dress fer church service, Sunday." Pansy reminded her.

"Thank you Pansy, I never thought of that." She said.

Thus far, moving had not been difficult; the furniture would be the big thing. Bartus and Ben would arrange that when the time came.

Carrie and Pansy could not tell which was the more excited, Gale or Lena, as they sat watching the girls.

"Lena girl yo goes and dances yosef a gig." Pansy laughed, clapping loudly as Lena danced.

Late, that afternoon, Mr. Barr rolled into 'White Oak' and seated beside him was the most astonishingly beautiful woman Bartus had ever seen! Despite her tied up hair, she commanded attention and he would never have thought her to be a slave; she could pass as white. Meticulously, she stepped down from the buckboard, stood erect, walked over to the back of the wagon and lifted her two sons. Hugging them close, she laughed, as one whispered, "Ma look at de bird! He wets everthin', he jist spittin' out wattah," the other said. Both boys shyly hid behind the long gray skirt of the coarsely woven fabric of her dress.

Pansy had clean clothes laid out for each of them and ordered them to follow her. The black wash pot boiled away; its lye soap just waiting to show power against lice, grease and filth.

Persimmon walked into the house with Pansy; she would get her bath first. Stripping her clothes and handing them to Pansy. She said, "Ma'am, I'll take them later, I am used to carrying on for my little family."

"I'se gwine do it." Pansy said bossily.

Persimmon, bathed, washed and rubbed her hair dry with the coarse, feed sack towel; she was anxious to see her husband. "He ain't been tole youse comin'. He gone be sprized, yes Suh, sho is," Pansy chuckled.

"He could never be more surprised than I, when Rolf and Scamp were sold; I thought I would die," she said earnestly. "I sure have missed him; our boys have, too."

"She sho look lak a white woman," Pansy told Bartus. "Gist an ole 'musty'. Her jealousy was overpowering. Bartus patted her on the fanny and that was all it took for Pansy to start smiling again. "She bes beautimus," she grinned.

Persimmon, dressed in the sack dress Pansy had brought from the pantry clothes closet; bathed her two boys. They did not have lice, she had always kept them picked off and washed their heads good with Octagon soap. Hugging them closely; she dressed them, while she crooned, "We are free, and Daddy, Uncle James, Scamp and Uncle Bartus are free!"

Pansy stood with hands on hips; "I'se free, too, has been free fo yeahs." She spoke hastily. She stood erect; commanding.

"You know, you won't ever have to wear shackles," she addressed her sons. "One day I will carry you to New Orleans and show you where I grew up with my Mama." The soft face gave way to a few tears as she spoke to her attentive children. They stood and stared up at her, their wide eyes had always seemed to penetrate her soul. "Yes ma'am," they answered in unison.

Pansy came in to give further instructions from Mr. Barr.

"Youse'll live wit me an Bartus till Carrie move out, den youse'll moves in, 'den Miz Carrie will train you tuh tak her place. She be movin' tuh Savanny, Youse sho gone has a tim wit Missy Barr," she mumbled, walking away.

At the supper table that evening, Persimmon fed her sons first; which was not a customary thing to do. It did not meet Pansy's satisfaction, one bit. She voiced it loudly, "No chillum evah, eats fust. Nevah, Nevah!" She shrilled.

The white horse drove the wagon up to the back porch. "Ben be home," Pansy said, dryly. A wagon with the workers pulled up right behind him. Persimmon first saw James, his head covered in hairs like little sandspurs all over. Next, she saw Scamp, "Where is Rolf?" She called out.

"Right here," He shouted from behind her; picking her up into the air and holding her.

"Mah wief, Mah woman." He cried! The boys landed on the floor, clutching his legs like leeches.

"Pappy, Pappy," they called him. He squatted on the floor, grabbing his sons. He held them for moments; crooning, his deep voice, like rolling thunder... "Ummmmm", on and on. "Mah Persimmon, Mah Newt, Mah Davit." He sang. "A man nevah hade a betta day. My fambly, we'se all free! Thanks be tuh de Massah; We'se free! The room had been enveloped with a sweet spirit; eyes poured tears, noses snotted. The family was complete; what a sight to behold!

Carrie was caught up in her own world, but had stopped by the kitchen for a moment. Young Persimmon asked if she could borrow a hairbrush; her long, wavy hair dropped almost to her waistline, it glowed, as the rays of the sun shown from the window that Pansy was peeking through. Persimmon was tall; her chiseled features were the stuff dreams are made of and her golden skin was shining after her bath. She had pulled her hair back and tied it with a rag; she was flawless. The combination of dark Rolf's muscular structure, his bald head and mustache was entertaining to say the least. Together, they were a black Nubian god with his soft bronze goddess. The boys were in between them in color. "A perfect marriage, for a perfect family!" John Barr would say later.

The demeanor of their faces were not hardened by their past; endurance, was their key. "*The windows of their souls shown brightly through the eyes of their children. They had known true love and care despite the devils snare. Suffering could not hold them.*" Carrie thought.

They were born to be great!

Pansy stood mesmerized by the handsome couple for she had only dreamed of such beauty herself. Bartus looked down at her; bouncing a small pat on her fanny. She smiled up at him; he was hers! She had more than she deserved and all she had ever wanted.

"God be goot, Ah Massah in heben be great tuh his chillun." Bartus prayed. "Sho is." Pansy echoed.

Seemingly, morning came almost as soon as the sun went down. Today, Carrie would introduce Persimmon to Eva Barr; she had only one fear and that was fear of the unknown. Being positive was the only appropriate thing to feel. She brushed her hair, forcing a smile to return itself, from the old blotched mirror on her dresser. Her deeply sunken eyes needed a little white powder; she put a small hint of red crape paper, dabbed in water, on her lips to bring life.

Her flower beds of pansies by her front porch commanded attention. The little faces turned upward, as myriads of small faces stared directly into hers. "Good morning little pansies, I'm glad you smiled at me today, I have lots of work to do but I will see you when I home. I always depend n you to brighten my life…" She turned back, stared into the window of Gale and Lena's room. "I love you." She thought. "There are no words strong enough to make you understand. You are part of me." She spoke softly.

Carrie, realizing she was about to go off on a tangent, stomped both her feet to bring stabilization to her thoughts. Breakfast was ready but she was not hungry; she knew she had to put something in her stomach. Her energy level was low and she realized she would never get to the top of the stairs without it, so she made it to the veranda, and sat down in the big wicker rocker until she could get her breath.

The weather was cool; winter would be here soon.

She would be in Savannah by then………….

Persimmon was waiting after eating breakfast with Rolf, Pansy, Bartus and Ben. Ordinarily, Rolf would not be allowed to take his meals in 'the big house', but; Bartus had bent the rules, until he and Persimmon could move into their own house.

Carrie ate a bite, and then met Persimmon on the back porch.

"Ready?" She asked Persimmon.

"Ready." Persimmon responded.

"Welcome to White Oak Plantation; may you and your family have many happy years here." Carrie offered. "Mrs. Eva Barr is a direct descendant of the Duke of Newburgh; her grandmother, Martha, was his sister and Mrs. Eva inherited this land as a wedding gift."

Persimmon shook her head, understanding well the language of 'old money'.

"Sometimes when aristocracy is involved, one can be hard to understand; Evangeline Tyne Barr is one of those. Basically, she has a heart of gold and dares not spare any expense, if she agrees, but; will put her foot down hard if things are not pleasing to her." Carrie admonished.

"I understand." Persimmon answered.

There was no time to tell her about all the conflicts she would experience; she would just have to experience them for herself, as time went on. Persimmon appeared to be aloof; this was good, for in order to survive; she would need to stay unattached.

"The stairway had become longer each and today it seemed even longer." Carrie thought. Her eyes would look at the long stairway for the last time. Arriving at the large doubled doors; she stopped and knocked.

"Entah," Eva's voice rang out. Her bed was filled with clothes; she was packing for her trip to New York that had been delayed, but, they would be leaving soon.

"Mrs. Barr, I'd like for you to meet Persimmon Reem. She will be your new companion, if you so desire." Carrie declared. "Persimmon is from New Orleans and lived with the Custoe LeBlanc family for over fifteen years. She has a high school education and has completed some studies at the University of New Orleans." Carrie finished.

"Ooooh, deah. How ostentatious and, what a lovely woman you ahre." Eva said.

"Ah have sooo many clothes ah'll bet are just yoah size. You may take yoah choice, you ahre so lovely." She said once again.

"Was it education, breeding or both that so delighted Evangeline Barr?" Persimmon asked herself, as they left the room.

Carrie picked up the breakfast tray, opened the doors and moved on to the next chore. The entire day was hectic for there were many things for Persimmon to learn and tomorrow they would start again with other tasks. Carrie was exhausted after the long day and fell asleep without a sponge bath or reading "Grimm's Fairy Tales to young Lena.

Lena took her book to her mother and Gale knew she would not fall asleep until she heard a bedtime story. Soon Lena was asleep with her black curls fanned out on her pillow, her mouth slightly ajar as she slept; reminding Gale of her daddy, she missed him; still. Her pain was only momentary; her mind had skipped many tracks lately for she was terribly lonely. She needed someone who spoke her language and Oprah was the only person in the world who understood her and would keep her secrets.

The next week came swiftly; Mrs. Eva Barr loved Persimmon and had given her an entire wardrobe. Persimmon fitted well into all the dresses.

They were ankle length on her and the bodice and waists fitted perfectly. She was about to recoup her past lifestyle; she sat and conversed with Eva for hours at a time. Eva's eccentric personality was a delight for her; even stimulating.

Persimmon had arrived in a safe haven; she would have her books and loved to read aloud to Eva Barr. Their love of music was much the same. "This is heaven," Persimmon said aloud. "It's a long way from hell." Her eyes blinked back the tears.

Already, she and Evangeline Barr were planning a trip to Atlanta to 'buy a few things', Eva needed for her New York jaunt.

Next, they would go to New Orleans….

PART 13

Savannah, Georgia

1855
"Have pity on them! For their life,
Is full of grief and care.
You do not know one half the woes,
The very poor must bear."

"The Poor"
Jane T. Worthington

The wagon was loaded to the hilt and there was no room for three passengers. Gale and Lena would possibly have to stay behind, without shelter, bedding or food; they both began to cry!

"Take some of the furniture off the wagon and bring it later, when you bring the organ." Carrie told Ben. "I'm not going to leave my family behind. We are all going together." She insisted.

Mr. Barr had come home from the saw mill; he was late going to the funeral home today and the loaded wagon had blocked the lane. Bartus had flagged him down and told him of the dilemma. John Barr walked around the wagon, assessed the situation and proclaimed; "Carrie you will ride with me. We will go on ahead of the wagon and find a house for you. The wagon will be slow; maybe an hour behind us. That will give us time to look for and locate something suitable for your family." He went on.

The ride in the carriage was comfortable with the break-away suspension of the wheels, gave way to the bumps and grinds of the rocky, pot-holed road. "It was a long, smooth ride." Carrie thought, gratefully.

Driving down the row, a distance from the docks, Carrie spotted young Missy, playing in the dirt at the corner of her front stoop. Missy's face lit up and she ran into the house. "Mama, Mama!" She screamed, pointing to Mr. Barr and Carrie as they stopped in front of Oprah and Adam's house.

Carrie and John Barr sat still in the carriage as Oprah came outside. She hugged Carrie and shook hands with Mr. Barr.

"The well of wattah is in dat house." She pointed to the last house from the end of 'The Row'. "It don't look lak much, but; it's sounder than the othus."

"Gale and Lena are on their way; they'll be here in an hour or so. Keep them with you until we are settled." Carrie said.

"I will." Oprah replied.

She was busy cooking supper; Adam did not come home for dinner, so; she cooked their biggest meal at night. This afternoon, she had rabbit stew boiling and decided to add more potatoes and carrots to the pot. She would also cook two waiters of corn pone, instead of her usual, one and there would be enough for all of them. Adam would be home around four o'clock and Oprah smiled as she prepared for her family and dear friends.

The last house looked nothing like one Carrie or John Barr would approve. The front porch was falling away, windows were broken out and debris covered the yard. Carrie's disappointment was overwhelming; hot tears flooded her eyes.

"I can't live like this; there isn't enough room for my family. The rooms are note sealed; look at the floor! They have rotted away." Carrie cried.

John Barr looked at the floor boards; they were separated, revealing the ground beneath. "We would be able to see the animals walking underneath the house." Carrie said, wiping her eyes. Knowing all along that crying did not help matters; she continued to sob softly.

"I'll go now and contact Mr. Brann. You let me handle it and you will have your house, just as you want it." He promised, patting her hand.

Then, pivoting on his bad foot; he forgot his own pain, as he pulled the carriage around and headed to town on the overgrown buggy trail.

Carrie was heartsick as she walked through the empty, falling down houses in 'The Row'. Feeling as though life had totally abandoned her; this was her hour of need so, she prayed. She wept for her mother, who had died when she was barely five years old. She cried for her husband who had abandoned her without meaning to; thoughts of his death bringing a sudden, sad memory to the present. Now, she would cry, for failing her child and grandchild. The weeping jags had finally caught up with her. All the suppression of her emotions flooded forth; they would no longer be denied!

The hoof beats of the horses drew her back to reality; Mr. Barr had returned and was walking toward the front of the house. He had seen R.A Brann and, purchased the property and would rebuild Carrie Grant's house, starting tomorrow. He ordered Ben and Bartus to leave the wagon, loaded with furniture; Bartus would ride back home with him, while Ben took the horses back to 'White Oak'. He pitched a large tarpaulin onto the porch.

"Tell them to cover the wagon and park it in Oprah's yard. If you want, Carrie, you can come back to the plantation tonight and if you want you can all stay there until we finish here." John Barr suggested.

"They can stay heah, suh." Oprah offered. "We will make room for them."

Carrie had never known life could be so hard, for today, cold hard facts stared her eye to eye. The children were loud; the house was cramped;

food supplies were short, and so were the tempers. She had spent almost a hundred dollars in the time it took to rebuild the house.

Mr. Barr had made daily visits to the work site. Across the entire front of the house, a porch stood, sturdy and inviting; the mock Victorian house was complete with gingerbread trim. R.A Brann and his wife, Fay, had been its creators. The floors and walls had all been replaced, with one wall being removed so that a parlor could replace the two small rooms. The kitchen had built in shelves and underneath the stove a backlash was built from floor to wall. A large round stovepipe was fitted to the outside of the house to evacuate the smoke. An extra bedroom had been built for Mama Sally and Carrie would write and invite her to come and live with them.

Mr. Barr had left Bartus in charge to oversee the completion of the move; along with any other needs Carrie may have. Bartus loved being a business man, traveling back and forth and helping to make decisions. Tomorrow he would measure the windows and go-and-fetch, between Mrs. Sally and Carrie, the supplies needed to make the curtains and when they were finished; Sally was brought to the house to hang them. Mama Sally would make new quilts and by winter, she and her neighborhood women could quilt three or four.

Happiness filled Gale and Lena and it was contagious; even Carrie was smiling and pleasant. Lena had her playmate again; Gale had Oprah to confide in, and Carrie had all of them, and Mama Sally, as well. It did not matter to her that she had lost five more pounds, because tonight Carrie was content. "Thank you, Lord." She said, gratefully.

Thanksgiving was near and Mr. Barr had sent several cords of wood to keep Carrie's household warm. Gale had taken over the cooking and, had become an old fashioned cook, with the oversight of Mama Sally. Carrie had lost interest in the wonders of life and, had taken to her bed a couple of weeks back.

Dr. Moore had a long talk with Gale and it had been a life-changing event for her. She now proved to her mother that she was capable of caring for herself and Lena. For the first time, Gale had become aware of the unselfish, self-sacrifice, Carrie had made for her. Now, her mother's comfort and happiness would become hers. She realized how hard it must have been to learn that her twelve year old daughter was pregnant by a vile rapist, who had never been caught.

"Mum, can I get you something?" Gale asked.

Carrie did not answer, for Dr. Moore had given her a sedative. Lately, she had become anxious and nervous and Gale would give her a pill to help her relax and rest.

Today was Thanksgiving Day!

Oprah had invited Gale, Lena and Carrie to share Thanksgiving dinner with her family. Gale checked in on her mother before she and Lena left home, a little after ten o'clock. The morning was brisk and cool as the two of the walked down 'The Row'.

As they entered the front porch, Adam extended his hand. "I would like for you to meet a friend of mine, Gale. He is in the Navy and his ship will pull out next week for San Francisco. He will be leaving for Spain in a couple of months." He went on.

"Gale, please meet, Mate Goolsby." He said.

"Mate, this is Oprah's best friend, Gale Grant." He continued.

Shocked and embarrassed, Gale shook Mate's hand, but there was very little talk. Gale was almost sure that Mate Goolsby was twice her age. After dinner, the table was cleared and dishes were put away; Mate walked Gale home to see about her mum, and Lena stayed behind to play hop-scotch with Missy.

On the way home, Mate Goolsby talked about himself, his career and his future plans. He had never married because, 'the right woman just never came', and he told her as he held the front door open for her.

Gale sat the food on the table and went into her mum's room; she had called to her but, there was no answer. Gale and Mate entered the room together. Carrie's mouth was wide open! Her pupils had completely changed and her skin was the color of ash!

"Oh, my God!" Gale screamed.

Mate Goolsby moved in closer and pulled the sheet up over Carrie's face and closed her eyes with his fingers. He put his arm around Gale, reassuring her that he would be there for her.

Settling Gale in the parlor, he went for help; vowing he would see her through this ordeal. He and Adam left immediately for Barr's Funeral Home.

John A Barr, II, was still on duty so he called Dr. Moore and hastily headed down 'The Row', toward Carrie's home. Uncontrollable sobs arose from deep within; others could not see them. He has lost an excellent worker but, more than that; he had lost a friend.

He would call upon his mortician to prepare her body for burial, for he could not bear to put her away. No years of training could prepare him for this day! Sadly, he drove his carriage home to 'White Oak'. His heart was heavy; knowing things had changed forever.

"There is death; and then there is death." He thought.

"No two are ever the same".

The next day, Bartus arose early; his was a day of great sadness, for he was on his way to carry the news to Sally Ogen. His heart was heavy, so he began to sing.

"We shall gather at the river,
Where bright angel's feet have trod."
"With its crystal tide forever,
Flowing from the throne of God."

His strong voice bellowed; as he drove, slowly. The squirrels scampered swiftly, seeking refuge, while birds flew in coveys out of the open fields into the deep woods.

"People and animals go into hiding when the Grim Reaper appears." He thought. Bartus himself had heard the story many times. "The animals head for the hills, when bad storms come." One of his owners told him, many years ago. Today was one of recollection and sadness, but, he knew he must control himself for Sally's sake. "Miz. Sally, gon' bees upsets, yes suh, sho is." He spoke aloud.

Sally had not slept for the last few nights. "The night owl cried all night long." She told Bartus.

"Don't know how I can bear it. I got a bad feeling, hanging over me. See the buzzards circling over my house? They've been that a way now for three days. It's a true sign of the death of a loved one." She explained.

"Lord, I never knowed Carrie was so sick. She's been looking peaked for a long time. Well, the good Lord gives and He takes away, too." She added.

"He sure took a good woman; He musta needed her to help him with something. Lordy, Mr. Bartus, I lose everybody; my son and now my daughter-in-law. Why don't He take me?" She continued. "I'm almost eighty; I have lived my life."

Bartus did not share in everything she said, however; he offered his condolences by going along with her, shaking his head in agreement and saying nothing.

Sally packed her clothes in a cardboard box and would go to see about Gale and Lena; they needed her now.

Three months after the funeral of Carrie Grant, the mailman brought six letters, all in one day. Gale read the backings on the envelopes and, never having taken care of business, she was not prepared to deal with the letters now. Mate Goolsby would be home in a month and he would help her. She laid the unopened statements on the mantle and forgot about them. She felt so alone, since Mama Sally had gone home two weeks ago.

Little Lena, loved Mate Goolsby, for he was everything she had ever longed for in a Poppy. During the weeks Mate was in the Port of Savannah, he spent all of it with Gale and Lena. He described to Gale, his thoughts concerning why marriage had eluded him. He had been afraid that he would never care enough for anyone to be tied down. Yet, when he met her; he had begun to change his mind, for she was the purest, most unspoiled woman, he had ever met. Her simple ways, were very attractive to him, as was she. With little Lena, he had found something to come home to. He would have a family and, in a few years he would retire from the Navy. Then he could settle down and never leave his wife and child, ever again; he promised. Many times, when he was on night watch duty, the billows rolled, seas were raging, but; somehow he had peace. His fondest memory was of Gale; she had walked down the aisle to meet him; holding to the hand of Lena. They smiled as they walked toward him and a warm glow washed over him; that had been two months ago today.

"I'm one happy man." He said aloud.

He had taken them both 'for better or worse'.

The memory Mate Goolsby had of coming back to Savannah right after Carrie's death, was bittersweet. It had been awhile since he'd seen his wife and child and he yearned to see them, but, on the other hand, he knew that Gale would not have reconciled her mother's death yet. She had become dependent and unable to function on her own and lately had been complaining of headaches. He could tell from her letters that she was having adjustment difficulties.

After Mate had been home for a couple of day; he discovered unopened letters on the mantle. After supper, he sat with Gale at the dining room table, explaining the process of bill paying.

"First, we look at the date of the postmark; next, we look at the return of the sender's name and we pay all the bills monthly, in this order." He spoke softly.

"You are so good to me, to help me. I've never done anything like this and I was afraid I'd make a mistake." She said as she began to open the envelopes. Inside, the message was always the same; paid in full by John A. Barr II.

"Silly woman, you have let these statements lay on the mantel and worried yourself sick over nothing."

"Come here, sweet woman." He pulled her close. "You are so beautiful and I am so lucky." He whispered.

Lena loved it and would sit between them, lost in her own world. She had a poppy, just like Missy and the other young'uns. Now, she could hold her head high, even as her scorners chided her. Many times Mate Goolsby had taken her on his knee, saying;

"Ride a little horsey, down to town. Look out little girl, don't fall down."

"Do it again." She screamed with joy!

He taught her to 'Jubal Cat Riding' on his foot.

"Jubal this and Jubal that; Daddy killed a yellow cat."

"Why did you kill the cat, Daddy?" She asked.

"Well Lena, I really didn't kill him, he was playing possum." He said, laughing. Lena loved the way he put her on his shoulders and would walk her down 'The Row'. The other children stared at her big, strong daddy as he walked with ease past their houses. Many nights, he would hold her, read to her and rock her to sleep by telling her of the many shipbuilding details that she loved.

Every day was special when Poppy was at home. "If Mate Goolsby stopped quickly, surely; she would run up his backside." Gale had said once when they took a walk to the docks. Lena was always present and Gale and Mate almost never had a minute together alone and she could be a nuisance.

Tonight, Lena would ask Poppy to sing about "Old Black Joe"; her request was granted and his husky mellow voice was heavenly.

"Gone are the days, when my heart was young and gay.
Gone are my friends, from the cotton fields, away.
Gone from the earth, to a better land, I know.
I hear their gentle voices calling.
Old Black Joe................"

"Lena this is a song written by Stephen Foster about slavery and hardships."

"Sing some more, sing it again!" Lena urged.

She sat in his lap as he explained about the injustices of slavery; while she looked straight at him, taking every word. There were times when Gale would sing harmony with him; what glorious music filled the air!

Lena's heart filled with love; as he stood tall and regal in his Navy uniform. When Mama Gale looked at him, Lena could feel the magic of their love. It poured forth, filling her with wonderment; what a good feeling to know. She was not a bastard, anymore!

These were her last thoughts as she fell asleep and in her dreams, she heard Mama Gale and Poppy, singing harmony, on and on------.

PART 14

Savannah, Georgia

1900
"Up in the old oaks pleasant shade
Where mossy branches swing
With gentle twitter lings, soft and low
Nestling with fluttering wings."

"Memories"
Margaret Bailey

The punishing heat of midsummer sun was most unbearable today, as workers moved hurriedly to and fro. John Alexander Barr II, had needed to expand and modernize his General Mercantile Company as well as expand, Barr's Funeral Home. He had retired to 'White Oak Plantation', several years ago and had left the businesses in the capable hands of his son, John Alexander Barr III. Today, he had come to oversee the 'going's on'.

"A stitch in time saves nine." He repeated to himself. The funeral home was in excellent condition, however; the volume of business had picked up considerably; it had outgrown the space.

The old horse stable, carriage shed and gear room was beginning to rot away. There was no need for a place to keep neither horses, nor carriages and he had made a decision to put the glass hearse on display. A small rotunda would be built to house the ostentatious carriage with the family crests. This idea had been Evangeline Tyne Barr's; in honor of her English heritage.

The automobile had taken its place and he and Evangeline had ordered a new 1900 New Orleans vehicle from Great Britain; her birth place. The seventy five years plus couple acted like newly weds once more. The horseless carriage was Belgian in design with a rear engine and vertical steering column. Licensed in England, the carriage was sought after by race drivers, everywhere. It was imperative that the garage be finished before it arrived. Dozens of workers from 'White Oak Plantation' were busy removing its contents and tearing down the antiquated shed. Ben Samuels would supervise the demolition and construction of each building.

During the fourth day of the demolition project, Ben Samuels brought to John Barr, a special find! A worker had found a sealed cardboard box in the far left corner of the gear room. Protected from the elements, it was in excellent condition. At first, Mr. Barr stared blankly, the; remembered placing it there. Ezra Carnes, Constable, had returned it unopened to him, the same day he had given to him written ownership to the horse. This was the white horse with one black foot that had been found wandering on his property. Ben Samuels had named the horse, 'Buck'.

Taking his knife from his pocket, John Barr, cut the cord from the box with one swoop. Lifting the lid, he pulled out a beautiful, hand tooled leather saddle bag, onto his desk. It was the fanciest one he had ever seen in these parts of the country. The letters J.A.B. were highlighted into its rich chestnut leather. Turning it upside down; he poured the contents onto his desk, exposing hundreds of gold coins; then a Georgia Rebel's cap. Inside the band was stuffed with old, dark brown folded papers. John set them aside, as his eyes caught a glimpse of a tin-type picture of a man, woman and crippled boy. As John was about to replace the contents; a vague memory came of a small crippled boy sitting on his mother's knee, began to illuminate before his eyes! They had been waiting for his daddy, John Alexander Barr I, to come home. He had seen the picture before because it had been on his mother's dresser.

"Bu---bu---but, why would it be in this saddlebag?" "How did it get here?" He wondered.

His memory ran rampant, back to Limestone Ridge, many years ago, when Oprah and Gale were raped; both within six months of each other.

"These memories are too much to bear." He tried to stand and his legs failed him; he slumped to his chair.

"The rapist was my brother; my father's bastard son!"

The loving thought of his Mother, flashed through his mind. The years she had waited up for her husband to come home, had worn her down. John wept bitterly as memories flooded his mind. She had died of pneumonia when he was barely three. These thoughts continued to plague him; even in his advancing age. No matter how many commendations he had received for outstanding service to Georgia, he would always be gimpy Johnny. Tears and revulsion filled his being once again; as tears spilled onto his desk. John took the papers belonging to James Adam Barr and ripped them into shreds. They were the only proof of James Adam Barr's existence.

Surely, Constable Carnes had not seen them or else he would have brought it to his attention. Perhaps, if he knew he took it to his grave, five years ago! It was for sure nobody would ever hear it from him. John went home early; he was burdened with the revelation and answers to years and years of unanswered questions. His thoughts played back and forth; surely, Evangeline would know what to do. He had to tell someone.

"Basically, John deah, there is only one thing to do. You must reveal your secret to both Lena Goolsby and Missy Mock; it could be of grave concern to each of them!" She spoke sweetly.

The next morning John Barr went over to see the two of them. Missy and Lena were sitting on the back porch at Missy's house drinking fresh iced tea. Without asking, Lena chipped ice and filled a glass with tea, then added a sprig of mint for him. John's visit took longer than he had planned.

"It takes quite a while to explain how Oprah and Gale came to live at 'White Oak Plantation. Your Mother's were young and innocent and all these years I have felt guilty for not protecting them from harm. I swear on the Holy Bible, I never met James Adam Barr before I buried him!"

"Mama died young and my sister Molly and I were alone; Daddy was only a name our Mother taught us to respect. Now, I understand why he was gone so much; obviously, he had another family. I'm thankful that I turned out to be a God-fearing man and not like James Adam."

John took two envelopes from his inside coat pocket, pressed them into their hands, tipped his hat and left.

For weeks, Lena and Missy stayed together, trying to fit the pieces of the puzzle together. Their secrets would be safe until Nicie was older. They knew the reasons for the monetary gifts from John Barr, II; they vowed never to spend them.

The next time Lena and Missy would see John Barr, II, was no more than three months later. They stood side-by-side, hand-in-hand as his son, John A. Barr, III, their playmate, lowered him into the ground. What a sad day it had been and he wept bitterly; just as he had eight months ago when he had buried Eva, his Mother. He had honored them both; all of savannah and much of Georgia had paid their last respects. Their last wishes had been resolved as Evangeline's plaques, ribbons and letters were read by the orphans, who attended her funeral. She had been humanitarian of the year, for years at the Orphanage.

The early 1920's brought an end to both Icons. Now John A. Barr, III would take the helm and carry the torch for 'White Oak Plantation'. He had been given concrete instructions concerning 'White Oak's' future. Evangeline Barr had requested that a little girl, who had wept at church, crying for a Mother she had never met, become the heiress of 'White Oak Plantation'. She reminded her of herself, as she boarded the St. Francis in Liverpool, years ago for America.

John A. Barr, III and his wife Victoria never had children; there were no heirs. Nicie Goolsby must agree to build a new orphanage to accommodate at least five hundred homeless children; if she were to inherit. Eva's antique trunk from Grandmother Martha Tyne and her brother the Duke of Newberg, would be sealed in glass, and stationed in The Orphanage of Georgia, located in Savannah.

PART 15

Savannah, Georgia

December 1926

"If any worth or virtue is in me
Let that live freshly, in your memory."

"Prospect of Death"
Anne Bradstreet

P remature darkness settled over the church as a throng of vehicles, carriages, wagons and buckboards had arrived. The young and old, well and ne're-do-wells had come to pay their last respects to an icon of 'The Row'; Lena Mae Goolsby. The solemn crowd stood outside the church as a 1925 Sunbeam convertible, turned sharply, entering the courtyard. Lines of horses tethered to the hitching posts, became frightened as the large six passenger car appeared, blowing its horn.

John Barr, III and his wife, Victoria had arrived to oversee the burial of Lena Mae Goolsby.

Charles, Nicie and Nell sat in the front pew; behind them sat Vincent, Crelon and Tollie Crane. Missy Mock, walked into the already filled church. Her eyes scanned the rows of seats and finally took her place quietly beside Nicie. She would not be denied the honor of sitting with her family; after all, Lena was her half-sister! Gritting her teeth, to still any sudden outburst that could arise, involuntarily; she clutched Nicie's hand. Inside, there was a deep, smoldering anger, consuming her; she snorted disdain as Nicie stared ahead.

The vestibule was full of plants, wildflowers and gifts from Lena's closest friends. Many flowers wired onto wooden stands, stood at each end of the coffin. In the center before the pulpit stood a hand tooled casket; in it lay, Lena Mae May, Goolsby.

Charles looked down at Nicie, their eyes locked, there were no words. Their eyes spoke the contents of their hearts. Throughout the service, Nicie watched Miss Missy Ward Mock, who was even tempered by nature, fall apart. She wept uncontrollably and Nicie laid her head on Missy's breast, in an effort to give and receive comfort.

Missy, felt alone since Lena had died. It was as though nature was provoking her resentment; steadily gouging at her last few days on earth! Lena had been six months older than she.

"The Grim Reaper is right around the corner. Lawd, I nevah meant it when I said, I'd be better off dead. I don't want to die and leave Nicie. I promised Lena, I would see to her. Let me live, Lawd." She prayed throughout the funeral. She had spoken these same wishes to John A. Barr, III, before the funeral.

"John-John is a year older than me." She told Nicie, in a whisper. "He was mine and Lena's playmate."

The music started and Missy swore this was the last funeral she would ever attend; except, of course, her own. As the funeral ended, Missy left the church ahead of the others for she had taken it until she could take no more. There were no more words to say, songs to sing, nor tears to cry; all she felt was anger!

Nicie had a hard time catching up with Miss Missy. Finally, she caught her and taking her hand, they walked toward the burial ground. The red clay bank of freshly dug earth stood on one side and a deep black hole was opened in the ground beside it. As Lena's coffin was lowered, a continuous shutter convulsed Nicie's body. She was embarrassed, as a small stream of water flowed down her legs, filling her new boots and puddled onto the ground. Missy Mock did not let go of her hand; instead, she spat a blob of snuff right on top of the puddle.

"Now", she snorted. "I was not ready to let her go; it was none of my doing." She said, spewing, sputtering her snuff with revenge. They left by way of a small grove of trees. Nicie, held to the soft black skin of the woman, Granma Goolsby had said was like a sister. Missy understood Nicie's accident and said nothing.

Charles Goolsby was so lost, in the eyes of Nell; he hardly noticed Miss Missy and Nicie walk up to the car and get into the back seat, sitting without speaking a word. There was no doubt in his mind that the two were kindred-in-spirit. One would have to be blind to overlook the shock on Nicie's face and the anger in Miss Missy Mock's.

Nell drove Missy home and opened the door for her and helped her onto smooth ground. Missy spoke seriously. "I will go over to Lena's on Friday; we have packing to do. I will need Nicie's help when she gets home from school. We'll make a weekend of it, I 'speck."

Without another word; she walked up her front steps, unlocked the door, replacing the keys in her bosom and pinned them safely onto her slip. Lena's keys were among them.

At last, Friday evening came and school was out for the weekend. Nicie rushed over to Granma Goolsby's house; Missy Mock was out in back, feeding the Dominique's and Rhode Island Reds, their nests were full of eggs. Nicie held her apron for Miss Missy to fill.

"Don't stumble and drop them!"

"Yes, Mama, I mean, no Mama." Nicie answered.

"We've got a lot to do, packing and cleaning." Missy reminded.

"You will be good help, Chile."

They would wash the clothes Lena had worn when she was taken sick. Missy starched them with flour mixed in a pot of boiling water from the wood stove. Next, she put two smoothing irons on top of the hot stove eye, heated them up and ironed Lena's dress to perfection; rubbing the iron with soap to make smooth ironing.

Nicie had watched each tender step; it was as if, Miss Missy was patting and consoling her old friend.

"Precious, precious." She said.

"The dress looked angelic, as it hung from a nail on the parlor wall." Nicie thought. Sadness crept back into her emotions, as Missy looked intently at the dress. Lena's voice of yester year seemed to cry out.

"Look at me, ain't I pretty!" Missy had heard this many times in the years they'd played together. They had grown up knowing they were special.

Later in the afternoon, Missy fried eggs and made hoecake bread for supper. Afterward, the dishes were washed and the warm water in the white enameled pan was comforting to Nicie's hands and spirit. Miss Missy busily hung the dishrags on the front of the stove to dry.

"Just as Granma Goolsby had done," Nicie thought.

"Chile, you're a big girl; taller than I was when I started to school and in more ways than one; much wiser. I don't want you to be upset over anything. Yo, Granma done all she could for you and evabody else. Her life was busy and she never got married; just like me, I never got married either. She loved one man; Mate Goolsby! He was already married to somebody else; her mother, Gale." She laughed with joy.

"Lena had promised at their wedding that she would love him forever, just as her Mother had. Pure and simple, Chile, Poppy was the only man Lena ever talked about."

"We wuz four or five years old when he came into our life. You know Chile, she was a little jealous, 'cause I had a daddy before she did. Yo Granma and I were always together. We have the same father, but; we never found who he was. The sad part was, we learned it from the gossip in 'The Row'. Out Mothers never discussed our beginnings; it was unheard of in our day."

"There were times when one of us would talk and the other would finish the sentence. We were sisters in the blood and sisters in the heart. She was six months older than me." She went on. "We were born at 'White

Oak Plantation'. Nicie gazed at Miss Missy in awe, "They really did have the same look, and their mannerisms were so much alike." She thought.

Missy went on with her story.

"Oprah, my Mother and Miss Gale, Lena's Mother, started to work as chamber maids when they were twelve years old. They operated the large fans to cool Mrs. Evangeline Barr, mistress of 'White Oak Plantation'. They were trained to listen to her commands, obey and never give an opinion, was to their advantage; it had not been a hard task for either of them. Listening to Mrs. Eva's complaints, whining and unnecessary demands was."

"Many times they were chastised with swats to the fanny, when they were slow to comprehend a command; they were expected to read her mind. At times they would go down and hide in the root cellar while Mrs. Eva slept. The root cellar was a cool place in the summer and a get-away, as well." Missy continued as Nicie sat quietly.

"They would giggle as Mama would mimic Mrs. Eva. 'Loahd, won't this coold weatha nevah cease?' 'Loahd, won't this hot weatha nevah cease?' Miss Gale would chime in. 'Oh, Loahd; Oh, Loahd', they both said in unison."

"At times, they were heard by Pansy, "Bettah git outtah heah." She would say. Pansy was Oprah's Mama and was the cook at the big house. They always did as she asked. She was not Mama's birth Mother but, had raised her, Missy explained."

"Lena and I were like our birth Mothers, strong, stubborn and sassy."

Nicie loved the story, her eyes were big, wide and staring, without blinking, as Missy finished.

"Tell me more, tell me more," she begged.

"No! No more stories tonight. We've got to get to bed, it is past eleven o'clock. Go wash up now," Missy demanded.

Nicie was wide awake, for she had heard the most interesting things about her family heritage, but, she had not yet heard the truth that her young heart longed to hear.

"I'm just getting started good, Chile. We'll talk again, tomorrow." Missy told her. She had not held back anything, thus far.

"Perhaps she would finish the story tomorrow," Nicie thought. There must be lots more to tell. "Oh, goody! Maybe, she knows who my Mother is." Delighted, she fell asleep.

The cool September morning was filled with a blast of North wind in 'The Row'. The tin topped slum houses clanged, as the loose tin blew up and down on their roofs. Missy built a fire in the stove and one in the fireplace.

"Dese ole bones get cold in the late fall; 'bout the time Thanksgiving is right 'round the corner." Burrr! She pulled up her gown in the back to warm her fanny.

"You know, Chile, I feel good around Lena's things; I feel close to her in this house." Missy went on. "You still got sleep in your eyes this morning and I'll bet you didn't sleep at all, last night." Missy quipped as she dressed for the day.

"Breakfast is ready; come over here and eat whilst I talk to you." She urged; slamming the stove door shut.

Nicie did as she was told as she was anxious to hear another of Miss Missy's stories about her family. She was beginning to connect to Granma Goolsby.

"Miss Gale, Lena's mother died from a stroke." The story went on. "She was a young woman, in her early years of life. I thought Mama Oprah would never get over her death. Mate Goolsby, her husband, struggling with his loss, finally went back to sea. "I can't stay, where I am constantly reminded of her sweetness, our house has become a morgue." He had told Lena. "So, Lena came to live with us and Mate returned to his ship and returned to San Diego, California. Lena and Mate wrote to each other every week, which took months to get the mail back and forth. The mail would pile up and, four and five letters would be delivered at once. Lena would go off by herself to read them."

"One day, a disaster happened; a malfunction in the old coal burning repair ship, caused an explosion, which started in the core of the ship. The flames exuded a poisonous gas, causing asphyxiation to some fifty or sixty sailors. Mate Goolsby was hit in the leg with fragments of steel. A large portion of his leg had been blown away; exposing the bone. He contracted gangrene poisoning and two months later, he was shipped home, to Savannah."

"A Purple Heart had been awarded along with the Bronze Medal and an Honorable, Medical Discharge. Lena had been called to a makeshift, tent hospital where tarpaulin gurneys lined the walls; it was a terrible day!"

"Lena began to gag as she smelled the putrid, rotting flesh of the wounded and dying. We had spent most of the evening, searching for

Mate Goolsby and finally found him. He had covered his head to keep from being recognized, embarrassed by his condition. Lena, being kind hearted, opened their house and brought him home. She cleaned and dressed the stump of his leg for years; but it never healed. She cared for him until he died."

"Mate had used crutches, made by Ben Samuels of 'White Oak Plantation'. He was never the same for the remainder of his life. All he talked about was Gale and, if his handicap was not bad enough, his nightmares were worse."

Vivid, repetitive blasts of fire played in his mind constantly. He remembered dragging his shattered leg through a ring of fire as he heard the screams of his buddies being blown apart. One of the dissected bodies lay motionless in the passageway and his mind had gone blank. Instinctively, he dragged himself to the upper deck of the ship where he was then rescued.

"Weeks passed and Mate began to regain his memory. Suddenly, he thought of his wife and child; he would never see them again." Missy said.

For months after he had gone home, he continued to have confusion and paralysis, but nothing deterred Lena; she would make him better! Poppie was her whole world, and she had cut herself off from civilization to care for him. She had never been able to convince him that Mama Gale had died.

"Moments before his death, he whispered; 'Baby, look into my sea bag; there is my retirement and an insurance policy, made out to you.' He gasped, "Lena Mae, Gale----! He called out."

"Lena never knew what he wanted to say. She vowed that day, that she would never marry, because Poppie was the only man she would ever love. To her, to even look at another would be to betray him." Missy continued.

"The retirement pension wasn't much; but, as frugal and saving as Lena had proven to be, she would have a good living. Lena was now twenty and had had several opportunities to acquire a job and to marry. She had made the decision to stay at home, for home was filled with loving memories. She would miss his stories of building ships for the US Navy and his many years of service; she had lived in every country and seaport with him."

"A few years later, Lean Goolsby had a visitor; a social worker who rode the train from Indiana to Savannah. She brought with her, two small, starving boys to live with Lena. The two year olds had been barely surviving when they arrived. The social worker had found Lena's address on a letter Lena had written to Mate Goolsby while he was in Guam. The letter had gone to his old address in Indiana after Mate had been shipped to Georgia."

"The desires of Lena's heart had finally been realized, for after weeks of investigation, Lena Goolsby became a mother."

"The twins, Clarke and Charles, had been recovered by the state, due to abandonment." She went on. "Their father, Theo Goolsby, had a bout with the bottle and their mother could not be located."

"As time went by, the twins became Lena's life; she was devoted completely to them. When they became seventeen years old, they enlisted in the Army." Missy stated.

"Nice Chile, Lena has some souvenirs in her trunk and they will be yours one day. We will look at them tomorrow." Missy concluded.

"My Mama, Oprah, died twenty-one or twenty-two years after Gale. The same death that had taken my Mother drove Lena closer to me. I had never really understood how Lena felt after the loss of her Mother, until I lost mine; I was so much older, too." Missy began to sob. "Lena was always here for me." Her sobs grew louder. "I never got married because she would have felt abandoned." She said, as the tears poured. "We shared a closer relationship than Oprah and Gale; folks talked for years about the way we stuck together through thick and thin. Other people looked down their noses at us because; we were the two 'plantation chillun with no pappy'."

"Nicie Chile, I won't use the bad word they called us, 'cause; Chile, you'll hear it soon enough," she said patting her hand.

"If we had both married; our husbands wouldn't have let us be together as much as we needed," she declared. "We always felt that we owed it to our mothers to keep their homes. They had made them during our childhoods, just for us, because neither of them had other children and devoted themselves to us alone."

"The years have taken their toll on the old cabins. They are worn, but sound still and they don't leak. I'd say, without bragging, that we have the best two houses in The Row." She laughed.

"You know Nicie; everything has a natural order; even death." Missy declared.

"Lena and I both knew that one day we would die; Gale went first, then Mama Oprah. Now, Lena is gone and I may have only six months to live." She spoke softly.

She laid her head on the back of Granma Goolsby's chair, choking back the tears as she rocked.

"You cain't die". Nicie cried. "I need you; you are so much like Granma, what would I do without you?" She blubbered.

The six year old crawled into Missy Mocks arms, her legs hung off her lap, touching the floor; each held the other with the tenacity of a junk yard dog.

"Missy cried forever!" Nicie thought. Would she ever get over it? She would laugh a little and cry out at times. Nicie's own tears had finally stopped; for she had expended every drop of moisture from her tear ducts and was quiet now. Disappointed, she began to feel outcast that she could not share in the party of tears. She was excited even though she could not process all that she had heard, because she was learning about her family!

Finally, both were exhausted and went to bed early. Tomorrow would be Sunday, Nicie wanted to slip away across the railroad tracks; there she would watch the people as they entered the church. She yearned to hear the bells ring in the tower, just as they rang in her head. "Oh yes, I want to hear about 'Amazing Grace', once more." She declared!

The coarse feed sack gown fell to the floor as she knelt beside the corn shuck mattress and prayed.

"Angels, you know I want to go to church tomorrow more than ever before. I need to be close to the beautiful words you sing to me. Amazing Grace is always there; the people sing to her every Sunday. I want to meet her, could I do it tomorrow?" Nicie begged.

"I hope somebody told you that my Granma Goolsby died. Certainly you would want to know; she was my very bestest Granma."

"I don't have anyone to call my own anymore, because my Mama and Daddy have never come to get me. What's wrong with me? What did I do to make them go away? Am I the only little girl in the world without a Mama and Daddy?"

"Sometimes I dream of them. We are having fun together; laughing and talking -----. Tollie and Millie have mamas and daddies." She cried harder.

Loudly, she prayed; "sweet Angels, it's just not fair! Please, Please, I want to belong to a family!" The once dry tear ducts had been replenished and tears poured onto her folded hands, draining toward her elbows. The hollow loneliness having been relieved, brought peace; Nicie slept. Missy Mock had not heard this as she was snoring from the bed that Lena

Goolsby had occupied for years. Nicie stirred in her bed, roused from a deep slumber by a horrendous, subconscious feeling; something awesome was about to happen! Afraid to open her eyes, she pulled the sheet over her head and slowly the feeling dissipated. She peeked out; darkness enveloped the room, the lumps on Granma Goolsby's bed, reminded her that Miss Missy Mock was still asleep.

Pitter patter, pitter patter; the rain tapped rapidly on the roof, leaves fell, floating across the view of the window lit up by lightening from the heavens. Nicie's heart kept the rhythm of the sounds as thunder boomed, making a deafening sound. Lightening flashed, etching the snoring lump of Missy, against the wall of the darkened room.

Nicie arose from her bed and walked over to the window. Standing directly in front of its panes, she watched the clouds pass and they appeared to have built in flashing lights as they moved rapidly with lightening. Then Nicie saw it! The clouds had clumped together; forming her Angels, holding hands, they had come to bring her comfort.

"Nice Chile, Nice Chile," they sang.

They floated past her window and dissolved into nothingness. Turning, they had smiled as their soft billows touched her window. Crawling into bed, she slept; a smile enveloped her soft, pink lips.

When the storm was over, extra problems arose as limbs from last nights winds had fallen from the gnarled old oak tree in the front yard. It had been planted years ago by Bartus Reem, of 'White Oak Plantation', for Carrie Grant and another one the same size on Oprah and Adam Mock's property, for Missy. A long rope, with an old buggy wheel was tied firmly in the tree tops. The swings had brought many happy hours to the children in The Row for years.

Missy had cooked a breakfast of a few smothered potatoes and water biscuits, which lay on the corner of the stove for Nicie when she arose. She was in a hurry to clean Lena's yard; knowing her yard would present the same, she hurried.

Missy was picking up the limbs and branches from the big oak, when Nicie appeared. They carried loads of limbs into the house, laying them in the wood box behind the stove. Afterwards, Missy poured herself a large cup of coffee as she busily cooked lard and flour gravy for Nicie. She ate heartily; brown gravy was one of her favorite meals and would have chosen to have grits too, but; never opened her mouth to complain. Pouring her second cup of coffee, Missy motioned Nicie toward the rocking chair. Sitting at Missy's feet, Nicie looked intently into her face, waiting.

The story continued -------.

"You know, Chile, your Granma heard from Charles and Clarke, almost every two weeks. They were good boys about writing; I'll say that for them."

"Never did I see a woman so happy, they shore brought her many happy days; Yes, mam." She ran on.

She took her snuff box from her apron pocket; pinched and pulled down her bottom lip and deposited the brown, dusty tobacco. Nicie backed up a few feet for she had been a witness to its brown fog floating into the air and there had been times she would cough until it rendered her breathless.

Missy Mock went on with her story;

"One day, somewhere around 1918, the boys came home on leave from the army. Mr. Vincent Crane was the same age as Charles and Clarke and they attended school together. I guess you would call them playmates." Missy got off track, but if Nicie noticed, she did not respond.

"Vincent Crane's sister had arrived by train and had brought two friends from New York with her. Crelon Ragan was a ballet dancer and her roommate, Senia Jones worked as a clothing designer."

"Chile, look on top of Lena's trunk and bring me that box of quilting pieces. I'm going to try to finish this, '*Step around the mountain*' quilt. Lena just didn't have time." She said, spitting her snuff into the fireplace. "We just finished a '*Wedding Ring*' quilt two weeks ago." She went on proudly.

"Where was I, Chile? Oh, yeah," she started again.

"Vincent needed an escort for Senia, since Clarke would take out Vincent's sister Grace. So later that afternoon, he drove the young women into the heart of Savannah in his 1907, Silver Ghost."

"Chile, that car was a sight to behold; he had inherited it from Fredrick Sims, his grandfather, who lived in Great Britain. It's the same car you and Tollie ride in now Chile, and when it was new; it was something else!" She said, smacking her lips.

"When they got to Broad Street, they stopped at a bakery for a sandwich, where they met the Goolsby twins, Charles and Clarke."

Clarke Goolsby excused himself, as he had to see his Army recruiter at the local board. Charles Goolsby was introduced to Senia Jones and they made arrangements to get together the following night. Afterward, the goodbyes and goodnights were exchanged; they waved to each other as the Silver Ghost sped towards Oglethorpe Avenue.

Charles walked down Broad to Victory Drive to the Army representative's office, which was full. He stood, looking out the window, as he waited for Clarke to finish his business and the twins walked toward Mama Lena's.

"We have picture show company for tomorrow night. You will escort Grace Crane and I will see Senia Jones and Vince will be with Crelon Ragan. These girls are friends of Grace's from New York." Charles said.

"Man, they are some lookers!" He said, taking a pack of Chesterfield's from his pocket. "Have one." He offered, extending the pack to Clarke. The sweet aroma encircled them as they stood on the street corner. The air was filled with smoke rings as they began their walk slowly towards home, in the cool Savannah night.

By six O'clock the next afternoon, Mama Lena has pressed both boys' uniforms with her smoothing irons while using a wet cloth. The young men dressed meticulously and no mother could ask for more handsome sons, standing tall and regal in their uniform. The boys were so identical that many times, even Lena got Clarke and Charles mixed up. In order to distinguish the two, she looked for a small brown mole behind Clarke's right ear. Lena was embarrassed by this, but if the twins ever noticed, they never let on. They were capable of making their own decisions and she was willing to let her sons have their own lives; it was good to see them having fun. At times, fear would clutch her heart at the thought of them getting injured or killed.

"It was World War I and this Great War had brought about many injuries and deaths."

Lena's fear was driven by the loss of her precious Poppy. "He paid the ultimate cost for our freedom!"

"Knowing her sons conscribed was a relief. They had always wanted to serve in the Armed Forces, for there was a mystique and honor that all servicemen exuded. When they chose the Army as their career, the Army allowed them to stay together; Lena took comfort in that." Missy said.

Vincent Crane's Rolls Royce purred as it moved down the dirt road and the fresh wash he had given it, would be null and void in a few minutes, she laughed. "But, who would care anyhow; certainly, not the six passengers, who were laughing and chirping away. Sounds of happiness filled the air as the long car pulled up to the curb. The movie theatre was crowded and the six of them were barely able to find seats together."

Douglas Fairbanks strode across the screen with sword in hand and the printed words flashed on the screen. Suave, debonair and gallant were words used by the ladies as Fairbanks fought the villain. They 'oohed and ahhhed' in most every scene and the guys were entertained by the ladies.

Charles had sat beside Senia, barely talking; Clarke reached over and kissed Grace on the cheek. She pretended to wipe it away, so he grabbed her, kissing her full on the mouth; the kiss lingering.

"Now, wipe that one away, will you." He dared her!

The others laughed, but not Grace Crane, her heart was beating ninety to nothing. She was flushed; not knowing what to say and it was awhile before she regained her composure. Vince and Crelon Ragan held hands and kissed lightly as he put the car into gear and they headed home.

Nicie was excited; she couldn't wait to hear the rest of the story and had listened intently as Miss Missy talked about the twins. As Miss Missy left the room to go to the outhouse, Nicie looked into the mirror. Pulling her ear forward, she discovered a small brown mole behind her right ear. Her heart beat rapidly as her thoughts ran past her heartbeats. "Clarke had a mole. I have a mole." She would not talk about it for fear of embarrassment.

Later, as Miss Missy entered the porch, Nicie was sitting on the doorstep, throwing cold bread to Buster, the Rhode Island Red rooster. The Dominique's fought for the last piece of bread from her hand.

Game chickens wandered around the edge of the buggy trail and on into the cotton patch; Nicie walked around the head of the woods. Granma Lena had taught her about the personalities of the different breeds and had showed her the stolen nests of Game chickens. "Don't touch the nests." She'd told her. "They will set and hatch off in about a month; chickens are like birds, they don't want anybody to touch their eggs." She went on.

Nicie did not find a hen's nest, but a rabbit burrow instead. Two very small bunnies crawled back into their soft downy hole as she approached.

"Don't worry, little bunnies, I won't hurt you." She said.

"Nice Chile." A voice called. Nicie ran speedily and found Miss Missy seated in the rocker; she was rocking back and forth, just as her story had.

"Twin boys, handsome too!" She spoke dreamily.

"Well Chile, the couples went out every night, leastwise; they were together."

Vince and Crelon were getting serious, as was Clarke and Grace, but Charles had met a girl at Fort Monmouth, New Jersey the year before. Her name was Mazie Ellis and she had stolen his heart; he could hardly wait to get back to her. Nicie shrugged at the mention of Mazie's name.

The last night the group was together, they sat on the veranda of Vincent Crane, Sr.'s house and collectively sang songs written by Cole Porter ate ice cream and drank coffee. When the time came to say their goodbyes, they had a glass of wine and a toast was made by Vince Crane.

"*To the United States Army.*" He proclaimed. "*Hail, Hail,*" the others responded. Charles and Clarke were heroes.

As the night ended, there were promises to write, sad goodbyes and sweet kisses, for two of the couples, while the other pleasantly shook hands. There were no regrets even though tears prevailed in the eyes of all, some were tears of joy, others; sadness. Tomorrow, Clarke and Charles' leave time was up and Uncle Sam had given the order.

The weeks crawled by, extending into months and every day, Grace Crane wrote to Clarke. Each letter included the same three words that no human being ever gets tired of hearing; 'I love you'.

They made plans to see each other when Clarke got a weekend pass and Fort Monmouth, New Jersey was within a few hours travel to New York City by railroad.

A surprise had been planned!

Crelon Ragan and Vincent had made plans to get married. "Hey, lets make it a twosome," he told Grace, and it was arranged. Vincent Crane had the longest distance to travel; Clarke Goolsby asked for and received approval for a two week furlough. Charles Goolsby asked for the same two weeks, to attend his brother's wedding. Crelon and Grace would plan their weddings for August 1, 1918.

"Nice Chile, not only was Charles the best man for Clarke, he was the best man for Charles too, because Charles married Mazie Ellis; there were three weddings at one time. Have you ever?" She questioned, laughing. She laid her head back and rubbed her belly; it was so contagious, Nicie laughed too and their laughter rang throughout the house. It was stilled as Miss Missy continued her story.

Nicie held her breath, Mazie Ellis, huh? She was aghast!

After each couple had two weeks together they went in different directions. Nicie did not completely understand, but said nothing. Missy paused, took a deep breath and continued to speak in low tones. Nicie was leaning into her, watching her nonverbal communications, as she went on.

"Charles and Clarke were shipped to France where the battles raged through the countryside for weeks. They were stationed on the border of Belgium, at Nord and in the spring of 1918, the tide of the battle turned. The Germans were driven back in defeat but, the area was a desolate, ghastly ruin. The town of Nord, France, on the river Lys, was destroyed, for it had been a base zone of the fighting all through the conflict, since 1914."

"For days, Charles and Clarke slept in foxholes, with guns and cannons firing overhead. They had been in France a little over two months without receiving mail from home. They both carried pictures of their wives in their pockets, close to their hearts. Mobilized units, stormed through the country on clean-out campaigns. French soldiers scattered about the fox holes, seeking to bring the American soldiers to safety."

"German Gotha planes flew overhead, bombing from the air and day after day, the boys dug themselves out, as the shells and mortar flew through the air. The dirt and sand seemed to bury them alive and they were hungry, tired and lonely; their canteens were empty."

"In a few days, a German bomber was seen descending from the sky and just moments later it had discharged its' load of ammunition. A blast of fire filled their foxhole; smoke and fog finally settled and cleared as Charles dug Clarke from his caved-in dirt coffin."

Missy could not go on; she began to moan and whimper words that Nicie could not understand.

"I need a little rest." Missy spoke softly as she moved from the chair to Granma Goolsby's goose-down bed where she lay spread-eagled, face down and moaning.

Nicie knew just how to help her as she ran to the stack of quilts on top of the trunk. Taking the one from the top, she stood in front of the fireplace, warmed it thoroughly from side to side and returned to the bedroom. She spread the quilt over Miss Missy Mock, tucking in the sides close to her body, patting her softly.

"Now," she said smugly. Missy slept.

Nicie balanced in the old White Oak tree in the front yard. Her heart was heavy; the grief she had witnessed was beyond comprehension.

"It was as if Missy had come apart at the seams." She thought.

"My goodness, I never knew Uncle Coot had a twin," she was baffled. "He had been in the Army, too."

She was puzzled; all she remembered was the day Granma took her by the hand, carried her clothes in a flour sack and walked her the distance to Uncle Coot's house. There had been no bed for her, so Uncle Coot had placed a pallet on the floor of the bedroom, where she slept the first night. Vaguely, she remembered Auntie Mazie shoving a thin quilt on the floor behind the stove; she had been barely three years old.

Later, Granma had brought a thick patchwork quilt to replace it. Granma had never explained her strange new living arrangements to her. It was as if children had no say in their lives.

"The grownups live in a separate world than children." She thought.

Once, she had watched as kitty-mama birthed her kittens in the hens nest. Granma had become irate and embarrassed and turned red-faced. "Chile, you ain't got no business watching such things. Go over to the corner and sit by yourself for awhile." She said shaking her finger in her face. "That kind of talk is not allowed in this house." She'd added. So, in the corner Nicie sat and watched as Grandma's hands in the cat's bed and watched as she picked up each kitten, one by one and, stroked them slowly.

Nicie never told her anything after that; two sets of rules had been written that day and they had been indelibly imprinted in her young mind. She could remember playing with Senia Monk on the swing, when Grandma called her into the house.

"You are not to play with those nasty Monk young'uns. I saw her brother peeing behind a tree at the corner of my yard." She'd said vehemently.

Then there were days when Granma would walk out of the house, sit on the back steps and light up her corn cob pipe. She would puff the pipe as if it were the single, most important thing on earth; her eyes would close in ecstasy, a dreamland that nobody else could enter. Until now, Nicie had never realized nor understood that these were the times Granma reflected on the past. Some of these were the stories that she had heard from Missy Mock, these last few days.

Uncle Coot had been kind and gentle to her and she had always known Aunt Mazie did not want her in her sight; at times her Aunt would 'throw a fit', without provocation. Nicie had learned to stay out of her way, for many were the times that Aunt Mazie would say hateful things to and about her and Uncle Coot's reason for not defending her, were unclear.

She had learned to say, "*Sticks and stones may break my bones but, words can never hurt me!*" Nicie repeated this over and over again as Mazie's harsh words were thrown at her carelessly.

Aunt Mazie would never know the hundreds of times she had struck out at the picket fence. That she was the object of her greatest anger and that she prayed for her to leave.

"Oh no! My anger was followed by relief." She thought, as the swing glided back and forth.

"Angels are a myth, you foolish girl!" Aunt Mazie once told her. "You jabber, jabber, jabber," she had said.

"She hated Granma and me. I believe she hated herself, most of all."

Suddenly, the buggy wheel swing stopped in midair and Nicie bailed out, landing on both feet. With her hands on her hips, she spoke decisively. "God won. My Angels heard my prayers and sent Auntie Mazie packing! She left in such a hurry her nail polish was left behind!" Nicie laughed. Justice had been done!

Uncle Coot is happy now that he has Mrs. Nell. We are a family who talks, laughs and cries together. She remembered the funeral and the rides she had enjoyed in Nell's car. Mostly, she remembers the way she had held her, a stranger, and kissed away her tears at the time of Granma's death.

"Uncle Coot would never have made it through all the funeral arrangements and sorrow, without Nell Bradley." She thought.

Missy Mock stirred from her bed. Sitting up she rubbed her eyes, replaced her spectacles and took a dip of snuff, moving slowly.

"Nice Chile, where are you?" She questioned.

Nicie stepped onto the porch followed by her dog Wimpy, who was hungry. The food supply was limited at Lena's, so she, Nicie and Wimpy would have to eat boiled eggs and buttered bread for dinner. It was already three o'clock and, if she didn't send the child home right away, Charles would be worried about her. Also, she would still have five and one half months to take care of Lena's business.

"I simply cannot be hurried!" She thought, locking the door behind her.

Nicie and Wimpy were playing 'Go and fetch' with a stick, as they walked. Missy watched until they were out of sight; then turned toward her home.

Uncle Coot was busy when Nicie got home, helping Nell clean the house. As she entered through the back door, she knew she had walked in at the perfect time. Uncle Coot and Mrs. Nell had been fishing and the beautiful browned catfish were large. They were so big they hung off the platter and, there were hush puppies too.

"We muddied the creek!" He laughed as he threw Wimpy a hushpuppy; Wimpy whined for more.

"Nicie, you would have loved it! We will take you next time." He declared. Nell laughed and giggled, rambling on and on about slipping down the creek bank as a water moccasin swam by.

Nicie faked a smile for convenience; hoping they didn't see that she was not the same little girl who had left for school on Friday morning. No; her entire life had changed over the last two days. The two wonderful people sitting at the table in front of her, paled in comparison to the pictures painted in her brain by Missy Mock. How could they know, that she had just lived through the Civil War, experienced Mate Goolsby's dilemma and World War I with Uncle Coot and Clark Goolsby? Knowing she could not make them understand; she ate a small portion of fish and went to her 'shed room', bedroom. She needed to be alone to absorb the stories of her family.

"Their blood is flowing through my bones." She spoke in awe. Miss Missy had told her the story, but how, she wondered, could she fit into this family?

Nicie could not wait to tell Millie and Tollie; there was so much to talk about. She would also tell Taryn when she came home again from Atlanta Academy. Tonight, she would plan to go to the docks and take the skiff to Fig Island, if she saw the camp fires. Regardless, she would see Tollie and Millie tomorrow.

In the morning, Tollie Crane's father dropped them off in front of the school, waving goodbye as he sped away. Nicie's eyes gazed as he drove away and she felt as thought she knew one of his innermost secrets. As she looked at Tollie, she thought, "How small she looks as compared to me." But, Tollie had never lived during slavery, the Civil War and World War I as she had! Nicie took a long breath, turned her back to her best friend and walked smugly into the classroom, alone.

The weekend came quickly and she was glad; she had not been able to concentrate on her school work. The teachers had reprimanded her on two separate occasions this week. Tollie followed Nicie around, "What's wrong" She asked. Nicie responded, "Nothing." She was not ready to share her innermost secrets with anyone; just yet.

Friday afternoon, Uncle Coot and Nell Bradley were going to the movies. "Come go with us." Nell invited Nicie.

"No, I have to meet Miss Missy; we have to finish packing."

Charles and Nell discussed the way she had avoided them and both chalked it up to the fact that she had always been quiet and somewhat withdrawn.

"She lives in her own world sometimes." Charles told her. They dropped the subject; laughing together as they pulled out of the yard, both waving goodbye.

The movie was not as they had expected, but that was not the reason they didn't stay. They had become so interested in each other, more so than neighbors lending a helping hand to each other or a friend. Shuffling down the theatre aisle toward the exit, Charles put his arm around her. Nell felt involuntary vibrations of excitement and emotions and her palms were sweating, although the night was chilly. Reluctantly, she withdrew her hand, rubbing both together, absorbing the moisture and replaced it quickly in his. Dusk deepened into night as Charles and Nell stood outside the theatre. The colorful marquee lights, blinking on and off, cast a shadow of her upturned face. Charles could see the outline of her lips and curve of her body; waiting ----. He looked at the sweet, half opened mouth, beckoning to him. He kissed her once, then twice; "I love the way you look." He spoke softly and simply. "Thank you." She replied. Cars flashed their lights at the couple as they drove by. He was upon her in a single stride; she was waiting.

"We are in a public place." Charles said, embarrassed.

"No apology needed, let's go to my house." She responded, hoarsely.

Neither of them had noticed the black clouds descending and blowing into the night; they were lost in each other! A blazing glow of reality conflicted with the nightly fantasies that had occupied Charles' mind, since the first time he had met Nell.

The death of his mother had taken priority over his emotions. At last, he was where he wanted to be and his thoughts ran freely. The headlights of the car beamed brightly onto the home of Nell Bradley; they had arrived! Holding the door for her as she unlocked it, gave Charles a sudden thrill. Nell led him into her parlor and sat on the divan as Charles built a fire. The warm glow of the fireplace created an illusion as the fire burned higher. Silhouettes of their bodies were reflected on the wall ten feet away. Cuddling and speaking softly, the couple's nonverbal communication was obvious as well. Cold rain poured, pounding the roof and rattling the windows from the force of the water and thunder. It was unclear whether the noises were the result of the weather or from the two bodies melting together.

The sun streaming through the curtains awakened the couple and Nell and Charles talked for hours, making decisions for their marriage in the very near future. First though, they would talk to Nicie for they would need her blessing.

Today they would eat lunch together at the Telephone Company and discuss important plans. Nicie would have her own room; a canopied bed with a ruffled bedspread and curtains to match, a dresser with a round mirror, French provincial chair, chest and wardrobe would be hers, to complete her needs. This had been Nell's room as she grew up and had loved its feminine adornments and had preserved them for just the right little girl. Now, she had found her and Nicie would be so happy! Certainly she had been, since she had met Charles and Nicie.

"I will be the best mother ever," Nell swore, crossing her heart.

At ten o'clock A.M., Charles and Nell left for Broad Street as a light rain was falling onto the car. The couple was divinely happy with their new found relationship; their promises had been made and sealed. Nell snuggled closer to Charles as he drove.

The next morning Missy went home to feed her chickens and Nicie walked to Uncle Coots. The house was empty and it was apparent that Uncle Coot had not been there. She trudged across the road from the picket fence, calm and cool as she awaited Miss Missy's return to Granma Goolsby's. She sat on the front steps, stroking Wimpy as he slept beside her, snoring lightly. At last, Missy arrived with a brown paper bag filled with teacakes; the cinnamon and nutmeg commanded her taste buds.

"Thank you." Nicie said, smacking her lips loudly.

"Sit over here, Chile. Eat our teacakes while I talk to you. First, I want you to know I am keeping my promise to Lena; she spoke softly. She wanted you to know who you are! There ain't no way to take short cuts in life's stories and at times, they can be long. I'm doing my best to make her proud. She knowed she was a'dyin and she was afraid she'd go afore you growed up enuf to understan' how life works; one way and then another. Lena had planned to tell you about your heritage, but, she passed too soon."

Missy choked up, pushed her rocker back and forth, and then went on with her saga.

"You know Chile, how people talk and, Lena knew you would find the truth, sooner or later." She coughed, and then regained her composure.

"There are only two of us alive who know the truth, John Alexander Barr, III and me. We made a pact a few years ago that; you and Charles would be told everything. Now the time has come and what I am about to tell you, may seem hard at first, but Lena and I had faith that Charles would go along with her wishes."

Missy rocked and the hickory rocker moved lightly over the creaking floor; her head rested against the rungs. Her story began where she had ended it yesterday.

"Charles, his commanding officer and Chaplain brought Clarke's body home from France. Lord, I thought we would have to bury Lena; and Clarke's wife as well, she interjected. Nobody in 'The Row' had ever before experienced so much suffering!" She spoke emphatically.

"Most of Savannah and even people from all over Georgia had come to see the United States Army, bury its' own. Taps was played by a young soldier from the Drum and Bugle Corp; while another soldier folded and placed the American flag into the arms of Clarke's widow. She was pregnant at that time; what that means is she was in the family way." Missy spoke in a whisper. Nicie nodded affirmatively.

"The widow was devastated. She refused to eat, could not sleep and cried day and night for weeks as her sadness took control of her life. Then, one day she became destructive; she destroyed her room, reducing it to shambles, as she threw her food that she refused to eat, against the walls. She also refused to bathe or come downstairs. Her family knew the young'un she was carrying was in danger and that she needed help. Each time they tried to reason with her, Vince and Crelon came to understand why they needed Dr. Roberts to help her."

Dr. Lem Roberts refused to medicate her. "It would be dangerous for the child." He'd said.

"Instead, he took her to a hospital where she and her baby would be safe. The baby was born on a Wednesday in June and brought to her Uncles house along with her mother. There were too many memories unresolved for the mother and she was returned to the hospital. Her baby stayed with Lena. There, the baby girl would be raised for the first three years." Missy said, patting Nicie on the head.

"Sometimes Chile, *Wednesday's child is full of Woe;* as the old saying goes." She quoted.

"Clarke's insurance policy had been made over to Lena and since he was only married for a month or so when he was shipped to France, there had not been time to change it over to his wife. The mail was slow and the twins rarely got mail, so they had no communication from home folks. Clarke never knew he was going to be a father." Missy concluded.

"Did the woman die?" Nicie asked timidly. A long pause followed the question.

"I, I, I don't think so, but; I do think its time for us to go home." Missy responded, not looking at her.

"Tell Charles to come with you tomorrow. We need to go over a few things together and decide what to do with some of Lena's belongings. These boxes are full and we need a place to put them." Missy explained, pointing to the stack in the corner.

"Yes mam." Nicie spoke softly, covering her anger!

On her way home she crammed her hands deep into her apron pockets. She had always known when she was not wanted but, had never been told why.

"Missy Mock talked in riddles." She said.

She then began to run toward the picket fence and with stick in hand, she struck it once, twice; over and over again. She kicked it so hard she could hear her own teeth rattle! Her jaws were shut tight; so tight that she felt as though they would shatter!

"All I asked was, did the woman die? She could have at least said yes or no." Nicie gasped breathlessly. "That would have been simple enough." She spoke, vehemently.

Spitting upon the ground over and over again as a rage of frustration seized her; Nicie began to cry. Tears filled her green eyes and fell freely as she slumped to the ground. Exhaustion claimed her body; while sadness took her spirit and guilt set in.

"I'm glad this ole picket fence can't talk." She thought. "Picket fence; I promise to never hit you again and one day I will paint you pretty and white."

Wimpy found her after awhile; with his tail wagging fondly, he licked the salty tears from her hands and face. In his language, he spoke clearly his understanding and acceptance of his little wounded mistress.

Nicie recovered just in time to hear a motor car in the distance; moving her way. A beautiful brown and beige 1925 Model T Ford car pulled up beside her, put on its brakes and came to a stop.

"Would you care for a ride, beautiful?" Uncle Coot called out to her.

Without hesitation, she stepped through the door he had opened for her. He bowed to her as she sat in the soft, kinda fuzzy seat; she rubbed it slowly. She was grateful for the ride and even more grateful he had not come by a few minutes before. She could not look at him as guilt and shame had taken turns washing over her; the two felt as rain and wind in a tunnel.

Finally, she asked, "Whose is it?"

"It's ours; yours, mine and maybe someone else's," he laughed, gaily.

"We're going to ride to the Savannah Cold Storage. How would you like a big banana split?" He questioned.

Nicie was taken by surprise! Only once had she tasted one and that was the day of Tollie Crane's birthday party and even then; she had only eaten a couple of spoonfuls. As quickly as she had become angry, she was now elated.

"Wonderful!" She cried. "I'm so happy, Uncle Coot!" She exclaimed, as the order was being filed. She sat, feeling giddy, as if she were awaiting a great surprise.

Uncle Coot said, "Nicie, I have a surprise for you."

"I know. Thank you, so much." She responded.

"No! No! I'm not talking about the ice cream." He stuttered.

Then placing his hand across the table, taking hers, he began -------

"You like Nell don't you?" He asked. Nicie gave an affirmative nod.

"I do too." He said. "I really do!" He spoke without taking his eyes from her face. They sat talking after the banana splits were eaten. Nicie was delighted with her new felt respect and was beginning to realize that an adult actually valued her opinion.

He held her hand gently, saying, "I value your opinion, Nicie. You are all I have in the world now." He went on.

"Nell wants to become my wife. I want her to, as well." He floundered. "Could we go by her house and let her tell you her feelings, about us?" He questioned.

"Will you go?" He asked like a little boy.

"Yes," Nicie said proudly. "I would like to."

"Taryn August would be proud if she could see me now!" She thought.

"Men are little boys who have grown tall; that's all." She quipped and hid her face, lest she become embarrassed.

"Uncle Coot, was your brother my daddy?" She asked, without looking directly at him.

"Yes, he was." He responded with shock! "How did you know?" He asked.

"I just figured it out by myself, but, I can't figure out who my mother is," she said sadly.

"Your mother is Grace, Vince Crane's sister." He responded quickly.

"The-, the-, then," Nicie stuttered. "Tollie is my cousin!" She added.

"She is your first cousin." Charles explained.

"I'm so glad your daddy's my brother. I was always so proud to be his twin; he was identical to me. That means we were exactly alike, Nicie." He said.

"I'm glad Tollie is my cousin, but Uncle Coot, I want my mother!" She spoke decisively. "Granma Goolsby was kind to let me live with you. That way, I could know what my daddy was like." She went on ---

Tears began to fall for the loss of the Father she would never meet and for a Mother who had not held her in years.

"I, I, I was the baby and Grace is my Mother? Miss Missy tried to find words to tell me." Nicie had solved the mystery. Nicie explained her tears as sadness and excitement enveloped her once again.

They were almost at Nell Bradley's house, so Uncle Coot blotted her eyes with his handkerchief. His eyes became wet as he listened to Nicie's point of view. He swore to make her heartfelt desire become a reality. Holding her close, he spoke. "Everything is going to be alright, baby; we will find your Mother."

Nell was waiting just outside the door as the car drove to the curb and she ran out to meet them.

"Charles, Nicie," she cried.

"Ch, Ch, Charles, a new car!" She screamed with delight.

Turning to Nicie, she said, "My goodness! You are growing up, riding in the front seat with Charles." She laughed.

"I love this car!" Nell said, rubbing the fender.

"Uncle Coot, May I call you Uncle Charles?" Nicie asked, peering over the hood of the new car.

"You certainly may, young lady." He responded. "Nobody ever called me Coot, except Mama."

"She called Clarke, Skeeter. It was a joke she always loved." He laughed.

Nicie called the name, Charles under her breath. She had never used his proper name before and somehow it rolled on her tongue, it made her feel grown up. Nothing could ruin the way she felt right now. Behind the two; standing straight, with shoulders back and chest out, she strolled into the house.

Nell had covered the table with a soft, pink embroidered tablecloth, centered with a crocheted pineapple. The green depression ware platter was stacked with bonbons. Grape juice was served in tall stemmed glasses. Nicie was not hungry because she had eaten every bite of her banana split, just an hour or so ago.

"I'd like to take mine with me. May I?" She asked.

"You certainly may." Nell Bradley agreed.

"I have something to show you, would you go with me upstairs?" She inquired.

The small girl stood at the bottom of the stairway, looking up. As she did so, she felt as though she were in Tollie Crane's house, once again. At the top of the stairs was a picture of a little girl with her dolly, sitting in a white wicker chair.

Nicie asked, "Is that you?"

"Yes, that's me when I was about your age." Nell Bradley responded.

Opening the door to the bedroom, she continued. "I've lived here with my Mama and Daddy most of my life; I married David Bradley when I was twenty. He passed away a few years ago; now I'm, I'm all alone." She stuttered, tears filling her eyes.

This was more than Nicie could stand. "Don't cry. Everything is going to be alright. You'll never be alone again." She spoke in a grown up voice. "Uncle Charles loves you. I love you, too." Nicie cooed. She put her arms around Nell's waist and patted her on the back, over and over again. It wasn't clear who was trying to console, whom; Nicie felt very grown up. Nell Bradley felt as she had long ago when she stayed in this same room.

Walking over to the canopied bed, Nicie touched it; sat and shook it. Never, in her life, had she ever seen such a beautiful room! There were dolls and teddy bears everywhere; she would have a hard time picking a favorite. Several minutes passed before she had chosen the ragged teddy bear and a dolly with fingers and clothes missing.

"I choose these." She said. "They remind me of me. I only want these two, there are other little girls like me and they have never had a real doll." She said, indicating her true feelings.

"What a lovely and unselfish little girl you are Nicie!" Nell was touched.

"I'm proud of you; you are so wise and one day soon we will ride downtown in Charles' new car and we'll buy wrapping paper. We will wrap a doll or a teddy bear for each girl and boy in 'The Row'. Won't that be grand?" She laughed. "Santa Clause is coming to town." She sang.

"Mrs. Bradley, you don't have to give me a doll or anything to make me like you, I liked you the first time we met. You helped me when I had no one; Uncle Charles was not home when Granma di, di, died." She spoke words that were hard to say.

"You opened your door in your housecoat and you were unashamed to run the long way to Granma's house. You just came when I called, like an angel." Nicie spoke positively!

"I had no idea you felt this way. I have but one wish; that we can always be friends. I, I, I, she stuttered.

"Uncle Charles and I had a long talk this afternoon." Nicie interrupted. "He told me that he loved you; I love you too." Nell was overcome with emotion; tears trickled slowly down her cheeks.

"My name is Lynelle and I'd like you to call me Nell. Charles calls me Nell."

"I must call you, Auntie Nell; this is the way Granma taught me." Nicie finished.

"Would you like to live here? I, I mean, would you like for us to be a family?" Nell asked hastily.

"Oh yes!" Nicie responded emphatically. Then, looking over in the corner, a brown bear, with a ragged ear, seemed to smile. It was as if he had approved of the conversation he had just witnessed.

"Why don't we go find Charles and see what he's up to? Are you ready for your grape juice and bonbon?"

"I sure am." Nicie responded, smacking her lips. The two new found friends had ended their conversation on a high note.

Charles Goolsby sat in the parlor with his head propped on a cushion, almost asleep; where the girls found him. He sat up saying, "I heard you two giggling, what was it was about? Was it about me? Have the two of you gone and plotted against me? Is this the way you women are going to treat little o me?" He laughed.

Nicie and Nell crawled onto his lap, one on each leg and both giggled like little girls. "Women are nothing but big, little girls." Nicie said; laughing.

"Yeah and I'm glad of it!" Uncle Charles responded.

"Seriously, Charles, Nicie and I have planned Christmas and we need to go downtown; would you drive us?" Nell asked.

"Sure will, if I can be Santa Clause." He added.

"That's a great idea! We will get Miss Missy to make you a red suit. Candy, toys and fruit will be given to each house in 'The Row'. There will be dolls and teddy bears for all the little boys and girls." Nell offered.

"It will be the grandest Christmas ever." Nicie said, excitedly. She was ecstatic!

The grandfather clock in the hall struck twelve and all the lights in the neighborhood were out.

"Would you like to stay here tonight?" Nell asked.

Nicie smiled, giving an affirmative nod; she did not want the night to end, she was too excited to sleep. Nell found Nicie one of her own gowns; no matter that it fell past Nicie's feet. They tied a ribbon around her waist and pulled it up, fitting it nicely. She had taken a bath in a real bathtub with running water and as she slid into the deep tub she had been overcome with fear, afraid she might drown! She held her head high above the water as the sweet smelling soap filled her nostrils and clung to her skin. For the first time in her life, she felt precious! She listened intently, waiting for her angels but they never came, for she did not need them anymore. She crawled between the clean cotton sheets, feeling every bit a princess and soon, she was asleep. A smile curved her lips.

A sprinkle of sunshine flared through the window shade; morning had come quickly. Hurriedly, she searched for her clothes and even though the dress she had worn last night was dirty; Nicie was prepared to wear it again. Stirring about the bedroom, she realized it looked different in the daylight; its beauty was enhanced. At the foot of her bed, lying on a gilded trunk was a new dress, a slip, underwear and stockings; along with shoes of black shiny leather. Rubbing her eyes at the unbelievable sight, she sang as she dressed.

"Amazing Grace, how sweet the sound"
"I once was lost, but now I'm found"
Amazing Grace, Amazing Grace"

Nell and Charles were dressed in elegant attire for today they would be married; they were waiting for Nicie. She had been too excited last night to hear about today's secret wedding. Finally Nicie stood at the top of the stairway, pausing to make her grand entrance. She hummed her song as she stepped downward, stopping here and there as she held her flared skirt outward.

"Come on down, Maid of Honor." Uncle Charles said, laughing.

"You look absolutely like a princess, my little darling." Nell told Nicie.

"This is a day to create memories forever." Uncle Charles spoke seriously as Nell flashed the Brownie Camera.

"Nell has asked us to marry her; we will become husband and wife, Nicie." He laughed.

He picked Nell off the floor and danced her around the room. Walking over to the third step of the stairs, he took Nicie in his arms and swung her around as the camera flashed again. Her white taffeta dress glistened in the light of the hallway as she pirouetted and danced with glee. Dancing into the parlor, Uncle Charles knelt before her. "Thank you my princess, for the honor of your presence, the dance was delightful!"

"My dream has become a reality!" Nicie thought. "Uncle Charles is the closest person in the world to my father." Her memory swung back to the sweet dream that had become a nightmare last summer.

"Give us fifteen minutes more." Nell said. Taking Nicie's hand they were off to her bedroom. Pulling the braids from her hair, Nell brushed briskly until Nicie's hair shown like a moonbeam. The golden hair, parted in the middle, fell in waves about her shoulders and her long bangs curled softly around her chin. As she stared into the ornate, gilt mirror, her eyes fell onto the picture there. Her heart leapt; Amazing Grace smiled back at her! She felt as though her angels had brought her this far, so surely they would help her find her mother.

Nell spoke first. "Now we are ready. All I have to do is put my dress on, and then off we go." Nell dressed as Nicie sat observing the ornate mirror adorned with two cherubs, strung with bows and arrows across their shoulders. They were ready and waiting for the special couple.

"Auntie Nell and Uncle Charles," she said aloud. Nell had heard and said, "Yes, I am the happiest bride in the world, Nicie. I have found a perfect family to spend the rest of my life with." Nell's eyes teared as she spoke. "We have plenty of room here for another person." She added, knowing she would explain later.

Nell looked radiant in her soft, off white lace dress and small lace hat. Uncle Charles wore a black suit with a white shirt and black bow tie. He stood tall and debonair as he escorted his women to the courthouse. If Nicie thought the couple were in a hurry; she said nothing about it.

The car was a few minutes away from their destination and Nell's upturned face glowed in the sunlight of the morning. Nicie sat in the backseat thinking and watching intently. "If my Mother is Mr. Crane's sister then, Tollie is my very own first cousin. What a revelation! We can be like Granma Goolsby and Missy Mock and grow old together." She was so excited; she suddenly gazed down at her hands and pinched them to be assured that she wasn't dreaming. The past few days had moved too quickly to absorb the details.

The car came to a stop in front of the courthouse and the three of them walked into the large building together. The Justice of the Peace had been waiting for them to arrive. Uncle Charles and Auntie Nell spoke their wedding vows, taking each other for better or worse. Nicie blocked the 'for worse' part, because she and Uncle Charles had already lived through the 'worse' part with Auntie Mazie; nothing could be worse than that! "Now the time had come for him to have a better life." She thought. She loved the grown up feelings she was experiencing. "I am not a Child of Woe! Granma was mistaken. If Taryn could see me now, she would see how much I have grown." Nostalgia flitted back and forth in her mind.

The next day the three went to Lena Goolsby's house to finish packing and clear her cabin. Missy Mock was at the chicken pen as the Goolsby's arrived, riding in the new 1925 Model T Ford.

"Lawd, Lawd I'd have never knowed you. You are all fancy, uptown folk." She laughed.

Charles put his arm around her, walking her into the house. The boxes were piled high and too heavy for Missy, Nicie and Nell to lift. Almost eighty years of riff-raff had been put away.

"Miss Missy, take what you want, Mama would want you to have first choice. Take any or all of what you see." He insisted.

Missy walked over to the stove, picked up the large cast iron frying pan and kettle. "These came from the 'White Oak Plantation', we were born there. My Grandmother, Pansy, gave them to Lena's Mother, Gale."

Walking over to the wall, Missy ran her hand down the dress; it's hanger being secured by a nail on the wall. "This will remind me of Lena everyday; I will hang it on my wall. She was wearing it when she passed." She said, choking back her tears. "We need to go through the trunk now ----."

They gathered around as Missy Mock unbuckled the leather straps, pushed the lid open to expose several crocheted and embroidered pieces on top. The next layer held a damask table cloth given to Lena's Mother, Gale as a wedding gift from Mr. and Mrs. John A. Barr II. Pillow cases and sheets came next; each had embroidered and crocheted edges, strung with tiny seed pearls by Sally Grant. At the bottom of the trunk was a cardboard box which held a hand-tooled leather saddlebag.

Charles held it, examined the handiwork and gave a whistle. "This must have been made before the Civil War. Look at the leather craft!" He exclaimed. "It is really something! It must be worth a fortune!" He finished. The initials engraved on the leather were J.A.B. Reaching inside the bag he pulled out a pouch containing hundreds of gold coins, some Confederate money, a Georgia Rebel's cap and a letter from Constable Ezra Carnes.

It read:

July 8, 1900
To whom it may concern:
This saddlebag was thought to be taken from a
Confederate Army deserter.
It was found at 'White Oak Plantation' on a
wandering horse by beaver trappers. The man
had been shot and was later buried in a Pauper's
grave by my good friend, John A. Barr, II.
These are the contents as they were found.

I remain your servant,
Ezra Carnes, Constable

"So", Missy sniffled. "Let the dead, bury the dead." Nobody dared ask what she was talking about.

"Now, I have a letter to Nicie from Lena." She offered. "I'm asking you, Charles to read it to her." Missy finished, wiping her eyes as she blew her nose on the tail end of her apron.

Charles Goolsby cleared his throat and began.

August 27, 1925
Dear Nice Chile,
I never could find words to tell you I knowed my time has come to
leave this world. Somehow, I never wuz good with purty words. If'n
you wuz to forgive a ole woman, I'd be much oblige. In the bottom
of my trunk is a sack full of gold coins, must be eight or nine hundert
dollars. I want you to go to school to be somebody. A somebody I
didn't ever git to be. My Mama had a 7 year of learning, that wuz
all I got too.

There's eight, ten year old War Bonds fer one thousand dollars each, sent to me by my little playmate's father, at 'Whit oke Plantation.' John A. Barr and his wife, Eva sent hit to me afore you wuz borned. Git yore Uncle Coot to put it in the bank soes you can go to school. I sen you to Coot soes you could be clost to your dead Daddy. I got a pitcher of yore Mama. Hit was took from my boy's pocket afore he dide. I saved the money my Poppa, Mate, left when he dide. It is all in the bank uptown. Coot, he would want you to have it. Clark was kilt in Franc, acrost the sea. Coot wuz ther. I will be gone when you read this will. I wisht I was strong enouf to tell you. I tried to gain strength but nevah did. Yore Mama got sick when Clark dide. Por soul nevah got over it. Fergive me fer being set in my ways. Give my corne cob pipe to Charles. He usta lip around and smoke it anyways. Kepe your Angels with you always. They sings so purty. I wants to borrow them fer awhile.

Give my sister and best friend Missy Mock anything she wants of mine. She wuz always ther fer me.

Coot will know what to do bout my house. Remember; Wendsays Chile is full of Woe. I was a Wendsays Chile too, but I made it an you can too. Coot will do all he can, I know. Keep singing Amazing Grace. One day you will find what it all means. Goodbye Nice Chile.

Till we meet agin, Granma Goolsby

Uncle Charles wiped the tears from his eyes, blew his nose on his handkerchief and looked away. He was unsteady on his feet as he took the picture of Grace and held it close to his heart. "His brother, Clarke would be proud." He thought.

"Who was the man with the saddlebag?"

"Missy Mock knew, but would never tell."

"It was obvious." He pondered.

Uncle Charles gave Nicie the small leather pouch. She pulled the drawstring, opening it and pouring the coins onto the bed; counting each. Later, she called out, "Four hundred and thirty-five coins." She replaced them quickly; nobody was listening.

Nell asked, "Nicie is there anything you want or would like to take home with us?"

"Yes," Nicie responded. I want the checked chickens, Buster the rooster and Grandma's quilts."

"We will build a chicken pen, won't we Charles?" Nell declared.

"NO, NO" I don't ever want to kill one. It makes me sick." Nicie spoke loudly.

Uncle Charles laughed. "Mama told me about that episode. Nicie, we don't have to kill them, baby." He promised.

"What will we do with the balance of Lena's belongings?" He asked Missy.

"I don't have a living soul who needs anything. All the people living here about could use almost anything and be glad to get it!" She exclaimed.

"Charles and I will take his Mother's trunk, packed as she left it. It will be a keepsake." Nell spoke, looking at Charles.

"You are so thoughtful, darling." He said kissing her cheek.

"If we have anything left, the Orphanage could use some clothes, pots, pans and whatever is left." Nell declared.

"Uncle Charles has enough stuff for the Orphanage." Nicie injected matter-of-factly.

"You are so right Ma'me. We still have all of it to pack and give away before I can sell the two houses." Charles said, winking at Nell.

"I have an idea, one that will help a family whose house burned last year. Hopee and Shados Golden are living with their grandparents because they have no home. Maybe they could live in ours until they find one." Nicie suggested. "My little room Granma Goolsby made for me could be used by two girls who need it." She finished.

"It would be a nice gesture to make it available to people in need." Nell offered.

"I was thinking about keeping both properties and improving them. Real estate properties are a good investment these days." Charles explained. "There's plenty of time to make a decision"

"Say, why don't we ride downtown? Then, we will take you home, Miss Missy."

"Yes," the others chimed in, "good idea!"

Nicie opened the shoebox Granma had left for her and inside was a corn shuck doll. "I played with this when I was your age." The note read, "This was made by Bartus Reem at 'White Oak Plantation'."

The only person who realized Pandora's Box had been reincarnated was Missy Mock. Silently she wished she had known long ago about the person who wore the Georgia Rebel's cap, from the Civil War. Knowing would have saved her the embarrassment she had felt as a child. Lena had shown it to her when she received it from 'White Oak Plantation'. She had also received the same note from John A. Barr II.

Missy had enjoyed the milkshake that Charles Goolsby had ordered. Now it was time to go home, she wanted to be alone and the moment she entered her front door was not too soon. She walked straight way to Lena's dress, hanging it on the bedroom wall. She stroked it tenderly as though she could bring it to life and spoke aloud. "Well Lena, here we are, old ladies now. Remember when we thought we would never die? What I never told you was… the day your Mother married Mate Goolsby, I knew I had lost a part of you. It pained me greatly. Actually I realize now that you taught me a much deeper love existed, through suffering and service, as you waited on Mate all those years. He was your happiness and I was a little jealous."

"The secrets of our birth will never part my lips; I never agreed with what took place against our Mothers. I wuz always thankful that you wuz my sister, even though we never spoke of it often. We should have proclaimed it to the whole world, but we kept one secret didn't we, Lena?" Missy spoke aloud.

"Yes, looks like we were borned a few months apart and we will die that way!" Her thoughts ran on.

"So, save me a mansion right next to you. Or, we could live together with our Mothers forever. I will be coming soon, dear soul." She finished.

She slept in Lena's hickory rocker, her head drooped forward; the sounds of snoring reverberated the paper fan lying on her lap.

In her apron was sewed a secret pocket behind its bib. Several envelopes were stuffed with Lena's bonds and hers as well. John A. Barr III had bought them yearly for years. Lena's was in her trunk and she had slipped them out before Nicie and she had opened the trunk together. Her scribbled not addressed Nicie as sole heir to her estate. She would keep them in her safe place; wherever I go, they goes with me. She scribbled on one of the envelopes; 'Nicie is my only kin alive! I loved her, sewed her clothes, fed her and took her into my heart to love forever. She was my 'Nice Chile', too. Lena was a little jealous of our relations, I am thankful we had each other and Nice Chile, too.'

It had been two weeks since Lena Goolsby's trunk had been opened. Nicie took the picture of Grace and placed it on her dresser. Running her fingers down her cheek and kissing her gently. "Where are you Mama? Why don't you come to me?"

PART 16

Savannah, Georgia

1926
Less beautiful than good and kind
Pure as snow was she
All gentle thoughts dwelt in her mind
By innocence and truth refined
Lauralie

"Lauralie"
Susan Pinder

The shock of Lena Goolsby's death touched John Alexander Barr, III with sadness. One of his little playmates was gone forever! Appointing Alvin Billy Coe's son, to direct her funeral, brought some comfort. He had been emotionally unable to attend either the preparation or direction of her funeral. However, he would attend services as a mourner.

For years he had sent generous donations to both Lena and Missy Mock at Christmas. Ten years ago he had purchased one thousand dollars in War Bonds for each of them and there had been a considerable increase since then. He had assisted in the hand writing of their Last Will and Testaments, pro bono. Remembering their past connections, he could never use Lena's burial money for himself. Instead, he had used it to purchase bonds for Nicie Goolsby.

There were no heirs to White Oak Plantation as he and Victoria had no children. "What better gift could I make than to leave my property to the grieving child I had witnessed, lovingly touching the old hearse as if it were gold. I watched too, as she walked throughout the funeral home, gently stroking the fabrics of the chairs; in awe of her surroundings." John had told Victoria.

White Oak had always demanded a caring conservative, to keep the workers, the Mercantile Company and the other small businesses thriving. Of course, Zinnie Coe's son, Billy and his family would inherit the funeral home.

The General Mercantile Company would go to Ben Samuel's sons, Cleve, Kirk and Neal. They had all worked there for the past fifteen years.

John was happy with his choices as he sat quietly at his desk. He lit a cigar, pushed his chair back and crossed his legs. The time was barely seven o'clock and morning had brought with it a cool feeling of Christmas; less than two months away. There was a certain sadness accompanying his thoughts. He was growing old and the pain of rheumatism had brought on a sudden attack in his legs, since the death of Lena Goolsby. He could not get her off his mind. He had offered her and Missy better housing years ago. Both showed no interest in making a change. Lena would not leave the home Mate Goolsby had made with his presence there and Missy loved her flowers and her present home.

John Barr sat for hours, reminiscing ----. Christmas at 'White Oak Plantation' had been a special event during those years.

Bartus Reem had made him a wooden wagon with wheels that rolled. He had taken months to whittle them, with a pocket knife, from yellow pine. It had not mattered that Billy's wagon was larger or that little Lena and Missy got most of the attention. He was happy to pull the wagon as they walked behind.

The girls carried their corn-shuck dolls with painted faces, just as mothers would carry their babies. Many times he and Billy pulled the babies in their wagons as the little mothers walked behind, carrying lace parasols, strutting down the wagon trails.

John laughed aloud, as he visualized himself and Billy as husbands to Lena and Missy. At times the five year old boys had been allowed to join a game of hop-scotch, double-dutch rope, ring-around-the-roses and London Bridges; see-saw was his favorite game.

John became tired and before exhaustion set in, he would complete his Last Will and Testament, and have it notarized and placed in his locked desk. He had discussed with Victoria, the educational needs of Nicie Goolsby and the financial care of Missy Mock. Victoria had recommended a private school in Atlanta.

"Certainly, Nicie will need a proper education." She had told John. "Management requires education and tenacity. Nicie Goolsby must have both." Victoria finished.

She could begin at the age of twelve; the school carried credentials for grades seven through eleven. "I will recommend her to The Atlanta Academy to save a place and boarding."

Today he would appropriate an account for Nicie's education. John did not need assistance to expedite his decision. His degree of law from New Orleans University would suffice. With pen in hand he worked feverishly as if a sudden, unknown urge pressed him onward. He thought of Billy's sons; all three of them were accomplished gentlemen. He personally had spared no finances to assure their education and stations in life.

Luke had become a minister; Alvin was co-owner of Barr's Funeral Home and Amos graduated from Howard University with a law degree. Currently, this inheritance would make him the senior partner with twenty employees at Smith, Dalph, Barr and Coe in New Orleans. Yes, Billy's boys had made exceptional men! John took pride in their accomplishments and was grateful for his part in their successes.

Approximately two hours passed and he had dotted every "i" and crossed every "t"; all documents were notarized and signed. His old friend Lena Goolsby could rest in peace; Nicie Grace Goolsby had become a very wealthy little girl, with just a few strokes of his pen. Missy Mock, his dear friend and heiress to one hundred shares of stock could rest easy also.

Suddenly, John Barr III felt as if the weight of the world fell from his shoulders. He closed and locked the door without looking back, then hobbled with the help of his cane to Barr's Funeral Home.

"I must remember to call Charles Goolsby." He muttered as he entered the door. Settling in his chair, he exhaled loudly, dozing softly; he dreamed of happier days -----.

The five year old mothers, Lena and Missy, whose dresses swept the ground, had again commanded the attention of young Billy and John-John as they slept.

PART 17

Savannah, Georgia

1926
"I am a pebble! And yield to none!"
Were the swelling words of a tiny stone?
Nor time, nor season can alter me;
I am abiding, while ages flee.

"The pebble and the acorn"
Hannah Gould

M onday morning, the high winds blustered around the corner of the house. The chimney roared its disagreement of the North winds. Nicie was ready as she walked onto the front porch, reading book in hand, and waiting for her ride to school. Her spirits were at a high water mark. The roar of the wind sang a song, while her black, shiny shoes tapped in rhythm. She glided to and fro, darting across the wooden floor.

Wimpy had greeted his mistress with great joy; suddenly he descended the steps, two by two. He crawled underneath the porch, whimpering, because he had never seen this action from her before!

Nicie stopped, listening intently as Auntie Nell and Uncle Charles readied for a new week of work. They seemed to be enjoying themselves. "Whatever happened to 'blue Monday'?" She wondered. Their conversations seemed droll to her, "They are always chatting about nothing." As they came through the door, Nell looked up, fluttering her eyes, gazing directly into her husband's for the first time in the last five minutes. Their genuine affection was apparent; one would have to be blind to miss it!

"Ugh, ugh," Nicie shuttered. "All this married stuff, they are glued together." She murmured. Hiding her face, she smiled as her heart seemed to swell; she took a copious intake of breath. She loved the change in Uncle Charles; she would never again associate him with Mazie! Most of all, she loved the change in herself.

The three drove toward the school and as they rounded a bend in the road, Tollie and Millie were walking to school; Uncle Charles stopped the car. They chatted lightly as he picked them up. Giggles from the back seat threw a 'monkey wrench' into the otherwise quiet drive.

Nicie longed to tell them her discoveries of the last two weeks. "No, they would not understand." She thought. Maybe later, there was plenty of time and basically she did not thing they would want to hear the saga of her family. Taryn would be the first she would talk to. She would understand and be happy for her, she mused.

Suddenly the girls began to whisper and laugh even more loudly than before as the car stopped at the front door of the school. The three young friends waved goodbye as they alighted from the car.

Nell called out to Tollie and Millie, "Come and visit us anytime you like."

"Bye Nicie, have a good day, study hard."

Nicie had a bright idea! She would invite both her friends to a spend-the-night party. Together they would wrap Christmas presents for the children in 'The Row'. It would be a special place for Santa Claus to come. She would introduce her secret friend, Taryn, to them and Uncle Charles and Auntie Nell, as well. All her secrets were demanding to be revealed and she was about to explode; she could hold them no longer! Yet, she must wait for Taryn to come home for the holidays before making her declaration to anybody. Her spirits were as high as a Georgia Pine!

Saturday morning breakfast was an event to remember. Nicie watched as Nell made waffles in a small electric waffle iron. The round cakes looked like checkered basket weave, stacked several layers high. She was enthused with the pancakes with checks; this invention was a clever one! "Who would ever think of such?" She wondered. "How yummy!" She said, pinching a bite.

The dainty cups of coffee were set before Nell and Charles' plates. Nicie asked if she could have one too. Actually, all she really wanted was to drink from the cup, pretend to be a grown-up, like Taryn. She had witnessed her new friend drinking with her little finger extended. "I would like lots of cream and some sugar please." She added. She would emulate Taryn's demeanor as she drank, sipping slowly.

Her short memory of Greta Garbo infused her. Granma had remarked during the movie, "Just look at her Nice Chile, one day you'll be a lady and drink from a dainty cup too." She had whispered.

Uncle Charles and Auntie Nell watched the role playing, looked at each other and smiled their approval of the moment. The three sat, sipping coffee together; Nicie was so excited! The coffee seemed to exacerbate the happiness and grown-up way she felt. She watched as the two actors touched their cups together and reiterated the same vows she had heard at the courthouse. Totally immersed in each other they talked in whispers, occasionally looking her way.

Nell Goolsby cleared the table and emptied the scraps into Wimpy's bowl on the back porch, where he appeared to enjoy the food, too. Placing the dishes in the warm water, piped into her kitchen sink, she sank them deeply into the water and the Maple syrup floated to the top, then dissolved into nothingness.

She and Charles had made plans over the last few weeks. Today, they would put them into action. She must hurry to finish cleaning the kitchen.

An appointment had been made; a very important one! Charles had told Nicie to go upstairs and dress her absolute prettiest.

Thirty minutes later, Nell and Charles were waiting in the parlor as Nicie entered the room. She had been lost in the mirror again; day dreaming of the day she had stood in a straight back chair on Grandma's back porch. The cracked mirror hanging high upon the wall had reflected the images of dozens of a small, pale girl with pigtails. She had stood, pulling them apart and brushing her hair one dozen times. For minutes she had twisted from side to side, posing. The green eyes stared back at her; the same green eyes she had seen in another place and time.

Today her ivory smooth skin glowed with happiness; she loved everybody and everything. In school her reading skills were considered to be the best in her class. A note had been sent home, along with her report card last week; she was graded 'Excellent'! Life was willing to give her a chance, after all; she smiled broadly then headed downstairs.

Her family was waiting and she had no idea where they were going or what the day would bring. Stepping down the stairway, her green and white checkered dress, with a soft lace overlay, bounced with each step she took. Needless to say, she took her time descending the stairway, the ruffled tail of her dress curled with yards of material. She was stunning but more than that, she knew.

Uncle Charles looked up and said, "There she is, come and give me a hug, big girl." He arose from his chair, picked her up, dancing her around the floor from the hallway to the parlor. He sang,"We are taking a trip today…. We're taking a trip today. Hi, Ho, La Dario, We're taking a trip today." His loud baritone voice was purposefully off key. Nell joined in the song, as did Nicie.

"Shhhh! Shhhh! we are disturbing the peace. Wheeeee, here comes the police. You're so silly." Nicie laughed.

"He is so much fun!" Nell injected, "And he is mine, I mean ours."

They ran to the car, entered and sped away. Driving through the city limits of Savannah, Nicie looked back as the two-lane black top stretched ahead. She had remained silent as long as patience would allow; speaking emphatically, "Where are we going?" "It's a secret," responded Uncle Charles.

At twelve o'clock, they stopped in Macon for lunch, which was short as was conversation; they left in haste. Nicie dared not ask again.

"We sure did come a long way to eat at Mama's Diner." Nicie gestimated, as she read the sign hanging across the door of the old building. Turning sharply, the car moved along, eastward toward Milledgeville, Georgia.

"Where are we going?" Nicie asked a second time.

"It really is a surprise, perhaps it could be the most eventful day of your life. I promise, you will remember this day forever!" Nell answered.

"Is it better than Christmas?" Nicie quizzed.

"Girl, it is better than all your Christmas's rolled together." Nell injected.

Suddenly, the car began to slow down pulling in toward the guarded gates. Two security officers conducted a random search of the car, asked several questions then, motioned to a third guard to allow entrance.

Nicie sat quietly taking in the view of the biggest house she had ever seen! The building rolled up and down the hills. Fourteen foot barricade fences were lined as far as the eye could see. Nicie's heart lurched in her heart! A graveyard stretched for acres just to the right of the buildings. There were all sizes of graves some were no more than two feet long.

Tears stung her eyes; she gazed at the markers as the car moved slowly. She turned to look backward until they were out of sight. They soon arrived and were ushered to a car park in front of the Administration building. Inside, it seemed as if they would walk forever; the long corridors ran North, South, East and West, luckily they had an escort. The indelible imprint into Nicie's mind was the people.

Some of the patients were allowed outdoor privileges; the concrete benches were lined with people, as 'birds on a clothesline'. All ages, colors and sexes of the suffering and debilitating souls, sat staring blankly; some were moaning, others laughing. A sad compassionate feeling enveloped the three as they walked, picking up their pace. These people's anguish became their empathy.

"God help them." Charles sniffled.

Nell squeezed his hand, "We have come here to make a difference. We will eliminate one special persons suffering today. Charles and I have a home and hearts big enough to resolve the needs of one tortured soul." She repeated, indignantly.

At last they were taken into a waiting room; the ceiling was strung with twisted, red crepe paper streamers. In the corner, on a homemade stand, stood a white pine tree, decorated with colored construction paper, cut into strips and glued together to make a chain. The only other adornment was a gold star attached to its top. The Arts and Crafts tables were filled with busy hands; this was their home, away from home. Somehow, even the bright colored paper of Christmas would bring happiness to some of the lonely souls. 'Joy to the World', played on the gramophone as the patients sang along; voices bellowed, hands clapped in and out of rhythm. Soon, Christmas would burst forth and there would be fruitcake, cookies, candy and socks, handkerchiefs, cotton stockings, as usual for each person; fruit baskets sat in every corner.

Nicie sat in awe of the goings on around her as she watched some of the patients responded to internal stimuli, sitting alone, with hands clasped tightly. She remained quiet while Charles and Nell had been ushered by a nurse into Dr. Roberts' office. Looking down the long corridor Nicie finally saw familiar faces. Coming in her direction were Vincent, Crelon and Tollie Crane.

Tollie ran towards. "What are you doing here?" She asked.

"What are you doing here?" Nicie questioned. "I am with Uncle Charles and Auntie Nell." She continued.

Quickly, the room filled with visitors. Some were waiting to secure passes for loved ones going home for Christmas and others were being discharged to family and friends. Nicie urged Tollie to the seat beside her; they were chatting with abandon as Nurse Brenda came toward them pushing a wheelchair.

She felt as though her heart would burst from sheer excitement. Not once, but twice, she looked --- seated before her was 'Amazing Grace'! This was the same golden haired, green eyed woman who hung over the mantel in a picture frame of gilded gold.

"Tollie, is it her? Is it her?" Sh-, She is the same woman Miss Missy gave me a picture of from Granny Goolsby's trunk." She stuttered. "Oh, my goodness!" She was speechless.

Grace Crane spoke first. "You are my baby, my Nicie Grace!" She spoke softly, extending both arms. Nicie fell at her feet. "Mama, Mama." She cried. "You are real! You are so beautiful! I have missed you all my life!"

Charles, Nell, Vincent nor Crelon heard the greetings; they were busy attending the discharge of Grace Crane. A confused Tollie sat with her mouth open, saying nothing. Finally, Charles buckled and strapped Grace's suitcases into the trunk of his car. Brenda, the discharge nurse, pushed the wheelchair down the walkway, directly to the car. As Charles opened the car door, Grace stood, walked the short distance, and got into the back seat beside Nicie.

"Bu, bu, but, I thought you were cripp---." Nicie stuttered. She was interrupted by her Mother. "You thought I was crippled." She laughed.

Suddenly, Nicie thought of Taryn. "If only she could see me now. I have a Mother just as she; but both of us lost our father!" She blinked back tears. At that moment Grace placed her arm around her, pulling her close. "There would be no tears today." Nicie swore. She had found her Mother!

"We have so much catching up to do, Nicie." Grace whispered. "I have my own private island to show you. I spent many happy hours there as a child. In fact, I buried my Grandmother Crane's old trunk there it is filled with my treasures. Nobody knows what is in it but me, your Father helped me to hide it securely. You and I will explore Fig Island together." She whispered emphatically.

"Oh, my goodness! Yes!" Nicie cried. "I love Fig Island!" Her head was buzzing with questions!

Charles and Nell chatted throughout the trip, unaware that secrets, plans and promises were being sealed in the back seat.

Grace took Nicie's hand and both made a fist, slapping them together twice and crossing their hearts; their secret code was born, Nicie exhaled loudly!

Finally, the vehicle pulled into the drive and Charles unbuckled the luggage from the car. Nell ran up the steps, unlocked the door and made a resounding declaration. "Welcome home, Grace Goolsby!" Grace looked around about, smiling broadly.

"I remember this house, it belonged t my childhood friend, David Bradley and his parents. I have been welcomed here many times." Nell had not heard, she was holding the door open, wide.

Vincent, Crelon and Tollie Crane pulled in behind Charles' car. They had brought with them an entire picnic supper. Nell had set the table in the breezeway, with the wicker furniture gracing the informal setting of the area. The phonograph played Christmas songs. A basket of fried chicken, potato salad, cabbage slaw, pecan pie and lemonade filled the table. A large Christmas arrangement adorned its center. Spiced oranges hung from the ceiling, scenting the house with festive aromas.

Grace Crane was the honoree and she delighted in being the center of attention. Her family indulged her with a patient audience of her real and sometimes imaginary conversations. If anyone noticed her solitary ramblings, it was ignored.

Nicie knew her Mother was delicate for she lacked the rosy health shared by others. Fig Island would help to bring her health back; along with Nell's cooking. She would gain weight, just as Nicie had, her ribs no longer showed through her dresses. Turning to look at her Mother, an old thought zipped through her mind. Many times she had promised her Angels to be the best daughter any Mother could have, if only she could find her.

"Mama, may I help you with your suitcases? Auntie Nell has made a beautiful room for you, next to mine. She and Uncle Charles have brought some of your personal furniture and pictures to decorate with." Nicie spoke excitedly.

"Sis, don't forget your room at our house." Vincent Crane reminded. "You and Nicie may come and go as you please." He finished.

"Yes, Grace, come often, Tollie can use some company and Nicie is the best. We have so much catching up to do!" Crelan injected.

"Auntie Grace, I am so happy my Daddy has a sister so beautiful. Nicie came to our house on my sixth birthday and she stared at your picture above our fireplace! You are more beautiful than your picture! When Nicie grows up, I'll bet she looks just like you." Tollie spoke last.

"Thank you Tollie, my dear, dear niece. You too are beautiful." Grace spoke softly.

"It must be a family trait." Vincent laughed. The room rang with excitement.

Christmas was rapidly approaching and this season would be one to remember. There were so many irons in the fire. The family discussed the prospects of a large family gathering for Christmas dinner; a Christmas Eve party in the yard of Lena Goolsby's empty house. The big Oak would be spread with tables and blankets everywhere. Open house would allow the neighbors an opportunity to select items that once had belonged to her. Santa Claus would come later in the night. The Goolsbys and Cranes would make a change in the culture of 'The Row' forever.

The picnic leftovers were packed and headed for the Crane's hilltop home. Nicie and Tollie said goodbye, waving as the car moved out of sight. Charles and Nell cleaned the kitchen and breezeway.

"Nicie, why don't you take your Mama for a walk? It always helps to settle a big meal." Nell suggested.

"Come," Grace responded, reaching for Nicie's hand.

Nicie would take her Mother on a walk to Bay Street and would, one day, introduce her to Taryn August. Just thinking about it made her heart leap with excitement! Hand in hand the two strolled and Nicie was careful to suggest a rest at times as they talked openly and freely. Finally they reached Bay Street, turning toward the wharf, with Grace leading the way, they picked up their gait. The wharf was almost empty, the workers were on Christmas vacation, but the two hardly noticed. They had a mission.

"Look," Grace exclaimed~ "There is my little skiff, Bobbin. It is still here, after all these years." Disbelief sounded in Grace's voice and was manifested in the greenest of her green eyes. Nicie did not answer; she was flabbergasted! The skiff belonged to her very own Mother! She had given it a name.

"Bobbin, perfect!" she cried aloud. "Oh, Mama, Uncle Charles taught me to row. We borrowed 'Bobbin' and went up and around Fig Island. I never knew she was yours. I thought she had no owner." Nicie shrieked with joy! Bobbin was hers all the while!

Grace broke the sudden silence of minds. "We will come back tomorrow and talk about our journey. I can see the sand hill where my trunk is buried from here. We may have to wait until after Christmas next week to explore our dreams. The waiting will be worth it, dear, I'm kind of tired, we must be headed back. We don't want them to be worried about us, do we?" She asked, taking Nicie's hand. They strolled more slowly going home.

The hallway grandfather clock struck eight; Charles had begun to pace the floor. "I will give them ten minutes. They have been gone since two." Charles' dejected look had given him away an hour ago as the sun went down.

Nell spoke calmly. "You know Charles, Grace knows this area 'like the palm of her hand'. Let's not ruin her first day home or Nicie's chance to be alone with her Mother."

"You're right Nell." He agreed.

Moments later the two entered the door chatting incessantly; obviously exhausted, they both yawned loudly. Grace Crane stood to her feet.

"I have retired early for years. At nine o'clock it was lights out for the patients. We got our baths from seven to eight thirty. We had only minutes for last minute reading." She said moving forward to the stairway. Nicie had taken her suitcases to her room and filled her tub with warm water. Grace's transition would take some getting used to; she had taken her bath, hugged her daughter and was ready for bed.

As she lay quietly, waiting for sleep to come, her mind went back to another time and another beautiful bedroom. -----

Grace floated in a cloud of dreams from the past; a high poster bed, draped with sheer curtains, hanging in ruffles, sat in the middle of her room. She was sitting in a rocking chair, the chair rocking steadily. Vaguely, she could see a small white cradle beside her rocker. Her baby, Nicie Grace lay sleeping as she rocked her back and forth. Suddenly, sadness crept in; she remembered the day! That had been a special day. Yes, it had been a special day, indeed! It was the same day Clarke's Commanding Officer, representing the United States Army came to the door. She could not remember the full details of their directive. However, he had placed a formal letter in her hand; suddenly, she stifled a scream. Sitting up in her bed; she wiped perspiration from her hot body and face.

"I am safe. I am safe. I have my baby with me." She whispered, reassuring herself; she slept.

Christmas Eve morning the Goolsby's and Cranes met at the old home of Granma Goolsby. Much 'to do' was made in preparation for the party. Many grown-ups and children in 'The Row' set up tables, decorated with crepe paper streamers and balloons. The special guests, Santa Claus and the children from the Orphanage, would arrive around two o'clock. Open house, with needy families making selections from Granma Goolsby's household goods, would start at four. Spreading tablecloths, Nell and Grace worked steadily, until suddenly, Nicie heard a loud snicker and saw red. She slowly moved toward her Mother, guiding her away from the gossiping mouths and prying eyes.

"Why don't we play hooky? You said you wanted to see your old home, we can go now and nobody will miss us." Nicie finished.

Walking away under scrutiny was unnerving to Nicie. Instead of blatantly acting out; she raised her shoulders, took her Mother's hand and moved down the dirt road. For just a moment she jutted her head upward and the tension in her spine eased. If Grace noticed she made no mention. Luckily, she had not seen the steel piercing look Nicie gave the two gossiping old hens.

The moment Nicie and Grace entered the home of Vincent and Crelon, there was a pause. Grace was stricken with fear, but despite her feelings, she kept in step with her daughter. Her senses were swimming, lips twitched; she had no words. With her back against the heavy wood of the door frame, Grace stood, taking a moment or two to steady her jangled nerves before entering. It was ridiculous to allow her past fears to affect her day. She'd sworn not to let them conquer her again. Taking a deep breath; she stepped over the threshold. Passing the living room, Nicie pointed at her portrait above the mantle.

"You look the same. That's how I knew you when they wheeled you in." She declared.

Slowly but surely, they climbed the stairs. "My bedroom was just as I left it." Grace thought, as both their eyes teamed to scan the bedroom at a glance. Tears stung Grace's eyes as the small cradle caught by the wind, from the open window, began to rock softly, back and forth.

Nicie recognized the stimulating presence of the rooms' effect on her Mother. Her incoherent rambling was barely audible; however, could not be understood. Turning sharply to stand before her, she looked up.

"I'm here Mama. I'll never leave you. We can't go back and change the past. It is part of our future and we will love harder to make ourselves stronger!"

Grace knelt before her. "My sweet child, if only I could see through your eyes! You are an old soul. It is strange for such wisdom to come from such a tiny girl. You remind me of my Mother." Wistfully, she kissed her.

Soon her disconcerting feelings vanished; Nicie was her best medicine. She was protected, shielded from disaster and no longer a hostage to her past; a bright future was hers.

Saturday evening, Charles and Nicie sat in the front porch rockers and reminisced about the events of the day.

"I've had the best Christmas ever!" Nicie spoke exuberantly.

"Yes, it has been quite and occasion and soon, I have to reconstruct my old house. The picket fence needs a little work, repainting and such -----."

A faint wistfulness in his voice made Nicie stop rocking. She straightened up; he had said all the things she had wanted to talk about, but had been afraid to.

"What do you think about the picket fence? Shall I tear it down, or fix it?" He questioned.

"Please don't tear it down! I will help you fix it back and paint it. Let me paint it and I promise to do a good job." Eagerly she urged.

"You will be held to that promise, big girl." Charles spoke seriously. Their conversation was interrupted by a young man on a bicycle. Ralph, the telegraph boy, skidding his wheels in front of the gate, pulled a telegram from his hat saying --- "A telegram for Mr. Charles Goolsby".

Charles gave him one dollar and sent him on his way.

"What do you know, Nicie? Mr. John Alexander Barr III is requesting a meeting, Monday at nine o'clock. He asks that you come along. It probably has something to do with Mama's funeral."

"While we are in town, we will stop by Barr's General Mercantile Store and pick up building materials. We need to make a list, so go get a pencil and paper; we are in this together, because these are our projects. Hurry up now, and you have to get to bed. Santa Claus comes tonight and we have church tomorrow." Charles said.

Sunday morning at nine o'clock, church bells across the tracks began to peal. Bright, warm sunshine competed with a frosty Christmas day. One hour later, the Goolsbys and Cranes filed slowly into one long pew, along with Missy Mock. Cousin Tollie, holding to Nicie's hand, smiled. Nicie held Grace's arm, staring into her eyes without blinking.

"I love you." Grace spoke softly.

"I love you, more." Nicie retorted.

The organ played, bells chimed and the choir sang. Ethereal wisps, silver tresses and gossamer wings, seemed to hover over the parishioners. Minister Neal Gold led them in prayer.

Nicie knelt beside the pew, bowed her head and prayed ---

"Angels in heaven, I will always love you for helping me find my Mama. Thank you for singing in my heart when I had no place to belong. I have a family now. Amen."

At last, Nicie understood who she was meant to be.

The choir filled the church with a heavenly melody. Nicie and her Mother were bathed in spheres of sunlight, radiating from the ceiling skylight. The Madonna and Christ-Child shone from the stained glass windows. The comparison was awesome!

"They are singing our song, Mama Grace." Nicie whispered.

Grace cupped her face gently as Nicie softly sang.

"Amazing Grace, how sweet you sound."

THE END